Grandfather, Father and Me…
Memories, Poetry and Good Food

Grandfather, Father and Me...
Memories, Poetry and Good Food

Editor
Donna Clark Goodrich

First Edition

Hidden Brook Press
www.HiddenBrookPress.com
writers@HiddenBrookPress.com

Grandfather, Father and Me…
Memories, Poetry and Good Food

Editor – Donna Clark Goodrich
Cover Design – Richard M. Grove
Layout and Design – Richard M. Grove

Typeset in Garamond
Printed and bound in Canada

Library and Archives Canada Cataloguing in Publication

Grandfather, father and me : memories, poetry, and good food / editor, Donna Clark Goodrich.

ISBN 978-1-627725-07-8 (pbk.)

1. Grandfathers--Literary collections. 2. Fathers--Literary collections. 3. Canadian literature (English)--21st century. 4. American literature--21st century. I. Goodrich, Donna Clark, editor of compilation

PS8237.G72G73 2013 C810.8'035253 C2013-905896-6

Contents:

Father Memories

Grandfather Memories

Men of Influence

Father Memories

A good father
is one of the most unsung,
unpraised,
unnoticed,
and yet
one of the most valuable assets
in our society.

Billy Graham

J. Graham Ducker

Painting the Crossroad

Mining companies in Northern Manitoba provided summer jobs for the older teenage boys for two reasons: to give them a bit of spending money and, in a subtle way, to keep them off the streets.

I was assigned to the paint crew. Our job was to paint pipes their identification colours of their contents: yellow for acid, blue for vacuum, and so forth. It was an easy mindless job.

I enjoyed the newfound freedom that came with having a few dollars to spend. After contributing one-third of my cheque to the family budget, I still had quite a bit left over.

Working for a living was certainly better than high school.

The new school year loomed.

At the supper table one evening, I announced that I was going to quit school and keep working.

Mother immediately launched into a long lecture, expounding how I was too young to quit school; my whole life was ahead of me; I had to have an education, etc.

I wasn't listening. I was waiting for Dad's reaction.

When nothing seemed forthcoming, my encouragement meter rose to new heights.

"So, you want to quit school, eh?" he intoned.

"That's for sure," I said. "I like painting much better. It's a lot easier than school."

"Um-hum," Dad agreed. At least it sounded like an agreement. "You realize, of course, those summer jobs end when school starts."

"Er, no, I didn't know that."

Dad carried right on. "But, that's okay. Maybe we can find you another job."

"Great!"

Dad spread the *Winnipeg Free Press* across the table, and turned to the want ads. "Let's see what you are qualified for. What skills do you have? You can paint pipes. Here, look through the listings for a pipe painter."

My scrambled search yielded nothing.

"Well, what else can you do?"

I could not think of anything.

My aspirations began to sag.

"They had you shovelling in the crushing plant for a while, didn't they? Maybe there is a need for diggers."

There wasn't.

My shoulders began to sag.

"I think there is a section for unskilled people. Have a look there."

My determined look yielded nothing. Even there, the minimum requirement was Grade Twelve.

Now it felt as if my ears were sagging.

"There is nothing here, either."

When Dad didn't offer anything more, I looked up and saw a small smile on his face. I knew I had been led down the proverbial garden path of self-realization.

"Well, it looks like I'll be going back to school."

That was the year I took my entire Grade Eleven by Manitoba Ministry of Education Correspondence, which led to completing University and a career in teaching.

Rona Evartt

Lessons from Dad

Dad always had a practical side when teaching. I may not have appreciated his methods at the time, but I can't argue with the results. Outdoor activities were a mainstay in our lives. He rode motorcycles for a California police department, and mini-bikes were our introduction into the hobby. It was our transition to the full-size model that presented my father with a challenge.

My younger brother, sister, and I had mastered the balance and power of the smaller model, but the added brake, clutch, and shifting gears were confusing. Frustrating time passed as he repeated instructions to our perplexed, innocent faces.

"The right-hand lever is the front brake, but you don't want to use that until you apply the rear brake with your right foot," Dad exclaimed. "The left-hand lever is the clutch. You pull that as you shift gears with your left foot, then smoothly release the hand lever."

Dad ran alongside until he was exhausted trying to instruct us. Sweat poured from his face after hours of attempts. We were beginning to get the shifting of gears as we sought the speed this new model provided over the mini-bike, but our stops were sloppy. Stopping safely was Dad's concern as he watched the back tire squirrel around on us over and over again.

"Not the front brake! You're gonna dump the bike and hurt yourself," he hollered.

This bit of instruction seemed unimportant as the skid looked pretty cool at our current rate of speed.

"Why does it matter, Dad?" we'd ask in unison.

"It does matter. You may need to stop very quickly, and you definitely need to stop safely."

Ron and I rolled our eyes.

"Look, if you don't get this right, you won't ride. It's that simple."

Now he had our attention. I could see the wheels turning in his head as he thought of a way to drill this important bit of advice into our stubborn heads. Suddenly he had an idea. We followed as he rolled the motorcycle from the flat dirt field from behind the house to our steep, gravel driveway.

"Rona, Susan, go into the house and get a drink. I'm going to show your brother first and then he'll get one of you."

I was the oldest and felt a bit slighted by Ron going first, but luckily Dad didn't have the typical chauvinistic attitude still dominant in the early 1970s about girls riding bikes, so I complied.

It wasn't long before my brother entered the house to summon me. His clothes were dirty and possibly torn. Dirt circled his eyes leaving clean the area where the goggles had been. His eyes were wide with something between fear and disbelief. Shaking a bit, he led me out the door.

Dad held the bike as I straddled the seat. I looked down the steep driveway wondering what was in store.

"I'm going down to the end of the driveway. I've marked a line in the gravel and I want you to stop at my outstretched foot. Wait until I get there."

Simple enough, I thought. I watched as my father and brother walked down to the end of the driveway, and waited for his signal. At his command, I let out the clutch and accelerated down the drive. Nearing his mark, I pulled the front hand brake. The front end locked up, the rear tire came around as if to greet me, and I went over the handlebars. Sprawled in the gravel, I looked up at my dad and muttered something to the effect of "What the…"

"Now, which is the front brake?"

"Uh, the right hand," I stammered.

"When you stop, which brake do you want first?"

"Uh…the rear brake?"

"Think you got it now?"

Yeah, I got it all right!

Now, Ron and I loved Susan as much as any brother-sister team loved their youngest sibling, but, let's be honest, we felt superior in our maturity. I need not reveal the many indiscretions brought to light at her mention as we received due punishment, while in our eyes she got leniency as the baby in the family. Exaggerated perceptions, I'm sure. I looked over at Ron as we simultaneously shouted with joy, "Susan!"

We pushed and shoved each other back up the driveway, racing to the house to retrieve Susan. I know our devious ambition wasn't lost on Dad as he moved her start lower down the drive making her acceleration much slower, catching her as the motorcycle slid.

To this day I wonder if he was just using a gentler approach with our baby sister, or if she didn't need as harsh a lesson as Ron and me. Superiority may not lay with birth order…

Theodore Christou

out reach

with grace you grant (me)
goodness; f a r m o r e
than i (your fool son)
sought; m o r e than (mere) man
you are, and (m o r e) a
man i m e a n to be
to honour you, whose
mean (and mind) the myths
of my heritage make;
i (in mirrors)
your gaze perceive and
(in my eyes) your stare
i see; my voice the
sound of your speech shows;
your words my (tongue and)
tone have styled, as i am
moulded in your guise;
intemperate blood
(of your breed) courses
(through me and) a l l through
my flesh; your name I
bear a b o v e my brow
and o n my chest i
cast our crest;
I n e e d you as
I n e e d air friend;
(dear father) m o s t blessed.

Theodore Christou

our conversation abstracted

i:

the beseeching and bespectacled moonlight implored my sighs to open; but i looked away; i had sworn never to sing of sighs again.

i swore once more; in spite of the light of the moon.

thou:

be still. be still my boy.

the time of moans; of sighs; of other sounds replete with -ōz- has passed away.

Karen Sue Chmielewski

Military Respect and Honor

My father, Edward (Ed) Chmielewski, was a seaman in the navy and thoroughly enjoyed a four-year duty in Pearl Harbor, Hawaii. The U.S.S. Perry minesweeper was his assigned ship and the crew went out to sea for months at a time on several dangerous missions sweeping the Pacific for live mines. That's where this story begins.

Three months prior to the bombing of Pearl Harbor on December 7, 1941, Ed was on duty in the torpedo room when the ship was rocked by an underwater mine and his back was thrown up against an engaged torpedo. The next thing he remembered, he woke up two months later in the Naval Hospital tagged as John Doe, because with the damage to the ship and the ensuing confusion, no dog tags or other identification could be found during efforts to get him to safety. Overnight, his hair turned white from shock. While in a coma, six vertebrae of his spine were surgically fused together. Within a couple of weeks of waking from this coma, he was told that he would be in a wheelchair for the rest of his life and never walk again.

However, Ed refused to believe his injury or let it stop his life. He walked out under his own power just in time to be present at the worst catastrophe in American history, the bombing of Pearl Harbor. This was an experience that he could never open up and fully talk about as he felt frustrated not being able to assist his navy brothers while trying to recuperate from his own sustained injuries months before.

The kicker here is that back on the mainland, in the town of Jackson, Michigan, his Polish immigrant mother Agnes had received word that her son was dead, lost at sea, because Ed was not identified in the hospital. She received his personal belongings and grieved over the loss of her baby boy. To make matters worse, her oldest son, Chester, was also missing in action and she was waiting on word for his whereabouts (he did come home safe). Needless to say, when she opened the door on a spring afternoon in 1945 and saw a man with white hair who looked like her Eddy Boy, although a strong and tough woman at 6'-4", Agnes fainted and hit the ground like a rock and the floor shook. She thought the figure in the doorway was an angel or a ghost because of Ed's premature white hair. It must have been a shock.

Ed was in pain for the rest of his life, but refused medical treatment. Yet he never complained as he spoke with pride about his honor to serve in the United States Navy for his country. Ed served God and his country with every fiber of his being and went on to lead a full, successful life as a court administrator and father.

Thank you, Dad! I salute you.

Brendalyn Crudup Martin

Daddy's Coin Collection

One of the few times I had my dad all to myself was when we worked on our coin collections. He started collecting coins when my brother Jun (short for Junior) and I were both young and would include us in his scavenger hunts for special coins to complete his collection. I was only six and Jun was nine.

I loved following behind my dad and because he liked coin collecting, it became my favorite hobby. Daddy tried to get Jun involved and for a while he saved his coins, but that didn't last long. Jun's first thought was money to spend on ice cream, candy or cookies; he was more concerned with spending the coins on treats than saving them in little blue albums.

Mom had a lot of other projects and didn't have time to devote to coin collecting, so that left me, Daddy's girl, and whatever Daddy liked, I liked. I saved my allowance and any money that I earned toward collecting coins. At the end of each week Daddy dumped his spare change on the kitchen table and we looked through every coin to see if there was a new treasure lurking in the pile.

Over time I saved more coins and added them to the pile. Sometimes we found Indian head pennies or Buffalo nickels. Other times we found wheat pennies and sometimes old silver coins, usually dimes or quarters, but sometimes half dollars and silver dollars. These were safely tucked away in the coin albums, to be replaced if we found others in better condition.

Sometimes we went to the coin shop and looked for bargains for our collections. Although my brother had given up, I kept going, treasuring this as the one thing where I did not have to share my dad with anyone. This was our time, when we marveled over the coins we added to our collections and talked about the history of the coins and why they were important to us. Not even my mother shared this interest with him; it was ours alone, and our collections continued to grow.

Daddy's collection held everything from pennies, nickels, and dimes to silver quarters, half dollars, and Morgan dollars. My funds were more limited and included pennies, nickels, and dimes with a few quarters and a Morgan dollar he gave me that I never spent.

My father passed away many years ago and I found his books tucked away in a closet. Through the years he had sold many of his silver coins, probably after he retired, but my mother remembered how he and I shared the love of collecting coins and she told me that now they were mine.

It wasn't until after her death, when I went through her things that I remembered I had left them with her. As I pulled the books from the closet, I was that six-year-old child again, surrounded by my father's presence as I turned the pages, looking to see what special coins I would find.

Alice Klies

Isn't It Ironic?

Up early in the morning, I walk toward the hallway to a bedroom door and peek in at the sleeping figure. I even check to see that his chest is rising up and then down with breath. Before waking him, I prepare a nutritious breakfast. I remind him of the day and time. After breakfast I encourage him to take a stroll around the backyard or maybe throw a ball to our golden retrievers.

Sometimes I sit down and play games with him or cheer him on to colour a masterpiece for me. When he colours something particularly well, I stroke his head and say, "Good job, well done."

Soon it's time for lunch. He loves peanut butter and jelly sandwiches, especially with sliced bananas tucked snug in the peanut butter. After lunch, I run a bath, trim his toenails and fingernails, and snip a little hair around his ears.

Today we have a doctor's appointment and afterwards we will go to the store to purchase diapers. Our supply is always running low and today they are on sale. The store is great fun because he loves to wander up and down the aisles. I usually find a few extra "goodies" in my basket before we check out. When we get back home, it will be time for a quick nap. He will be tired.

Home at last and after a busy day, naptime starts to look really good to me. I tuck him in with a kiss and within minutes he is sound asleep. I relax for some downtime and I reflect. I've done this before and here I am once again, only this time it's not my four-year-old son, it's my ninety-two-year-old daddy. I settle back in my chair. I smile because I know that sixty-five years ago my daddy took care of me.

I remember the patience my daddy had when my gait seemed slow. I can still feel his strong grip holding my hand tight as I took step after step, teetering from side to side, knowing he would not let me fall.

When I have to repeat myself, I recall how often Daddy had to read and re-read a storybook to me. When he tells me the same story or joke over and over, I think about how many times he listened to me sing the same silly song twenty times a day or hear the word "why" from my lips constantly.

I watch food dribble from his mouth. I clean up a spill or broken glass and I pause, yes, to remember the many times Daddy must have wiped the chocolate from my mouth or pulled out a broom to sweep up my messes. He certainly washed plenty of my colouring masterpieces from the walls of my room.

Daddy can no longer hear well. I am forgiving because I know I turned a deaf ear to him many times, especially during my teen years. I can almost see the expression on his face when he used to say, "Alice, are you listening to me?" My heart aches a little when I realize how often I didn't listen to him.

During bath time, while the water runs and I lovingly sponge his back or soap up his hair, I understand how his back may have hurt while bent over a tub playing with a giggling little girl and a plastic ducky.

Daddy sleeps the greater part of his days now, and instead, stays awake much of the night. Does this sound familiar? I close my eyes and lay my head back on the chair rest. I breathe in deep, holding back the tears that start finding their way down my cheeks, and I ponder and realize how hard it must have been for Daddy the first few months of my life when my pattern of existence was much the same. Isn't it ironic?

* * *

Daddy passed away peacefully at ninety-three. When I could finally go into his room and sort through his things, I was blessed to find a notebook of poems and prose he had written without my knowledge. The following is one that gave me needed peace.

> God is with me this day. He has shown me the way to the beyond that everyone must face. There is a time for happiness and a time for the sadness we must face in our lifetime. I feel that God has left me a place.

I walked out of Daddy's empty room with an armful of memories that encouraged and assured me that I can look forward to embracing him in heaven.

Elynne Chaplik-Aleskow

Golden Hands

"Golden hands" was the way we spoke of my grandfather Isidor Chaplik. One of his sons, my father, Rubin Chaplik, inherited his gift. Both my father and grandfather were meticulous craftsmen. My dad invented and patented the first automatic coffeemaker for restaurants. Until my grandfather's retirement, my father worked alongside his father in a family factory that my grandfather built from scratch when he came to this country as a teen from Russia. All my uncles were part of the business but it was my father who shared his father's talents. My grandfather and my father could build almost anything.

When my parents decided it was time for our family to move from an apartment to a home, my father designed our house and oversaw every detail of its construction. He even included a soda fountain which my mother eventually begged him to empty of its goodies because my sisters and I spent so much time tasting and devouring.

One day while shopping, my mother saw a chandelier which she loved and wanted to hang in our home. When she learned the price, she quietly shook her head and, almost in shock, left the store. That night she told my dad about her find and its price tag.

About three months later, my mother drove to pick my father up at the factory. Dad motioned to her to come inside and follow him into his workroom. There, hanging in all its beauty and glory, was the fixture my mother had wanted.

"Did you buy it?" my mother asked.

"No," my father answered. "I made it."

Stunned, my mother smiled at my father while alternately staring up at her gift.

"Golden hands," she said. "Thank you."

My sisters and I grew up with the realization that we lived with a man who could fix anything. A woman can get spoiled easily with that good fortune.

My dad would bring home all kinds of toys, my favorite being a model train. The problem was that we could never get close enough to play with these toys because my dad was playing with everything. There was one exception. I recently realized that although I am right-handed, I can only play left-handed pool because my father, who was a lefty, taught me how to play on the billiards table he bought.

My dad was a Renaissance man, a human being who loved life with a passion and joy that were awe-inspiring. He was the father of four daughters, and watching him master his varied interests was a lesson my sisters and I enjoyed learning. From photography to flying his own plane, his joie de vivre was a gift he shared with not only his family, but with all who knew him. My father joked that he took to the skies through his love of flying because he lived with five women. We always laughed at that joke and were happy to see him enjoy his true life's passion.

My father believed in himself and his talents. That example of determination, focus, and commitment was a life legacy he gave to us. He was our protector and mentor, a creative inspiration in all he did.

From his father, my dad learned many lessons: love of family; a work ethic that was solid and uniquely successful; pride in being Chaplik; generosity to others in need.

My mother, sisters, and I were grateful for this special man in our lives and the honor of sharing his genius. His warm charismatic smile and his larger-than-life energy touched many.

My father was also blessed with a beautiful singing voice, sounding very much like Bing Crosby. Yet, the artist whose signature song my dad loved and sang over and over again was Frank Sinatra's "My Way." My dad was a true individualist and original. This was one of the greatest gifts he gave to me. I have tried to live my life "my way" as he lived his.

* * *

On December 20, 1974, my father and youngest sister Ivy, who was sixteen, died in a plane crash on their way to meet my mother who was waiting for them in Florida. Investigators concluded that an air traffic controller made mistakes in information given to my father.

My dad's legacy lives on through his daughters. There is not a day that goes by in which we are not inspired and motivated by his philosophy of living and loving. My dad lived it his way.

Helen L. Hoover

Daddy's Fudge

From the day of Larry's and my marriage until my dad died in 2000, we lived within two to three miles of each other. We visited back and forth, played games, took trips together, ate meals at each other's homes, and helped one other when needed. Our lives were intertwined with his life and activities, including my mother and then a stepmother. We enjoyed his friendship, encouragement, and humor, never exchanging harsh words. When we were with him, we felt accepted and loved.

"Helen's dad never seemed to disapprove of me, nor gave any indication he would have preferred she married someone else," Larry tells people.

Since everyone has personality traits, habits, and quirks that others dislike or find annoying, it is quite a testimony that Dad kept his mouth in check over those thirty-eight years. Consequently, Larry and I didn't have the added stress on our marriage of dealing with the disapproval of a fault-finding parent. We try to follow his example in the treatment of our children's spouses. If we disagree with the actions or words of a daughter-in-law or son-in-law, we discuss it among ourselves but not with our child.

* * *

"Will Granddad have some of his fudge ready for us?" Grant, our five-year-old son, asked as we headed to my dad and mother's home for a Christmas meal and gift exchange. The mouth-watering fudge, that only Daddy successfully made, was a treat for anyone who came to their home for the holidays. He usually made two or three batches of the candy so he had plenty to share. He never doubled the recipe.

As we stepped through the front door, we could smell the chocolate delicacy as it cooked. Then the beating began. He never seemed to tire of beating the mixture until it was the right consistency. Whew, my arm got tired just watching. Our anticipation mounted, as we waited for the fudge to cool and then cut into small bite-size pieces.

I knew that weeks before, Dad had gone to a friend's property, which had black walnut trees, and picked up the nuts. After getting them shelled, he spent hours picking out the nut meats. That was a time-consuming job in itself, but he considered the walnuts an important ingredient. Pecans could probably be substituted, but he never considered them for "his fudge." The fudge making was definitely a labor of love on my dad's part.

I tried making the fudge a few times, but gave up. Mine never compared with his. My family learned to enjoy the treat only at Granddad's house.

We haven't had any of Daddy's fudge for thirteen years now. We miss the yummy confectionary, but we especially miss the unconditional love my dad extended to his family.

Daddy's Fudge

2 cups sugar
1 cup milk
2 tbsp. cocoa
1 tsp. butter
1 tsp. vanilla
2 tsp. cream
¼ cup chopped black walnuts

Mix sugar and cocoa in a large saucepan. Stir in milk. Add butter. Cook, stirring constantly, until a drop forms a soft ball in a cup of cold water. Add vanilla and beat until grainy. Add cream and chopped black walnuts. Pour into greased (with butter) 9x9-inch baking dish to cool.

Linda Rose Etter

The Last Surviving Guinea Pig

My father, Robert John Etter, was born the same year insulin was discovered—1921. When he was two-and-a-half-years old, my grandmother took him to the University of Michigan Hospital where he and four other brave young boys with diabetes were put on tables and experimented on by injection. Guinea pigs.

When Dad was about four years old, he was able to stay home most of the time under the excellent care of his mother who carefully measured and cooked his meals to the doctor's directions. She also tested his blood and urine and injected her little son four or five times daily. My grandparents were told that he would probably not live to see twenty years old.

My dad remembered his grandfather, who came from Germany, sitting at the kitchen table, eating an apple and reading his Bible every morning. Due to their faith in God, prayer, and my grandparents' good care, my dad lived to be seventy-three.

Dad and his brother, Roy, who was two years younger, loved to play baseball. Uncle Roy was able to play on the high school team but because my dad was a diabetic, he wasn't allowed. The views on diabetes have changed over the years. Today diabetics aren't barred from sports.

My parents gave birth to me in 1950 and my dad started rolling a ball across the floor to me when I was old enough to sit up. By the time I was twelve, my dad's dream of seeing his daughter play sports came true. Now I realize how hard it was for him to travel to my games and manage his sugar levels but he was determined to be at every one!

Dad died on my forty-fifth birthday before he turned seventy-four. He was the last of the five boys from the University of Michigan guinea pigs to die.

He was a wonderful father who taught me about sports, woodworking, and life. The most important thing that he taught me, however, was about knowing God and the importance of prayer and daily Bible reading. God was his strength and He enabled Dad to stay disciplined and positive about his health. Without this, Dad wouldn't have lived long and I wouldn't have been born. I am thankful for his godly example in my life.

Cassandra Wessel

Breakfast, Beds and Blue Laws

As a child my sun rose and set around Dad, but his PTSD from World War II caught up with him as I entered my teenage years, tarnishing his halo a wee bit. In spite of that, I cherish my memories of our time spent together. Nearly every Saturday my father would give my mother a break by taking over her kitchen to grill flapjacks and sizzling bacon served swimming in syrup. He used a melt-in-your-mouth buttermilk pancake recipe from his mother, along with his own recipe for homemade syrup. Since these were not written recipes, he followed his mother's "dab of this and that" method.

Saturday morning, Dad would chase Mother from her kitchen and I would climb upon one of the breakfast barstools to watch. While he would attempt to focus, I would chatter away, making him lose track of what he was doing. Then he would chase me off to go watch TV with my brother, but I always snuck back to watch him pull the pancakes together.

First thing he did was check the refrigerator for a quart of buttermilk. If there were none, he would hop in our station wagon and drive to the supermarket. Usually I jumped in the car with him. At the store Dad would never admit he needed help finding the buttermilk, nor would he ask for directions if he were looking for a new store. Eventually we would return home with the buttermilk in a quart glass bottle that Dad would set on the counter. He would then line up the white and buckwheat flour, the baking powder and soda, the shortening and eggs. Reaching beneath the countertop, he would locate Mother's electric mixer and set of bowls, putting them on the breakfast bar. He was finally ready to make his famous buttermilk pancakes.

When Dad had finished making breakfast, and we had devoured it, he was done in the kitchen. He figured he had cooked so someone else could clear up, namely me. From scraping to drying dishes, Mother oversaw the whole process which took most of the fun from splashing in dishwater. She fairly praised me for my efforts, but in spite of the fact that my skills scarcely measured up to her standards, I helped with household chores. Much later in life, she admitted to often redoing my tasks like ironing Father's shirts, sweeping floors, and making beds.

Dad took an interest in my bed-making skills. Since he had been in the navy during World War II, he was a bit of a "petty officer" when it came to inspecting how we made our beds—bottom sheet pulled tight enough to bounce a quarter, top sheets and blankets tucked into hospital corners. I really tried to meet his standards, but a blanket corner would inevitably sneak onto the floor. Dad simply tousled my hair and showed me how to do it again.

When Saturday chores were finished, Dad rewarded himself by reading the newspaper or a magazine while classical music played in the background. But he would always turn off his hi-fi so Mother could see her favorite TV show. At the end she would hustle us off to the bathtub for our weekly scrub and hair wash. Afterward she would set out our Sunday best as Dad polished all our shoes until you could almost see yourself in them. Being a navy man my father really knew what "spit and polished" meant. He wanted us to be at our best when we worshipped God.

In our family the Sabbath was strictly observed. A person would have thought my mother invented the "blue laws," prohibiting nearly everything. In this she basically had Dad's support, but his reasons were practical, not moral. The Sabbath was his only full day free from any and all work and we observed it by going to both Sunday school and church. Since Sunday belonged to the Lord, listening to radio preachers like Billy Graham and classical music filled our afternoons. Never was music such as "rock and roll" or games such as football or cards permitted on the Lord's Day. Similarly, even if businesses had been open, we would never have dreamed of shopping on the Sabbath.

Since the weekend was Dad's only free time, he relished spending it with his family in a variety of ways, not the least of which was making pancakes on Saturday morning. To this day, I remember Dad as I use his pancake recipe.

Dad's Pancake Recipe

Ingredients:

2 tbsp. shortening or lard
1 cup buckwheat flour
1 cup white flour
2 tsp. baking powder
1/2 tsp. baking soda
1 egg
1¾ - 2 cups buttermilk
Spray oil

Variation:

2 tbsp. canola oil
1/3 buckwheat, or 1/3 cup oatmeal
1 2/3 cup white flour
2 tsp. baking powder
1 tsp. baking soda
1 egg
1 7/8 cup milk
2 tbsp. plain yoghurt
1 tsp. white vinegar
Spray oil

– Measure about 2 tablespoons shortening into a small pan and melt it on the stove, letting it cool until warm, but not congealing.
– Pour cup buckwheat flour into small bowl, and set it aside.
– Scoop cup of white flour into small bowl, setting it aside.
– Measure out 2 teaspoons baking powder and ½ teaspoon baking soda into small dish, setting them aside.
– Sift together flour, baking powder, and soda into the largest bowl making a hollow in middle of flour mixture.
– In a smaller bowl, beat 2 eggs using mixer. (TIP: A wire whisk would work instead of an electric mixer.)
– Beat 2 cups buttermilk into eggs.
– Combine cooled shortening and milk mixture, mixing well.
– Slowly pour liquid into hollow of dry ingredients, mixing as you pour until there are no lumps. (TIP: You can use a wire whisk for this step, but a mixer set at low speed or a spoon can also be used.)
– At this point, remove beaters (or whisk) from batter and mixer. Place into sink. (TIP: In order to catch drips from beaters or whisk, slip small saucer beneath.)
– Lightly grease griddle. You can use shortening or spray oil.
– Turn burner to medium or medium-high heat. Set griddle on heat source.
– Sprinkle dash of water onto griddle. When it sizzles and pops, griddle is hot enough for batter. Another test for griddle readiness is to drop a teaspoonful of

batter onto it. When it bubbles it is ready. (TIP: If griddle begins to smoke, lower heat and set pan off to side on trivet. When cooled, wipe griddle clean with paper towel and recoat with oil. Reheat skillet or griddle. If griddle is too hot, pancakes will burn on outside and be raw inside.)
– When griddle is at correct temperature, dip 1/3 cup of batter at a time onto it forming 3 pools of pancake batter. Flip when pancakes are evenly bubbling. When bottoms are golden-brown, lift with spatula and slide onto a plate. (TIP: To check for colour and doneness, peek by lifting a bit of pancake edge.)
– To bake a single pancake covering the whole griddle, turn heat on stovetop burner between low and medium, cook until bubbles form all over the pancake top, then flip and cook until underside shows golden brown in colour.
– Serve pancakes hot with steaming syrup, or topping of your choice like honey, ice cream or whipped cream, nuts, or fruit. Repeat cooking process until batter is used up. This makes about a dozen pancakes depending upon the size of the pancake. (TIP: Surplus pancakes may be frozen. Pop into a toaster, toaster oven, or microwave to reheat.)

Dad's Homemade Maple Flavored Syrup

1 cup white granulated sugar
1 cup brown sugar, any type
1 cup water
1 tsp. Mapeleine maple flavoring or 1 tbsp. molasses for flavor

– Pour sugars into pan. Add water. Stir until melted. Heat until liquid boils. Lower heat and let bubble gently to syrup stage.
– Add flavorings and simmer for 5 minutes.
– Serve hot or cold.
– When cooled, syrup may be stored in glass canning jar.

Glenn Kletke

Watering

It's late afternoon and the landscapers
have finished their work, a yard completely
made-over, one of them gathering up
rake, hoe, and other long-handled implements
while the other, in a moment of pride and triumph
sits on the front steps and holds a hose
to water the new and lush and deep green sod.

As father would sit on a summer evening
on his cracked and repainted concrete steps
twin iron railings enclosing him
while the park across the street sent him
the distant and muffled cheers of a baseball game
watering one side of his front yard, then the other
until sun, baseball teams, fans, and cars slipped away.

Last of daylight and his lawn full of sparkles
as if he were inviting the silent and reluctant stars
to come down from heaven's bleachers to join him.

Christine Henderson

More Than Daddy's Little Girl

I consider myself lucky to have been born as the last child to my parents. By the time I was a toddler they had become more at ease with being parents and were a little more flexible or maybe just tired of putting up a fight. Whatever the reason, I was somewhat spoiled by both my parents and grandparents. This meant that my recollections of growing up differ from my older siblings' memories. When they were younger, my dad was putting in a long commute to work and by the time he got home it was almost time for them to go to bed. My experiences were different as he was home for dinner early and had time to spend with me.

I would definitely say I was Daddy's little girl. When he picked me up and sat me on his shoulders, it was as if I owned the world. Once the training wheels were off my bike and I did my first solo ride, he encouraged me with his mantra "You can do it." If I was having trouble with my math homework, Dad would help me through it until it made sense. He helped me to believe anything was possible. Although it was clear that he was my father and not my buddy, he let me know he wanted to hear what I had to say.

By the time I was midway into high school, my other siblings were away at college. I don't know if I thought I was more intelligent and worldly having college age brothers and sisters, but I no longer wanted to be considered Daddy's little girl. It seemed to me that I should now be more akin to his equal.

To the consternation of my mother, this entailed us having rather heated arguments at the dinner table, although my dad and I would more likely have called it merely a vigorous discussion. Politics and religion were not banned from our chats and those were our usual topics. Our talks had their rules though: Dad couldn't say, "I'm right because I'm your father" and I couldn't say, "You're just not keeping up with the times."

Our dialogs followed a loose debate style. When I wanted to make a point, it couldn't merely be my opinion. Dad would say, "Think before you speak. Give me reasons why you believe what you are saying." I had to back it up with logic and facts. At times that was hard for me to do. When I couldn't provide the grounds for my viewpoint, Dad would then table the subject until I did.

Looking back I'm sure at times he was probably laughing inside about the way I made my points but he never showed it. However, decades later I still get teased by my brothers for some of the things I was espousing at the time. My dad, though, made sure I was given the proper respect. He taught me, without knocking me over the head, the concept that I needed to learn to make my own decisions. He didn't want me to be his puppet; nor did he want me to follow the crowd because "everyone was doing it."

Knowing how to make my own decisions paid off when I went away to college. I could stand on my own. While many of my friends were partying a little too much because it was the first time we were away from home, I moderated more. I didn't feel like I had to stay out ultra late or do stupid things just to fit in with the others. My training with my dad also taught me how to debate my professors and come to my own conclusions rather than just parroting their philosophies.

The only downside to being taught to be independent, according to my mother, was the fact that I didn't feel I needed to stay in my old neighborhood. When I got married, my husband and I moved across the country for his continued schooling. Though I might have felt uncertain about being in new surroundings at first, it wasn't long before I made it my home. I didn't feel homesick because I could always pick up the phone to call my dad and say, "I was thinking…"

I will be forever grateful to my dad for teaching me to think on my own. As a result I have been self-employed for years. I've had to be responsible for my own actions and to create my own success. I've also tried to encourage that independent spirit in others. I've done this through the years with the students I have taught at Sunday school. Like my dad, I don't want them to believe something because I say it. I want them to investigate and understand why they believe what they do.

Parents may give their children all the toys or material possessions they could want, but that's not what really matters. When you teach your child self-confidence and self-determination, you give them the opportunity to create a better life for themselves.

Thanks, Dad, for believing in me so I could believe in myself.

Nancy Dobbins

Stepping into the Unknown

The reflections from below caught my eye as I peered out the car window.

"Daddy, look—a lake! Can we stop and swim? I'm tired of sitting in the car. It's boring. There's nothing to do. It's taking forever to get to California!"

My brother and sister pleaded, too, so we headed down the mountain towards the lake. The tires screeched on the gravel as the car swung to a halt. I ran out to the edge of the lake. Dad's hand grasped mine.

"Daddy, let go! I wanna play! Can we get a beach ball somewhere?" But it never happened. He kept striding forward—into the lake.

As I pulled and jerked, some swimmers edged up to him, their faces creased with concern.

"Let her go," they demanded. Their eyes flashed fire. Then my dad spoke. The wind caught his words. Their faces softened and they turned back to toss their beach ball. I chewed on my hair, as my thoughts jumbled.

My dad just continued to squeeze my five-year-old hand and strode across the lake. With each step, I wailed and jerked.

"Daddy, stop! I'm gonna drown!" But he didn't stop. He set his face with grim determination.

A second group splashed over to us. Their blotchy faces and their challenging tone seared my mind with chaotic thoughts.

"Let her go!"

Dad spoke and their glares turned to wobbly smiles. I stared. My face turned red. I pulled harder. My piercing screams echoed in the lake. Silence fell. Faces scrutinized us. My father still refused to let go.

A third group surged through the water. A serene white-haired man followed in the rear. "Let her go," the group demanded.

The white-haired man lightly placed his arm on one swimmer and pushed into the group. "Let me handle this," he said. His look of love and kindness soothed my spirit. I gazed at him in wonder, open-mouthed. He spoke gently in low tones to my father. My dad's answer was caught by the wind.

Then the group held hands and closed their eyes. Their words were muffled by the wind too.

Dad let go of my arm and walked to the center of the lake, beckoning me to come to him. As I walked to him, I looked around me in wonder. "But Daddy, I'm not drowning."

"That's right, honey. Look around. Who's swimming?"

"No one. They're all standing up."

"You know why? The lake is shallow."

"What's 'shallow,' Daddy?"

"That means 'not deep.' See? The water comes only to the middle of my leg. Do you know why the people's angry faces changed so fast? 'Cause I told them 'She's afraid of the water.' They all smiled 'cause they wanted you to get over your fear.

"Remember the group that stood in a circle? They prayed for both of us. They wanted you to get over your fear too.

"Now can you see why I wanted you to hold my hand and walk across the lake? It was to help you get over your fear. Before we even started, I saw everyone standing. Then I knew the lake was shallow. I could see the end of the lake 'cause I'm taller than you."

He grinned and his eyes danced. "Can you make yourself as big as me? Stretch and see." I strained and stretched as high as I could.

"But Daddy, you know I can't."

"Here, let me help you." His hands plunged into the water, splashing me playfully. He beamed, then lifted me high above his head.

Later, I earned my "Guppy Swimmer Badge." I beamed with pride every time people saw it. It meant that I could swim in the deep end of any pool. Without my father's grit to break my fear, I couldn't have done it. He helped me step into the unknown with victory.

When I was five, I couldn't see where my steps would lead me. My father could. I misunderstood his purpose in taking me where I thought I'd be hurt, but his determination helped me conquer a major fear.

Later this helped me in my spiritual life. Sometimes I resist my heavenly Father like I did my earthly father's steps. But I found that God can see beyond my limited vision and He knows what's ahead. When I put my hand in His, He faithfully guides me.

Claudia Loopstra

The Better Offer

After Mom died in 1995, I drove one hundred kilometers, twice monthly, to my hometown to visit my father. He and Mom had lived in Sunset Haven nursing home for six years.

Dad turned ninety-two in March 1996. By then, he'd lost a lot of weight. His face had become so thin he could draw his chin up to his nose. The absence of teeth helped with this achievement. He seemed to enjoy the amusement he created among the nursing staff. Despite his physical discomfort, my father's sense of humour stayed with him until the last few months of his life.

"Watch this," he'd say whenever staff gathered nearby. Dad would suck in his lips, jut out his white-whiskered jaw, and raise his chin to meet his nose. He would hold this position until the staff applauded his feat.

My father always enjoyed his ability to make people laugh. Playing the clown to a captive audience was a favorite activity.

Dad was both funny and smart. Although he had only an eighth-grade education, he was a voracious reader. His mild dementia did not impair his spelling ability. The nurses on Dad's floor bragged about how he would win all of the spelling bees during patient activity time. You'd think it had been their own personal achievement, the way they went on about him. I often wondered if my "whiz kid" dad had been creating some heavy betting.

"Spell estimate," my daughter's fiancé said to Dad once when Melinda and Tim were visiting. Melinda had told Tim about Grandpa's spelling bee successes.

"E-s-t-i-m-a-t-e."

"Spell severance," urged Tim.

"S-e-v-e-r-a-n-c-e."

For the next five minutes, Tim kept tossing out increasingly challenging words.

"Spell supercalefragilisticexpealidocious."

"Go to hell!" Dad said as he spun his wheelchair around and headed for his room.

Tim looked bewildered.

"I warned you not to mess with Grandpa," Melinda admonished.

* * *

During his last year of life, one of Dad's chronic conditions was constipation.

"Dad," I said, during a visit, "I know you're feeling terrible because your bowels haven't moved lately, and you may have to have an enema which you hate. Would you like me to pray with you about it?"

He turned from me and gazed straight ahead as though waiting for me to make him a better offer. I was a firm believer in the power of prayer and he was not. He didn't refuse, so I took his hand in mine, closed my eyes, and asked God to relieve him of his discomfort.

When I opened my eyes, Dad sat staring at me.

"That's a lot of shit," he said.

"Time for me to go, Dad," I said as I gave him a hug and squeezed his arm. "Love you—see you in two weeks."

"Yar," he responded.

What a character.

* * *

May 4, 1997, the night before Dad passed away, Melinda and I sat with him in his room. Although he had slipped into unconsciousness, we took turns holding his hand and singing "Jesus Loves Me." Above his head was a wall plaque displaying the 23rd Psalm. We read it to Dad, hoping it would somehow bring him comfort.

When we'd said good night to the nursing staff, Melinda and I drove to a local hotel. We had asked the nurse not to call if Dad died during the night. There would be much to do in making funeral arrangements, and we needed to sleep.

On May 5th, I awoke at 7:00 a.m. and made the phone call.

"Your father passed away at 2:00 a.m."

I held the phone still for a second.

"I'll be there shortly to collect his belongings."

The loss of my father didn't bring tears to my eyes. He'd been a difficult man, an alcoholic, and although I'd forgiven him for the turmoil he'd caused in our family, I didn't cry over his death.

When Melinda and I walked to the elevator at the nursing home, we met Dad's nurse coming off her shift.

We're going to miss your dad," she said as she embraced me. "Your dad—he was so much fun and so—religious."

"Religious?"

"Yes, he was always singing hymns. 'Abide with Me' was a favorite."

"It was?"

Golly, he had more sides to him than a Rubik's cube. HAD he considered Jesus the better offer?

* * *

For Dad's funeral, I arranged for a cousin, a choir member, to sing "Abide with Me."

The day before the service, I received a phone call from Larry, a hometown funeral director. He had once been my boyfriend.

"Hi Claudia," he greeted. "We can't bury your father tomorrow after the service. The ground is too soft. We'll have to hold him here until we're given the go-ahead at the cemetery."

"How long will that be?"

"No more than a week. I'll call you."

Three weeks later—still waiting.

I visualized my Dad and Larry in the mortuary, having a beer together, while swapping jokes.

Day twenty-two, the phone rang.

"Hi, Claudia," said Larry in an overly upbeat tone. "Your dad has to be buried tomorrow."

"Tomorrow! I don't think I'll be able to get pallbearers on such short notice. Everyone will be working."

"Don't worry. We'll take care of all the details," he said.

He was never trustworthy when we dated. Can I trust him now?

I proceeded to phone my family. As I suspected, no one could make it. When I called Larry and left him a message, he didn't return my call.

It figures.

May 28th was a warm, sunny spring day; the day of my sister's birthday and Melinda's wedding anniversary. We were all dressed up as though we were about to celebrate both.

A small group gathered at the funeral home. The mourners included my brother, Carl; my sisters Patricia and Shirley; Melinda; my parents' two best friends, Violet and Scotty (who were well into their nineties); Rev. Thorpe; and me. Of the ten, only two men were from the funeral home.

The others must be waiting at the cemetery.

Dad's casket was already in the hearse. We were told the order in which to follow the lead car. The procession began up the three city streets that led to the cemetery.

As we slowly travelled along the route, I commented to Melinda on the fact that cars had pulled over and stopped as our procession passed "Your grandfather would be beaming if he could witness the respect that had eluded him all of his life."

I took my daughter's hand in mine as we both continued to stare out of the window. On the day of his burial, I wanted to remember only the things that I had loved about Dad.

The minister—a man in his seventies—greeted us as we got out of the car. He held the Anglican *Book of Common Prayer* from which he would read for the committal of Dad's body. Although Dad rarely went to church, Mom had gone every Sunday. When Rev. Thorpe had conducted my mother's funeral, he had consented to do Dad's when the time came. Now he stood respectfully solemn by the hearse as he waited for the pallbearers to remove Dad's casket.

Two men from the funeral home opened the back doors of the hearse as we all gathered around. "Would the pallbearers please step forward for the carrying of the casket?" one man requested.

Silence.

I looked at Shirley who then looked at Patricia; Patricia turned and looked at Carl, who looked at Melinda, who shrugged her shoulders and looked at me.

Melinda and I stepped forward in unison as though we had been rehearsing this very moment.

Counting the men from the funeral home, the number of pallbearers had reached four. Two more were needed.

Carl stepped forward next. We all looked around. Shirley and Patricia were huddled together as though they were in the middle of an Alaskan winter deep freeze, while Violet and Scotty seemed to be taking it all in their stride.

The minister handed his prayer book to Scotty and stepped forward to become the sixth pallbearer.

There we were, an unlikely group of pallbearers, gingerly stepping our way through the thick grass to Dad's place of burial.

A voice came from behind me. "Psst. You're standing in the wrong place."

"Huh?"

"His feet have to be the other way. You have the head where the feet should be," said the guy from the funeral home.

"Let's turn now, Melinda," I whispered.

"My heel's stuck."

"No, it's not! You're fine. Move slowly."

Finally, we lowered the casket and set it down over Dad's grave.

Rev. Thorpe turned to Scotty who handed him back the prayer book, and he began—

"For as much as it has pleased Almighty God of his great mercy to take unto himself our dear brother departed; we therefore, commit his body to the ground…"*

* *The Book of Common Prayer, 1962, Canada, p. 600*

Millie Barger

Dad's Old Sweater

I remember the sweater my dad loved best to wear,
It always hung on a peg under the kitchen stair;
He liked to wear that sweater when he went into town,
Just an ordinary sweater of deep, dark brown.

Whenever he came home, we kids raced to meet him,
We hunted through his pockets as we'd fondly greet him.
Peanuts were the treasure we looked for in that sweater;
Sometimes we found chocolate drops—they were even better.

Later, when all alone, I'd slip under the stair,
And search in the pockets of that old, brown sweater there.
I sniffed the good aroma that lingered on and on,
Sometimes finding peanuts that supposedly were gone.

When fancy turns the clock back to childhood's mem'ry store,
I think of Dad's old sweater, then I see him once more
Bringing love in his pockets when he came home from town,
In an ordinary sweater of deep, dark brown.

Diane K. Ellenwood

Just Ask

You might say I was a bit of a grandpa's girl growing up. Oftentimes I would shadow him as he busied himself around the house, at one time nearly getting myself plastered to the wall that he papered. Grandma caught him just in time with a shout, "Watch out for Pete!" I'd hide under the table and use Grandpa's shoelaces to learn to tie my own. Later, I could hear Grandpa say, "Now where did Pete put my shoelaces?" Couldn't he see I left them near his shoes?

If you ask my siblings, however, they might tell you I was Daddy's girl. I went to work with him when I was three and four years old. Soon I learned all the tools in his toolbox by name and could hand him the one he needed for the job at hand.

I learned early that all I had to do was ask my dad for what I wanted and he always said yes. I was so good at asking and getting that my sister would send me to ask for her too!

When I was in my junior year in high school, the principal wouldn't give me my report card. I had been to the school several times before I went to my dad and told him. My dad called the school and told them he expected to see the report card in the mail in two days or some heads were going to roll! In two days, my report card was delivered by the postman. What I tried to do on my own, my father was able to do with one phone call. He had the authority; I just needed to ask.

Many children don't have a father in their lives today. Too many times their stepparents don't want them either. And I wonder, how are they supposed to relate to a heavenly Father, if they don't know what a father is?

John 15:16 says that "whatever you ask the Father in My name He may give you." Like my earthly father, He has the authority. All I have to do is ask.

Diane K. Ellenwood

A Father's Heart

He lays his hands on their heads and prays
He wipes away their tears each day
He promises his child as long as he lives
Protection, devotion, and care he will give

A father is found on his knees to pray
Each night they sleep safely as they lay
He blesses his children as they grow
For in his heart he comes to know

The life that he lives, his children will see
When they are old, it is what they will be

Don E. Cunningham

Secure in My Father's Love

As a young child I was very insecure when the challenges of life confronted me and I depended on my father's protective arms. Four instances of his comforting and guiding influence linger in the recesses of my mind.

I remember going to a semipro baseball game with him, and sitting to his right along the third baseline. One of the players hit a hard line drive that came thundering toward me. It hit me in the stomach and I rolled off the front row bleacher, writhing breathless on the ground. As I tried to regain my breath, tears started to flow down my cheeks. Without mentioning the tears or telling me boys don't cry, Dad helped me to my feet, brushed me off, and said, "Don, I am so proud of you. Look at you. That big slugger hit the ball as hard as he could and you're standing up. I bet that would have knocked me down, too, and I might not have gotten up as quickly as you did. You deserve a bag of popcorn." He walked over to the horse-drawn, red popcorn wagon and bought a bag of butter-coated popcorn. He turned the pain into gain!

We lived about halfway between Powers and Whipple Schools. All of my brothers and sisters attended Powers. The school district was considering transferring me to Whipple to balance out the classroom count. I was petrified of going to a different school than my brothers and sister attended.

Dad went to Dr. Trehurne, the superintendent of schools, and pled my case. At the superintendent's urging the school board decided to leave the border between the schools where they were. Dad saved the day not only for me, but for another frightened young boy on our block.

The third time my father rescued me, in what to me was one of the most frightening experiences, was when my favorite childless aunt and uncle invited me over to their house to spend the night. It was the first night I had ever been away from home.

After enjoying a great dinner, playing games, and listening to the radio my aunt tucked me into bed for the night. I fell asleep, but was awakened in the middle of the night by a nightmare. My aunt and uncle ran in and tried to comfort me.

It was well past midnight when they phoned my father. Since we didn't have a car and the buses had stopped running for the night, he walked the three miles to their house. The minute he entered the house, I ran to him—my fears gone. He thanked my aunt and uncle for calling him and apologized for my behavior. Then he picked me up in his arms, wiped away my tears, and carried me all the way home. It was my first and last overnight stay.

My friend, Johnny, and I enjoyed going up to the Boston and Maine railroad line to wave to Johnny's father who was a fireman on a steam-powered locomotive. When diesels began to replace them, he was promoted to engineer. We loved going up the tracks to wave to his dad and hear the sound of the thunderous locomotive, the blast of the whistle as it approached the trestle, the sucking feeling of the cars as the train roared by. One day while we were waiting for the train to roll into sight, we began pushing each other around near the trestle. I fell backward and split my head open on a concrete abutment. I held my hand over the bleeding gash while we rushed home. My father, who had just returned home for lunch, picked me up in his arms and ran a block and a half to the emergency room at the Leonard Hospital. The emergency room personnel cleaned the wound, sewed it up, and bandaged it.

We returned home, ate lunch, and Dad took me to work with him. He showed all of the workers in the bank and police station my bandaged head and bragged about how brave I had been. He even told the bank president, Mr. Cobden, how proud he was of me. Once again he took something that could have made me feel insecure and turned me into a hero!

The following Saturday, Mr. Cobden invited my father and me to his mansion, and took us down into his huge basement. A large olive drab green bike was hanging from one of the beams. He took it down and asked me if I would like to try riding it. After he adjusted the seat for me, I got onto the bike and my father and Mr. Cobden took turns steadying it as I gradually learned to ride. When I finally was able to balance on it by myself, Mr. Cobden told me his son was away at college and had no further need for it. He knew his son would want a brave young lad like me to have it. I was elated, and thanked him for it.

He smiled at me and acknowledged my gratefulness. Then he walked into another area of his basement and came back with a wooden pogo stick. Handing it to my father, he said I could also have that. What a blessed day it was! I was secure in my father's love and the beneficiary of a rich man's blessings. How I cherished my bicycle and pogo stick. A few months later my father died, leaving me with these tokens and memorials of his love.

Debbie Schmid

Safe in Daddy's Arms

In the wee hours of a crisp December morning, a nurse placed me in my father's strong loving arms for the very first time. Three days after Christmas, Daddy's little girl had arrived. And the glow on his face was evidence that he adored his precious daughter, cradled safe in Daddy's arms.

Twelve months later, on Christmas Eve, a picture of us together portrays the story of a frightened little girl. Santa's bright red suit and long, white flowing beard was truly a dreadful sight! Although my face was painted with fear, Daddy was smiling as he held me snug. Almost one year old, but too young to understand; I was safe in Daddy's arms.

At four years of age, while carrying me out to the car, Dad accidently slipped on the ice and we tumbled down a flight of stairs. Consequently, my front tooth was injured in the process, and shortly thereafter, it turned black and fell out. My injuries could have been so much worse, but that blustery winter night, I was safe in Daddy's arms.

As a result of my congenital heart/lung disease, I often struggled to survive. One afternoon while fighting for life, Dad rushed out to the garage and hauled my oxygen tank into the house. Despite my resistance, I remember him frantically working to secure the face mask over my nose and mouth. Once he got me situated, I stopped gasping for breath and calmed down. Then Daddy picked me up and held my frail body close to his heart until the paramedics arrived. On the brink of death, I was safe in Daddy's arms.

During the winter, when it was too cold for Dad to work outdoors laying brick, I remember him in the kitchen making homemade chicken noodle soup and freshly baked cinnamon rolls. More often than not, I sat on the counter so I could get a better view of his creative cooking. Oh, what special treats he made!

Over the years, Dad and I also planted a summer garden. When the crops came in, we canned homegrown dill pickles together. After the pickles cured, I remember snuggling with him on the sofa. While watching sports on television, we often devoured a whole jar of pickles, just between the two of us! Dad and I agreed: They were better than any bowl of popcorn we had ever tasted.

Riding with him in his red antiquated Diamond-T truck was exciting and fun. The horn went "Oooga, Oooga" as we traveled down the snowy country roads one frigid winter morning. When we got to our destination, he wrapped me in blankets and gently carried me into a house where he was building a beautiful stone fireplace. To this day, I thoroughly enjoy sitting beside a warm fire, while thinking about the tender moments we shared together.

As time would have it, years passed and I became a teen. Unfortunately, Dad was absent more often than not during those pivotal years in my life. If he happened to be home and sober at the same time, he was attentive to some of the things I was wrestling with. As a result, I felt at ease talking to him about the painful struggles I was going through.

One summer evening, while walking from work to the train station to meet my neighbor so I could ride home with her, a classmate stepped out from behind a tree and threatened to kill me. The knife was pulled and the chase was on! If I hadn't run in front of the train and over the tracks before the train stopped at the station, I may not be here today. My adversary was momentarily blocked, giving me an opportunity to run between traffic and hide under my neighbor's parked car on the other side of the tracks.

When I got home that night, Dad was relaxing next to the fireplace in his bright orange recliner. The moment I entered the house, he knew something was terribly wrong. When I told him what happened, anger burned in his eyes. He immediately got up and rushed out the door.

A few weeks later, Dad hugged me tight. He told me that the evening I was chased, he had gone looking for my enemy. When he found him walking along the side of the main road towards town, he pulled over and chased that young man through a cornfield! As they ran, my dad shot bullets into the sky and kept yelling, "If you ever threaten my daughter again, I'll hunt you down with my rifle!" No need to worry about me. I was safe in Daddy's arms.

Approximately twenty years later, my late husband, Tom, was diagnosed with lung cancer. As we faced the heartache of Tom's illness, I struggled to take care of my dying husband, our young daughter, Kylea, and our family business. At that juncture in time, Dad was retired, so he came to Tucson to help me out. Even though I was a grown woman with a family of my own, the moment he embraced me, my heart melted and I felt comforted. Once again, I was safe in Daddy's arms.

In early December, six-and-a-half years after Tom's passing, Kylea and I were blessed with the opportunity to travel back to Illinois to spend some quality time with my dad and stepmom. When the plane landed at the Chicago O'Hare International Airport, large fluffs of falling snow graced our arrival. Every evening during our stay, we sat around a warm fire in the fireplace, talking about the joys we remembered while sharing our lives together.

Even though at that time my dad was going through another round of radiation, he kept reassuring me. "Debbie, I feel good about this. Everything is going to be just fine." His positive attitude in the face of cancer was such an encouragement to me.

But when it came time for us to return to Arizona, Dad was terribly ill and failing fast. Although his weakened hug was one of inner strength and courage, I knew in my heart the end was drawing near. While holding each other close, I suspected that this would be our last embrace. Even so, I was still safe in Daddy's arms.

Two weeks later, the pending call came. This was the third time in seventeen years I had lost a significant man in my life due to lung cancer. This dreadful disease first claimed the life of my maternal grandfather, then my husband, and eventually my dad.

In a hurried rush, my daughter and I packed our suitcases and began our long drive from Arizona to Illinois. The further north we got, the more the chill of winter set in. That year, Christmas Day was spent in the minivan listening to Christmas carols, munching on finger foods, and praying we would find another service station open for business before running out of gas.

Prior to taps at my dad's final resting place, I was blessed with an opportunity to share these same memories with family and friends. Three days after Christmas, exactly forty-five years after our journey together began, it was time for my final good-bye. Although Dad is now gone from my sight, he will always live on in my heart. From the day of my birth until the day of his passing, I was his little girl, safe in Daddy's arms.

Dill Pickle Recipe

Wash small cucumbers with brush under cold water. Pack in canning jar using small piece of garlic at bottom and top of jar. Add pinch of powdered alum and sprig of dill to each jar. Fill jars to the top with boiling solution of 1 quart cider vinegar, 1 cup salt, and 3 quarts water. Seal jars at once.

Cinnamon Rolls Recipe

1 cup milk
1 pkg. dry yeast
½ cup lukewarm water
1 tsp. sugar
6 cups flour
1/3 cup sugar
1½ tsp. salt
1/3 cup shortening
1 cup lukewarm water
brown sugar
cinnamon
powdered sugar
milk
vanilla

Scald milk (do not boil). Set aside to cool to lukewarm. Add dry yeast to half cup lukewarm water to which sugar has been added. Let stand for 10 minutes. Sift flour into large bowl. Add sugar, salt, and shortening. Add milk, yeast mixture, and 1 cup lukewarm water. Mix all together. Put on floured board and knead until smooth. Put in greased bowl and set in warm place to rise until doubled in size, about 1½ hours. Knead down and let rise again. Roll half the dough to ½" thickness. Spread with soft butter. Sprinkle with brown sugar and cinnamon; about ¾ cup. Roll up like a jelly roll and cut into 1" slices. Put on greased tin and let rise. Bake 30-35 minutes in 350° preheated oven. Spread with powdered sugar icing while still hot. (Icing consists of powdered sugar, milk, and vanilla.)

This dough also makes plain dinner rolls without cinnamon and brown sugar.

Carolyn Brown Copeland

My Father Never Told Me He Loved Me

Following the death of my grandfather, my father revealed a vulnerable side of himself never before expressed when one day, shortly after the funeral, he tearfully blurted out, "My father never told me he loved me."

The confession marked the end of a sixty-eight-year father/son relationship and I wondered somberly: Why do fathers and sons find it so hard to voice their love for each other?

The love existed. I knew it did. But how do you convince a person of that reality when the source of the love is forever silenced?

My grandfather, though small of stature, was head of his family—a typical authoritarian patriarch of the Old World German tradition. Not the jovial, fun-loving grandfather whose lap you climbed into when you came for a visit. He farmed for a living. After a long, hard day in the fields, he was exhausted. The last thing he wanted in his lap was a fidgety grandchild. Grandpa might be best described as "steady" or "responsible." During the height of the Depression years he eked out a living for his family of ten children on the bare necessities of land.

Warmth, love, and emotion were not his qualities. These, I think, he felt belonged to the female members of the household, for he had grown up in an era when it was not masculine to "show emotion."

Thus, it was no mystery that my father wondered if his father loved him. Perhaps all his brothers and sisters wondered the same thing. But only my father expressed the concern to me.

Dad was the oldest of the ten children, and in the qualities of love and emotion, he was uniquely like his own father. Hugging and kissing his wife or his children, or telling them how much he loved them, were acts he avoided. Yet, before the advent of television, I recall playing board games and card games with my father during cold Wisconsin winter evenings. I wondered now if his father had ever played games with him, or if there was no time for such "foolishness" in his young life.

When I first heard Dad's misery over this deep disappointment in life, I wanted to lecture, "If it was really so all-important for you to know, why didn't you ask?"

Grandpa was not young when he died. He was ninety-three years old and had been ill for many years. The opportunity to make the initial overture toward love was just as available to Dad as it was to Grandpa. "Why didn't you make him voice his love?" I wanted to demand, but I didn't because I had been taught to honor my parents. And talking in such a manner would not have been respectful.

Instead, my heart went out to him in his grief, remembering when I, too, wondered if my father loved me. I was just fifteen when I confronted Dad. It was not a confrontation of love, it was a jealous challenge. "You don't love me at all," I accused, charging that he only loved my younger sister, a baby at the time, who was receiving an overabundance of his attention.

Tears welled in Dad's eyes—the first time I had ever really seen him show that kind of emotion. He wrapped his arms around me—awkwardly—for he was not accustomed to expressing sentiment in any physical, tangible way. For a moment, he just held me close, the rivets of his bib overalls biting into my cheek. Then with a huskiness in his voice, he said the words I'll never forget, "I love you all the same."

Not that he loved me more or less than my brothers or my sister, but that he loved us all the same—no favorites. In my youthful adolescent rebellion, those were important words to hear.

As my mind flashed backward to that incident, I wanted now to reward my father for that simple confession of love—to return to him the hope that love, although often unspoken, still does exist.

And so I challenged my father, "Did you ever tell your dad you loved him? And have you told your sons you love them? Does that make the love less real? When you die, will your sons also wonder if their father loved them?"

He didn't answer, of course. I didn't expect him to, but I thought I saw a flicker of understanding in his eyes. He loved his sons the same way his father loved him, yet he, too, found it difficult to voice that love. For the first time in his life, perhaps, he understood love from his father's point of view.

Several years have passed since my father and I held that conversation. I know that Dad still hasn't told his sons he loves them. As death draws near, will he discard the custom that brainwashes men to believe masculine love toward one another should not be expressed, or is the ghost of tradition so firmly ingrained that, like his father, he will die with the words in his heart, but not on his lips?

This summer while I was home for a visit, Dad announced to my oldest brother, Harold, that he wanted to take him and his wife, Jean, out to dinner for Harold's birthday a few weeks away. This may not sound like much of an overture of love unless you understand that Dad dislikes eating in restaurants, but he knows Harold loves to try new eating places.

It is only a small crack in the wall of tradition, but tiny cracks have tumbled mighty buildings.

Patricia Anne Elford

There You Are!

It was a moment of joy for a proud father. Each morning, he scooped their daughter, Patricia, up into the wooden highchair. Each morning, he exclaimed, "There you are!" as he plunked her down on the seat. One morning, during the daily scoop, she beat him to it. "There you are!" Her very first words.

Her father was there for her, not just then, but for as long as he lived.

Who talked with her and listened while he prepared the tea in the cream and green enamelled pot before Mom's busy day began? Who once read to her nightly, snuggled up in the big chair, from the one-a-day children's Bible story and story time books?

Who walked her gaggle of girlfriends home with her after each birthday party Mom had so carefully planned? Who taught her to love the pet cats and took on the task of burying them when they died? Who taught her to walk on stilts he'd made and to shoot hand-whittled arrows from a bow he'd fashioned? Who taught her how to use a jackknife? Who put the worms on her hook for catching sunfish and trout with the bamboo poles? There he was!

Who fastened the cleats onto her worn shoes using a shoemaker's anvil, created a just-right doll's wardrobe with a door handle made from an old shoe's tiny buckle, built her a desk, a bookshelf, then a hope chest? There he was!

Who played arithmetic games with her to help her with her personal challenge? Who taught her to play crokinole, checkers, and card games? Who taught her to skate on the backyard rink and pointed out Orion in the clear sky? Who helped her to know one tree from another and which tree gum was good to chew? Who taught her which plants could be used to heal and what would fight a bee's sting? Who walked her home from the Teen dances, but went home another way if she had an escort? There he was!

Who waited in frigid, soggy, or scorching weather to meet her at the bus or train each time she returned from the city? Who reminded her of her commitment when her marriage was failing but welcomed her home when it ended?

He practised active listening before the phrase was coined. He practised compassion. He practised loving presence. Despite life's trials, he made it easy to believe in an even greater Creator Father.

One night, years after she had remarried, she awoke in the middle of the night. She was frozen, icy cold in her very being. She couldn't get warm, no matter how many blankets or cuddles her husband provided.

The next morning, too early for comfort, the phone rang. Her husband answered. Her mom asked him to break the news that her father had died. He'd died at the very time Patricia had been too cold for warming. Beyond all comprehension and understanding, as he'd died— even then— there he was—my father.

Debbie Carpenter

Weekend Walks with Dad

Some things that happened in my youth
Have surely slipped my mind.
However there are moments
I will never leave behind.

I think of bygone days with Dad
And camping in the pines,
When stories told around a fire
Sent shivers up my spine.

I reflect on Christmas morning
When I'd open up my eyes
And find that he had planned for me
A wonderful surprise.

And other times I won't forget
While thinking of my dad,
Were weekend walks with little talks
And all the fun we had.

We'd roam the desert singing songs,
We made up our own words.
Sometimes we'd stop and listen
To the singing of the birds.

We'd hope to see some wildlife
Appear along the trails.
Our favorite things were rabbits
For we liked their cottontails.

Then my dad would share with me,
The things that he had read,
About the desert way of life
As on and on we tread.

Like all good things the time would pass,
Our stroll would have to end.
We'd keep these happy memories
Until we walked again.

Donna Clark Goodrich

Singing for Our Dad

In days gone by we'd gather 'round
The piano we once had,
We'd sing the songs we children liked,
Then up would speak our dad:
"Sing this one song," he used to say,
"I sang it as a lad."
He'd hum a bit of a favorite song,
And we'd sing it for our dad:

> *Amazing grace! how sweet the sound,*
> *That sav'd a wretch like me!*
> *I once was lost, but now am found,*
> *Was blind, but now I see.**

The years passed by; we moved away,
Then a call came on the phone,
"Your dad is sick," and once again
We gathered at our home.
"Please sing for me," his voice was weak.
"The words I do not know,
But let me hear you sing again
As you did so long ago."

> *Precious mem'ries, how they linger,*
> *How they ever flood my soul,*
> *In the stillness of the midnight,*
> *Precious, sacred scenes unfold.***

A year went by, then one more call.
"Your dad won't last the night."
We caught the plane, but he was gone
'Ere we could end our flight.
But though he's gone, those words he said,
I still can dimly hear,
"Please sing for me, just one more time,
This song I love so dear."

When I get to the end of the way,
I will rest at the close of the day,
And the toils of the road will seem nothing,
*When I get to the end of the way.****

Yes, now he's gone, but one glad day,
We'll meet him on that shore,
Our family all will gather 'round,
And we shall part no more.
We'll laugh and cry and reminisce
Of memories we once had.
And then, for all eternity,
We'll sit and sing with Dad.

Will the circle be unbroken
By and by, Lord, by and by,
In a better home awaiting
*In the sky, Lord, in the sky.*****

* *"Amazing Grace," John Newton*
** *"Precious Memories," J.B.F.W. & Lonnie B. Combs*
*** *"When I Get to the End of the Way," Charles D. Tillman*
**** *"Will the Circle Be Unbroken," Ada R. Habershon*

Connie Johnson

Reflection

You were the one with thick wavy hair,
I was the daughter with a head of natural curls.

You were the one who fixed flat tires in the driveway,
I was the one who sat in the sand and asked,
"Why ruff up the edges? How much glue? When can we put in the air?"

You were the one who said "No" followed by a silent lecture,
I was the one who felt bad and understood every unsaid sentence.

You were the proud one riding the John Deere tractor, cutting, raking, bailing hay,
I was the one ready to hike and bird, leaving dishes and kitchens far behind.

You were the one showing off your new car, complaining, "It isn't red."
I was wearing red, thinking someday I too will drive a car.

You were the one who nightly dished out whisker rubs between spoonfuls of cornflakes,
I am the one remembering your laughter as I fill my bowl with Cheerios before bedtime.

You were the one who wanted cowboy boots and hat for your birthday,
I am the one, years later, collecting hats and boots, even one red pair.

You were the one who taught yourself to play the harmonica,
I am the one who listens to those distant notes, as I write.

Gail M. Murray

This Was My Father

Dedicated to William F. John Carr
February 7, 1915–April 12, 1996

This was my father
strong and robust
tanned and smiling
patient and dependable
at home in orchard and barn
tending crops and animals
driving the tractor,
gathering hay,
ploughing fields
in harmony with the natural world
living compassion.

This was my father
helping with homework
encouraging with gentle praise
picking me up from Brownies
and later from high school dances
previewing college calendars
guiding a future
proud of his daughter the graduate
teaching on financial matters
fostering a business sense
laying the foundation for success
beyond school and family
a loving father
always there; selfless, strong.

This is my father today
silent and sightless, wheelchair restrained
frail and vulnerable, attention span fleeting
mind wandering, conjuring fantasies
beyond nursing home blandness
escaping daily monotony
his life a jumble of memories without index.

With childlike anticipation he asks
"What did you bring me?"
As a little girl, I'd ask that same question
as he'd scoop me into his sturdy arms.

Flavour is all he has left
the sweetness of chocolate
the tartness of tangerine
textures of flaky piecrust and aged cheddar
smooth summer fresh berries
little treats gratefully acknowledged
Still there is the recognition
he identifies my voice
knows my love surrounds him
reflected in precious moments on sunlight patios.

"We're having a nice time, aren't we?" he offers
He is lucid today, initiating and following conversation
together we enjoy life's small moments
glimmers of bygone years touch my heartstrings
for inside lives the strong loving father
this child once knew.

Jaclyn Piudik

Kisielin

for my father

When our speedboat pulled my father
across the surface of the lake on his skis
he carried himself as if this were the life

he truly wanted, as if his voice were
not lost behind the whirring engine
of a 70 horsepower motor in this resort

town being overrun now by Hassidim
reminding him of his childhood in Poland.
The ice skates he carved from pieces of

wood, he hid somewhere in the forest
so his father would never know that
he was gliding on ponds, swinging

on trees, falling in creeks, when he
should have been milking cows, reading
Torah, learning to be a cantor so that

he could cant like his father couldn't.
But he stashed food to eat on Yom Kippur
in those skates tucked under a fallen

tree trunk. Perhaps if he weren't such a rebel
he'd be wearing black robes in Jerusalem,
davening, chanting prayers in his mother tongue.

Under the wig that she wore, his mother
seemed to speak to another. She sat
next to the hearth mending worn out socks

with the holes he skated his way through,
saying nothing. She saw the skates on her walks
to the village, heard the shrieks on the swing

as her son flew amidst the branches of
the only wonderland a poor boy could know
in that Eastern European town where
milk doesn't grow on trees.

Richard M. Grove

Proud with a Flashlight

I stood with a flashlight,
poised,
pointing into the deep,
cool, black hole,
where my dad was working.
It was late and well past dinner time,
all others had eaten long ago,
but we men were still working.

I was proud to be a man,
with my dad at that moment,
even though only 13 and still quite a boy.
I was proud,
to be of service even with a humble task.

My job was simple,
shine a beam of light
into that six foot deep hole
where my dad was crouched
so he could hook up the plumbing
that was rooted deep beneath the surface
in the primordial earth
that fed from the barn.

He was dirty and hungry.
I was tired and hungry.
I was proud,
to be a man,
with my dad that night.

Connie Kinnell McKinney

Daddy's Shoes

a letter to my father

Dear Dad,

Perhaps, you did not know I saw you do it. But, I did. Perhaps, you did not realize that such a mundane act could touch a child's heart in some way. But, it did.

You see, children notice things and they learn from their parents; from their weaknesses, true, but also from their strengths. You taught me something special without even knowing it. So, sit down for a bit and I'll tell you about it.

Some of the favorite things in my life, as I grew up, were the little traditions we wove into our weekends. Do you remember the Sunday night trios? They were the three "Ps" known as pizza, popcorn, and Pepsi, along with the TV trio known as "Lawrence Welk," "Lassie," and "The Ed Sullivan Show." We enjoyed these traditions for many years. I have to let you know now, Dad, that Lassie was enjoyable and Ed Sullivan was OK, especially when Topo Gigio appeared, but your three daughters still can't quite understand your fond attachment to Lawrence Welk and his bubbly band. To this day, a bottle of bubbles blown into the wind dredges up memories akin to some long lost episode of "The Twilight Zone."

As for that mundane act I mentioned earlier, well, it was included in another traditional trio you performed every Saturday. Perhaps you don't remember the routine now, but this is what a little girl's heart remembers her father doing. First, depending upon the season, you would always drag out the little push mower and mow our yard, or perform some other necessary task. Next, while you were still covered in a healthy dose of sweat, you would get out a big bucket, drag out the garden hose, fill the bucket with soapy water, and wash the family car. Sometimes, you would even let your girls "help," but I'm afraid those were times we probably got cleaner than the car! Finally, you'd come in and get cleaned up, then get out your dress shoes and polish them to a pretty shine. I knew what this meant. It meant that you were getting ready for church the next day. So why was this simple, even mundane act, so special? After all these years, it's time to tell you what you taught me so long ago.

You and mom were always faithful to take your little brood to church every Sunday. At the time, I didn't always appreciate going, especially if the pastor got a little too long-winded in my opinion, and I'd wind up looking long and hard at every line and part of each stain-glassed window. But, the routine taught me faithfulness to goodness and to God. Watching you polish your shoes instilled in me that, on the next day, we would be going to a special place, to worship a special God and His Son, Jesus. It prepared my heart to believe in God, whom I found out also had a Father's heart for me. One special Sunday, after a children's sermon, I asked Jesus to come into my heart. He did and I was reborn into His family. That day was my second birthday and I'll never forget it. Now, I have and enjoy two fathers—my earthly father and my heavenly Father.

Today, we live in a world where suits and jeans, polished shoes, and flip-flops may often co-mingle in the same church, worshiping the same Savior. I've learned, in God's eyes, this is all right. For He is still the same Father who "so loved the world." He looks right past the outside person and straight into the heart of each of us. He always has. I've learned He delights in the heart that comes to Him, as lovingly as the little girl who wanted to be near her daddy as he polished his shoes.

I may never fill your shoes, Dad, but my heart will always treasure the memories you gave me; memories that prepared my heart and taught me to follow in the steps of my heavenly Father. I love you both now more than words can say. Thank you.

Your daughter,
Connie

Deb Kemper

Ed

"Sis, how ya doin'?" My father, Ed, squeezed his six-foot-four-inch frame into the passenger seat of my MGB. The side that was still intact.

"Hurt right now," I replied honestly, pinned between the console and the door crushed into my side when an old Mercury Comet slammed into me.

"What happened?" Ed's voice gentled.

That was odd.

I couldn't turn to get a look at his face because a brace supported my neck. "Brakes failed. Ran through the intersection." I tried to get a deep breath, still unable to get adequate air since the impact.

The man who drove the Comet stayed in my line of sight, wringing his hands. He already had apologized twice. He and Ed were friends.

"They're bringin' the Jaws of Life to cut ya out." Ed glanced up as an EMT tapped his right shoulder, protruding outside the tiny car.

"Ed, let me in there. I wanna check her vital signs."

"Sure, Jerry, come on." He levered his frame out of the car he swore was more like putting on and taking off lead coveralls than getting into a vehicle.

Jerry propped himself with one knee in the floorboard. "I wanna check ya again, make sure everything's okay."

I hadn't seen Jerry before, when he slipped the neck brace on me after he climbed through the hatch and broke the back on my seat to gain access to my imprisoned body.

He recorded my blood pressure and oxygen level. "Lookin' good. We should have ya outta here soon."

"Okay, I'm not going anywhere." My eyes shifted back and forth, hoping to catch a glimpse of my father.

I heard his voice.

"Hell, I can't get in that contraption; I can't even get a cigarette outta my shirt pocket." His audience chuckled.

* * *

Everybody knew him, most liked him. If he was present, he was the life of the party. The one they clustered round, to listen to his stories. He was amusing as long as he didn't drink hard liquor.

Ed was an alcoholic, had been since his early twenties, before my birth. Now, in his mid-fifties, after two bouts with lung cancer and numerous other health issues, he primarily drank beer. At least a half case a day. Even when he worked as a cabinetmaker he drank.

Somehow he functioned with a buzz. He could not bear silence or sobriety.

I often wondered why, then. It would be decades before I understood him.

We worked on projects together, built bookcases, a table, painted rooms, poured concrete pads. He taught me how to handle power tools, how to sand fine wood by hand. He taught me the patience of slowly wiping on stain with a cotton rag to get an even coat.

He'd been absent most of my childhood, yet I knew him. Not from information gleaned from family; I just made a connection with him somehow. We were rarely awkward with each other, accepting ourselves at face value.

Ed spent time in prison, in psychiatric wards, even a year in Florida's state mental hospital, Chattahoochee. The experts declared him sane. He declared himself too ornery to do right.

Ed married more than two dozen times. Not a lot of women, one he married frequently—Barbara. I didn't understand why. She appeared to have more sense than to allow herself to be sucked into the vortex he created when he drank heavily. She was mostly kind and pleasant unless she was furious with him. She divorced him every time, occasionally holding on for years before she flung her hands in the air and declared her limit had, once again, been surpassed.

One woman Ed married three times. Jeanne hated me. She blamed me for his indifference to her and heavy drinking. She didn't seem to grasp that Ed was who he was, not a project, but a man. Often I think women look on men as an improvement venture. Ed wasn't going to change for anybody, least of all a woman.

* * *

Twelve years ago I came home from dinner and a movie with my husband to find numerous messages on our answering machine. My mother, sister, and aunt all left voice mails.

My father died. Ed finally wore out his body. He had stomach cancer and wasted away to almost nothing.

We hadn't seen each other in eight years. We rarely spoke on the phone, as he was usually drunk when he called.

My husband, Ken, and I left our Missouri home to drive to Florida. I wanted to fly. I felt like I needed to get there quickly but we drove. Ken gave me the time I needed to come to terms with the death of the man who played a role in my being.

I met a half-sister I'd only heard about. She lived locally and handled all the arrangements for the funeral before we arrived. She was the one by his side for the few months he lingered, cleaning him, feeding him.

He called her by my name toward the end. So sure it was me holding his hand, reading to him.

I apologized to her for his mistake. I grieved that he denied her existence for sixteen years only to have her with him when he needed someone, and then deny her again. It broke my heart for them both.

She looks like him. I don't.

Surrounding influences shape us—good, bad, and indifferent.

I learned a lot about crafting from a master. Ed could see what waited inside a piece of wood, lingering until the artist seized its potential. He brought wood grain to life, capturing its best qualities.

People challenged him. He tended not to bring out the best in us.

* * *

The preacher, whose brother was one of Ed's many best friends, approached me at the funeral. He overflowed with assurance that my father had accepted the Lord as his Savior before he died. When he found out I was Deborah, not Edwina, my much younger half-sister, he became brutally honest. "I don't know why but it seemed like it never…took…with Ed. I was out to his place every week for two years."

I nodded and smiled inwardly. "Ed didn't want to change. Don't despair. It really isn't up to you who accepts and who doesn't."

I don't know if I'll see him in heaven. It'll be nice if it happens.

* * *

Because of our time together I'll always appreciate the beauty of fine oak, hickory, or maple furniture. I have to touch it and wonder about the man or woman who first envisioned its possibilities, what prompted the first cut. The knots in pine and cedar, while lovely, are evidence of weakness in the wood. Still, in a master's hands, they can be strong and useful.

I believe we're like that to our heavenly Father. He sees all of our roughness through the lens of his love. He sees us as we are, and what we can be, but loves us anyway. When we let Him, He shapes us into exquisite, loving examples of His mercy and grace.

Ed's Florida Cornbread

1/3 cup oil
1 tsp. salt
1½ cups corn flour
1½ cups water

For Hush Puppies:

2 tbsp. dried or fresh onions
½ tsp. baking soda

Pour oil in 12-inch cast iron skillet…heat in oven at 400 degrees. Stir salt into corn flour then add water, stirring until smooth. Add more water, a tablespoon at a time, if needed, until batter is loose, like cooked oatmeal.

Pour into hot oil and bake until edges set, about 35 minutes. Flip it and return to oven to brown the other side, about 30 minutes. Serve hot. It isn't good cold and can't be successfully reheated.

The cornbread is fantastic alongside a pot of greens or beans. Fry it on the stovetop by dropping spoonfuls into hot oil. If you want hush puppies, add 2 tablespoons of dried or fresh onions and ½ teaspoon of baking soda. Ed used beer in place of water for hush puppies. Drop into hot oil set on medium high heat. Remove to a warm plate covered with paper towel to drain.

Jan K. Potter

Always There for Me

"Now! Pull the line—pull the line!" Dad hollered.

I jerked up the fishing pole, but lost him again.

"That fish must have eight or ten of your worms by now." Dad shook his head and sighed.

"Well, try again." He put another slimy creature on my hook and I tossed the line into the pond one more time. I had entered a local fishing contest for kids, and found myself taunted by a lone trout. He kept stealing my worms and slithering away before I could catch him.

We watched and waited. Then I heard Dad shout "Now!" and simultaneously felt my pole jerk. Dad had reached over and pushed up my hand.

"You got him! Now reel him in." Dad instructed me in each step as we watched the huge trout dangle from the line and swish his tail, trying to break free.

People turned to watch as I made my way past the crowd to the judges' bench. Fourteen inches! I tied with a boy for first place. We both won a new fishing pole and appeared on local TV news in Cheyenne.

I didn't know whether or not I should feel guilty that Dad had helped. But I did know that he was there for me. And that became the recurring theme of our relationship.

Dad loved to fish, camp out, and take our family on vacation every summer. I have fond memories of Yellowstone Park, counting down for Old Faithful to shoot her spray straight up into the air; being careful to stay on the path close to Dad and away from the boiling hot springs.

I loved the fragrance of pine, the sweet smell of fresh rain in the forest, and the sound of the wind swooshing through the trees. Bacon crackling and the rich aroma of coffee brewing on a campfire. I remember lying in my sleeping bag at night, hearing the pounding of a waterfall and the occasional whistling and clacking of a train; drifting off to sleep, wondering if a bear might raid our camp and creep into our tent while we slept. Afraid, but not really fearful because Dad was close by. If anything happened, I knew he would take care of us.

Those trips were such a special part of my childhood, but there was much more.

I have fond memories of reading Bible stories at night and kneeling at the couch to pray. Before Dad could get up, I jumped on his back to play "horsey." We ate our meals together as a family, and Dad always said grace. His regular church attendance also set a lifelong example for me.

I remember standing along the street watching the horses and clowns go by in the Cheyenne Rodeo parades. Dad would make sure we stayed far enough back so we didn't get trampled.

I can picture Dad on a ladder, applying fresh paint and wallpaper when we moved to another house, which seemed rather frequent. Dad liked adventure and changed occupations several times: army sergeant, architect, band director, forest ranger, salesman, teacher, repairman. He fixed everything that needed fixing—leaky faucets, broken bracelets, TV sets, automobiles. "Do-it-all dad," "Jack of all trades," and master of several! I could always rely on Dad and I believed he could do anything.

When we moved to Colorado, every Sunday afternoon Dad took our family for a drive—usually in the mountains, or around the majestic red rocks at Garden of the Gods. We looked over the city from the top of Pikes Peak; hiked up Helen Hunt Falls and felt the water spray our faces; walked around the grounds at the beautiful Broadmoor Hotel, as though we actually had a room. Dad made sure we were all included in the outings.

I remember the raw wood scent of the basement steps in Colorado Springs as I cautiously descended them into the cool cellar and sat next to Dad, just to be near him while he worked on projects. He "helped" me make a transistor radio with transparent Plexiglas for the science fair at my junior high school. He showed me how to explain to the class the positive and negative charges of the electrical current, using stick figures drawn on poster board.

Dad made sure we got places on time and he always kept a watchful eye to see that we got home safely. One night when I was in high school, I found him sitting on the couch waiting up for me after my blind date. I sailed through the front door, slammed it behind me, breathed a sigh of relief, and exclaimed, "Never again!" I was thankful that he didn't quiz me, because I was too embarrassed to explain how I dodged the guy's advances all night and escaped his final attempt to kiss me good night. Dad just listened to my feeble attempt to explain my gratefulness at finally being home, and then he went to bed.

I think of Dad's sacrifice. In spite of a meager income, he encouraged us to attend college and helped pay our way. He was willing to give or give up almost anything for us. When I came home from college on summer vacation one year, I put a set of red American Tourister luggage on layaway at the department store where I worked. Dad knew it would take me two or three years to pay for it at the rate I was going, so for Christmas he surprised me and paid it off.

I felt comforted by his faithfulness in "sticking with it" through long, hard times. Traveling to the burn hospital in Texas to be with my brother after his helicopter was shot down in Vietnam. Caring for my mom in the midst of her mental illness the last ten years of her life.

Dad moved in with us shortly after he turned ninety. I drove him to doctor appointments and the grocery store, cut his toenails, put clean sheets on his bed, and cooked his dinner. We went on Sunday afternoon drives and to summer band concerts. I often read Bible stories to him at night. It's odd how our roles had reversed. Once my daddy took care of me and then I took care of him.

When Dad was ninety-four, he fell and fractured his pelvis. After a couple of brief hospital stays, he went to live at a care center for more intensive medical attention. I visited him frequently—read to him, took him on short drives and "wheelchair walks," and sat with him watching goldfish swim around in the pond where he lived. It was hard watching him lose so much of his physical capabilities, but mentally he stayed fairly sharp. Sometimes, though, he would become confused and make statements that made perfect sense to him but not to anyone else, like when he told me that some of the Bible verses were written by Mark Twain. Or when he said he ate some beef stew and blew it out his ears!

He was hard of hearing, and sometimes his comments were pretty humorous. When asked, "Do you like pie?", he replied, "Do I want a fly?" A social worker at the center asked him, "How are you feeling?" and he said, "How was my funeral?" I never could figure out how he came up with this one: I asked how he was and he said he couldn't seem to get balanced. I asked, "Do you think you're gonna fall over?" and he said, "Go to Hollywood?"

Dad died at the age of ninety-seven. I still miss him.

He wasn't perfect. He could be passive, was somewhat of a hypochondriac, and I often thought he saw the world through weed-coloured glasses. But one night, a few friends and I were having a chat about our dads. All four of the other women in the group told how their dads had been mean, or abusive, or self-centered, or stingy, and how they had lifelong poor relationships with them. And I thought, Wow! I am so thankful that I had a loving, caring, kind-hearted dad. My dad who was always there for me.

Ruth Clarke

The Last Word

For our parents' fiftieth wedding anniversary, my sister, Marion, and I planned a celebration that they wouldn't forget. My father never forgot anything anyway, as we learned that night. We'd invited one hundred guests—who all came—and seated them in a horseshoe shape, surrounding the head table where my mother, father, we children, and our spouses sat. We had asked several of the guests to speak throughout the evening, reminiscing about attending Howard and Grace's wedding, practical jokes that had been played on them when they moved into their house, and other memorable moments they recalled throughout the years. We'd chosen people whom we thought were the best speakers; folks we thought had the "gift" of the gab, for my father was a storyteller and he loved a good yarn.

The event required long-distance planning for Marion and me; I lived in Vancouver and she lived in Bobcaygeon, where my parents resided and where the dinner party would take place. My geographical distance turned out to be propitious; I lived near the Pacific Ocean and the bounty that it provided: salmon. Our menu included smoked salmon among the appetizers, and barbecued salmon as the entrée.

The cocktail hour was quieter than we'd anticipated. The people with the "gift" were looking distracted, clutching their notes and drinking fruit juice and soda water, most unusual for the crowd we had invited. But our parents didn't seem to notice and were mingling with everyone, delighted to be the centre of attention.

The salmon was a hit; no scrap was left on any plate and few leftovers in the kitchen for the hosts to take home. When the first course dishes were cleared, the lights were dimmed, and the voice of Dorothy Lamour drifted over the speakers singing "Thanks For The Memory." While she sang, five waitresses entered from the kitchen, each carrying a flaming Baked Alaska dessert. Everyone sang along and watched as their desserts were served.

The room was large but the ceiling was low and we had decided to dispense with a microphone. When the dessert plates were cleared, I thanked everyone for coming and told our guests that several people among us wanted to share their remembrances about Howard and Grace. I introduced a man whom everyone already knew, but not necessarily his significance to the occasion. He cleared his throat and stood.

"Fifty years ago today, I stood up for Howard when he married Grace, though my role as best man might have been disputed." He coughed and waited for the chuckling to subside before continuing. "The wedding was held in the gardens of Grace's parents, Roland and Lib Thurston, at Locust Hill Farm. It was a sunny day, like this has been, and the gardens were beautiful, as was the lovely bride." He turned to Howard and Grace, his cheeks darkening.

"After they said their vows and we signed the marriage licence, the bride and groom mingled with their family and friends on the lawn, while a few of us stole away to take care of some business we'd been planning." He coughed again. "We'd stashed cans and chains to decorate the car, and someone had raided the garden for some onions that we fixed to the radiator. Sorry, Howard and Grace, after fifty years, I must own up. Forgive us for the smelly ride to the hotel." There were more chuckles and guffaws, giving the next speaker time to stand.

"When Grace and Howard moved into their matrimonial home, it was still pleasant weather," the former Reeve of the town began. "It was a Saturday night, well after bedtime and we saw that their house was dark, but we knew they were home. I think I can point out most everyone in this room who was there." He stalled and looked around smiling.

"Our wives had made sandwiches and cakes, and we brought crates of beer and a couple of jugs and hid them in the hedge that separated their home from the barn. Others brought pots and pans and when everyone had taken their places around the perimeter of the house, we commenced our chivaree, banging and clanging and carrying on, until the porch light came on and Howard and Grace stood at the door. They'd taken the time to put on some clothes—I don't expect they'd slept in them. They must have expected something like this would happen, since they'd been part of shenanigans like this themselves. It was a tradition." People nodded their heads and smiled, probably recollecting their own experiences.

"However, something happened that night that we didn't expect. Howard kept a goat on the other side of that hedge and while we were carrying on, that damned old billy got into our victuals! When we finally went to gather them up, he butted one of the men and had him down on the ground, standing over him, all the while chewing on a sandwich. He wasn't a pig though, and left some for us. Congratulations, folks."

When the room settled down, other nostalgic and sentimental recollections were offered; each person warming to the relaxed atmosphere that was growing after the nervous initial speeches had broken the ice. And as we'd planned, Dad got the last word. He was well into his cups, but he stood calm and erect, without notes, as he looked around the room at his friends and smiled.

"Grace and I thank you all for coming. And we thank our daughters for organizing this great celebration. But even though it was fifty long years ago, a couple of you stand to be corrected." He looked to his best man and grinned.

"You got it right about the chains and cans, Norm, and they were indeed noisy. But it wasn't onions you put on the manifold, it was limburger cheese." Then he looked at the former Reeve.

"Yes, Grace and I knew that you had something up your sleeve and we expected to be chivareed, but it was a ram that got those sandwiches. We never had a goat."

To the waitresses and the kitchen staff standing at the back of the room he offered thanks. "Your service tonight was wonderful, and we thank the chef for preparing such a lovely meal. But I have a recipe that you might consider when next you serve barbecued fish. This recipe was handed down to me from my father, and perhaps his father before him, though I can't attest to that. It came from the lumber camps and was probably the original recipe for planked fish—since we had an abundance of cedar. This recipe is Planked Carp."

Planked Carp

Depending on the size of the carp, you will need planks of cedar large enough that the carp doesn't droop over the sides. We used cedar shake, like the cedar shingles for roofing before asphalt became popular. Soak the cedar planks in water overnight, so they absorb moisture and don't burn when they're on the barbecue. Gut the carp, cut the head and tail off it, peel the skin off it, and feed it to the dogs or cats that are standing watching you. Then put the carp in a brine of salt, brown sugar, lemon juice, and spring water. Leave it in the brine for about four hours. While it's in the brine, cut up six lemons in thin slices and as many garlic cloves. When you take the carp out of the brine, it will be shiny from the salt water. Set it on towels to remove the excess moisture, and while it's drying, start your fire. Then, make a paste of brown sugar and Dijon mustard, adding the slices of garlic. Add liberal amounts of salt, pepper, and chopped parsley and paste the carp both inside and out. Arrange the slices of lemons inside the carp so the juice will soak through while it is cooking.

Check your fire again and see that there is a good bed of coals beneath the rack. Take the slabs of cedar out of the water and overlap them; then set the carp on top of them. When the coals are ready, set the carp on the slabs over the coals on the rack. Depending on the size of the carp, allow for about ten minutes per inch, to cook through. Turn it once and allow for the same amount of time on the other side. While the carp is cooking, you can make a salad, slice some bread, and set the table.

When the carp is finally cooked, deliver it to the table. No doubt the dogs and cats will still be around, waiting for their share. And after that, give them the surprise of their lives. Drop the carp on the floor and eat the cedar slab.

Connie Poole Wesala

Without Wasted Words

"What was it like growing up in rural Louisiana in the twenties?" It's only one of the many questions I wish I had asked my dad before he died. My father was an introverted man who rarely spoke about his feelings or his past. He expressed few emotions beyond loud pronouncements regarding politics, his Cadillac, or his lousy golf game.

I knew he was a good man and a hard worker. For someone with a sixth grade education, he provided for us extremely well, and I knew that he had come home from "the war" with memories he relived in dreams most nights.

I remember my father best through the eyes of a camera lens. Boxes of old black and whites, taken with our Kodak Brownie, sit in my office. There are dozens of me as a child with a beaming, proud father kneeling beside me. In the large pile are also many group photos of my parents with close friends they visited on Friday nights.

Among them was an older couple who had adopted Dad as a young, recently discharged soldier with a wife and infant, struggling to make ends meet, far from his rural Louisiana roots. This couple lived on the outskirts of our small Oklahoma town and were the closest "grandparents" I had. I spent hours in my pretend world at the old treadle sewing machine while my parents played Canasta with Charlie and Hazel in the next room.

Dad's tattered, dog-eared albums are filled with photographs of evenings with his work buddies and their wives—card parties, Fourth of July get-togethers, and lightning-bug-filled evenings where I, an only child at the time, played frenetically under star-filled skies.

My parents' closest friends were Dale and Maxine, and our picture albums are full of homing pigeons, chicken coops from the year the "dads" decided to raise their own Sunday dinners, and handmade wood and wire shortwave radios they had more fun with than we kids did. While Dad and Dale won at the card table on Friday nights and the wives chattered, I sat with my best friend and her brother browsing through the "Monkey" Ward catalogue and cutting out paper dolls from magazines.

It seemed like I lived on the fringe of my parents' lives, and Dad was an important, yet vague, apparition moving about my universe like the sun—keeping us fed, clothed, and warm, and providing us a roof of shelter, protection, and discipline. In those days mothers were omnipresent, nurturing, teaching, and loving, while dads were out there keeping the bearings oiled, the brakes working, the tires aired. They were the engines of the family's life and as such they seemed somewhat foreign and distant.

My father was the "fixer." He tended broken legs, drove me to the emergency room on a regular basis, and disengaged my right thumb from the mixer blades which he bent with ease. Back then, I thought he could bend steel beams. As my high-strung mother reacted frantically to each of these events, my father quietly walked in and took charge.

He sprung open the rollers of the old wringer washer to rescue my little sister's arm; he wrapped her hand in gauze when she fell through the front glass door; and he drove like an ambulance driver to the hospital. He found Mr. Peepers sitting in the tall elm tree out back and put my aqua and white parakeet back in its cage as I cried with relief. He could fix anything around the house and in our lives. Without wasted words.

Dad could sit silently in his worn brown rocker recliner for hours. We listened as Claude, his golfing buddy and best friend, relived each stroke of their afternoon round. Dad's contribution to the conversation was an occasional nod or grunt.

At some point, his reticence to talk, to share, to be actively involved in my life began to create a wall that I had difficulty breaking through. As most teens do, I began to see myself separate from my parents' views, resisting my dad's southern ideas about race and politics and social issues. When I went off to college, I wrote to my mother nearly every day, always adding a postscript, "Say hi to Daddy."

After mother died at age fifty-seven, Dad seemed to withdraw even further. He focused on surviving as a sixty-year-old widower; involved himself in travel, church groups, and even an adult choir, though he couldn't sing on key to save his life. He was shy in groups and roomed alone, but he filled album after album with his ventures around the country and an Alaska cruise—the dream trip of his life.

A different man emerges in photos taken with his brothers during our annual family visits to Jena. It was there he seemed most alive—in his element—surrounded by laughter and fun and Friday night fish fries under the tall Louisiana pines of his childhood. Each evening, before I headed to the kitchen to help with the dinner dishes, I watched as the men left the long rustic wood table on the back porch and retreated to the front where they sat on the horsehair seats of the old straight back chairs, tipped precariously against the side of the house as they smoked and told tall tales and laughed and cursed and spat. I now wonder if his quiet reserve became a refuge when he returned to the city. I'll never know—for I never asked.

Daddy seemed a miser for many years, convinced he didn't have enough money for a new pair of shoes or a new sweater from Dillard's. I was surprised when I began receiving large annual checks in his later years, gifted to avoid probate. And it was with total disbelief after his death to find myself the recipient of a good amount of stock shares and insurance money. Why? I wondered. Why did he not spend and enjoy what he had? Why wait to give it to his two girls? I know the answer to that question, of course. A sense of duty, of responsibility, drove my dad's life, and he would not die without leaving his family financially sound.

That generation of men, the World War II survivors, knew what it was like to give everything they had for their country, their wives, and their families. Many made the greatest sacrifice with their very lives. Those who came back, alive but scarred, returned with a sense of duty.

At my dad's ninetieth birthday celebration, my sister and I watched as people entered the church social hall. I saw the years melt away as old Army buddies started up conversations they'd begun long ago.

People streamed in for several hours, checking out our tables of photos, awards, and memorabilia. There were church friends and ministers from the past, former work colleagues, card group members, and old neighbors. Some knew my father simply by the Oklahoma Gas Company uniform he wore for thirty years. "Hey, Louie," they called as they entered the room, gave him a hug or a handshake, and thanked him for his help.

I watched in amazement that day. Here was Dad surrounded by all these people who remembered him, thought of him, and cared about this shy, quiet man. It was then I realized I hadn't really known my father. I was his daughter, not a friend or colleague, not a work buddy or choir member. They knew someone different than the old black-and-white photos from my childhood. They knew and respected a man who was gentle and caring, who gave beyond his means, who worked harder than anyone else, who gave his all for others.

Even today, I'm a bit ashamed that I didn't know him better, but I am generous with myself. Do we ever know our parents outside of their role as parents? Do we ever stop disagreeing with how they raised us or their politics or their flaws? Can we understand that what we saw as miserliness came from the hardships and lack of money during WWII when they were young adults themselves?

There are a hundred questions I would ask my dad if he were here. I'd be more interested. I'd care more. I'd want to know. I hope that he is playing Canasta across from my mother on Friday nights with Claude and Virginia, or Pitch with Dale and Maxine. I hope he sees Charlie and Hazel often. And I hope he sits around sharing stories with his brothers on an old battered porch much like Granny's.

My questions will have to wait for the other side. Meanwhile I have my photos and Dad's look of pride as he holds the hand of his little girl in her Easter bonnet in 1947.

Gloria I. Taylor

Gone, But Not Forgotten

We planted a honey locust for you
Just as straight as a tree can be
And just like you…
Tall and strong, always on your watch.

Soft and sweet as the yellow blossoms in summer
That fall from its fern-like branches.
The fragrance lingers
Forever.

Shane Joseph

Outliving the Cat —my dad's many lives

My dad's many lives began at the same age that his father died of a heart attack. At thirty-seven, my dad lived in fear, scared that he would not outlive my grandfather. Dad smoked, suffered from hypertension, and was overweight, despite having been a bodybuilder in his twenties. I was entering my teens and there were three younger siblings—not a time to die, especially when Dad was the sole breadwinner.

So Dad took a walk in the dusk one evening, threw away his cigarettes and matches, and didn't touch another smoke again. If he had withdrawal symptoms, there were no signs. If he suffered, he did so in silence, and we never knew what he went through—relief, is my guess.

When I was in my late teens, Mum rushed into my room one dark morning, screaming, "Your father is dead at the top of the road. A car has hit him." I dressed hurriedly and rushed to the scene of the tragedy. A car had crashed through a fence and was half inside a house that straddled a bend in the main road. "Drunk driver," I was told by onlookers, "fell asleep at the wheel." Dad, who had been walking to the bakery to buy bread for the family's breakfast, had been swiped by the car, tossed over a barbed wire fence, and deposited not far from the wall from which the rear end of the still-smoking car stuck out. The ambulance was yet to arrive. Dad was not dead but groggy, and he had broken his hand. I bundled him into a taxi and took him to the hospital emergency room. The nurses, occupied by much larger calamities, did not pay much attention to his injuries. "He'll mend," they said. And he did.

A few years later, I was now employed and was returning home from work one late evening in the pelting tropical rain. As I rode down stately Ward Place, a wide boulevard bordered by large colonial bungalows, I saw a bus skidded off the road and embedded in the wall of a nearby mansion. It reminded me of my dad's previous accident and I wondered whether, by some quirk of fate, my father had been involved again. When I arrived home, Dad was sporting a fractured arm—he had been on that bus. I learned not to speculate after that. His complaint was not so much about his injury but the fact that someone had stolen his glasses in the confusion.

Flash forward a few more years; I was working for an airline in the Middle East. Dad was working for the same airline in the old country, Sri Lanka. The news flashed across our CRT screens that terrorists had blown up an aircraft on the runway at Colombo airport. Knowing how thin the security at that airport had been when I had worked there, I sent Dad an intercompany telex, seeking information, even cajoling the puny security arrangements back home. He answered promptly, "Don't criticize. I was on that plane."

It turned out that Dad had been on a business trip to the Maldives, and per his habit, had boarded last. The plane was behind schedule by twenty minutes due to a late arrival from its previous point of departure. As he was entering the cabin, the bomb—timed to go off while the aircraft was in midair—exploded, throwing him out of the plane and onto the mobile stairway. His allocated seat was blown to bits. On the stairway, struggling to get to his feet, he realized that he had lost his glasses, again. He was not to be deprived of those expensive lenses this time, so he began groping for them as fire and mayhem raged around him. He claims that an angelic voice kept urging him to "Get up. Please get up"—which he did, but only upon finding his glasses. Then, invoking "the speed of Carl Lewis," he ran for the terminal before any further explosions occurred.

He didn't count the number of times he was stopped by mobs who were burning Tamils with tire "necklaces" in Colombo as he ferried his staff to and from work through the curfews and civil unrest in the mid-eighties. "Occupational hazards," he tosses off in his laconic way.

He faced another crisis before coming to Canada. His spine started to give way and the diagnosis showed that he had suffered an attack of polio as a child which had been put down to a bout of fever. He was given two options: (a) status quo and end up paralyzed within five years, or (b) undergo an operation with a 50 percent chance of success. He was admitted to the hospital and prepped for option (b) but suddenly had a revelation: "I gave up the cigarettes through will power, I can beat this," he resolved. He discharged himself and scurried home before the doctors could arrive at the operating theatre. He took acupuncture treatment instead. That was over twenty-five years ago—he is still walking.

And I did count this other life, years later, when Dad—retired from an airline executive's job in Sri Lanka and working as a security guard in Canada because he wanted to be independent—was walking to the grocery store with his shopping cart. A van came out of a corner and hit him as he was crossing the road. His legs went under the vehicle that stopped just at that moment. The frightened driver disembarked to see his victim rising, dusting himself off, and straightening out his twisted cart. The driver gave Dad his license and insurance details and offered to take him to a hospital, or to his home or to wherever he wanted. At this point the hapless driver was willing to offer his firstborn. Dad shrugged everything away, made sure that all his bones were working, and said, "I must be going now, my wife is waiting for me." He walked the kilometre home, dragging his misshapen cart. Mum was livid at his nonchalance. "At least you could have asked the man to buy you a new shopping cart."

Tragedy struck again when a botched cataract operation caused him to lose his sight in one eye, with the other also losing most of its function around the same time. My dad, a man who had read copiously all his life, was robbed of one of his greatest pleasures. It broke my heart to watch him sitting in his armchair, with reading material by his side, untouched, waiting. Waiting for what? Or was he suffering again, in silence? But that good angel who had spoken to him on the stairway of a burning aircraft came calling once more: A cornea donor was found and a year later Dad recovered most of his sight; at least, he could read the library's large print books again.

But the years do wind down body parts and the next time it was his heart, the same organ that had malfunctioned for his father at thirty-seven and his younger brother at fifty-seven, felling them both. He went in for stents and came out smiling, willing to go for a jog, if his failing knees would allow him. "Good for another fifteen years," he said.

As my dad crossed into his eighties, a decade longer than the "three score and ten" he says men are granted according to the Bible, he assumed a new life: caring for my mother who began to have health issues. The man who had never boiled an egg or made a cup of tea when I was a child suddenly became cook, cleaner, and caregiver in the tiny apartment that he shared with my mother. He even figured out how to program his TV/VCR, although he never bothered with the internet—to him it was another nuisance.

And so the old soldier marches on, outliving lives, gathering others. I wonder how a man who would rather live a placid life with his nose behind a book could have so many adventures that younger men only dream of. And I have described only nine of them, the same as a cat is reputed to have. But knowing my dad, I'm betting he'll outlive the cat.

P.S – I spoke too soon, Dad has beaten the cat! He has begun a new life: After years of protest, he has finally embraced the internet and tablet technology and is "surfing" like an athlete on steroids. He grins. "I should have done it ten years ago."

Rona Evartt

Girls Can Be Marines!

Dad was the envy of all in the neighborhood. If the other fathers had free time after work or on weekends, we never saw them. My dad, on the other hand, was the good-natured catcher in the cul-de-sac baseball games, or the project manager for our latest building effort. And Mom was the refreshment team leader as well as first-aid provider for the many mishaps. This could be frequent as Dad was the biggest kid on the block. Children would knock on our door and ask if my father could come out and play. If parents had known of all the ideas he came up with, they might have been more involved.

My brother could never complain about being the neglected middle child; he was the only son of an only son. Dad did all the usual "guy" things and, fortunately for me, shooting, camping, fishing, and motorcycles were family events. Hunting was reserved solely for just the two of them. I was envious that all the fun stuff seemed to be reserved for the male members in society. I was luckier than most, though.

My brother and I were inseparable. I enjoyed the roughhousing of the boys' play over the droll dolls popular in the late 1960s. I could throw a football or baseball as well or better than any of them.

* * *

"I can too be a marine!" I cried as I ran to follow my brother and his friends down the cul-de-sac.

"Girls can't be marines. Only guys," they shot back.

On this day we were mimicking what we witnessed in the nightly news reports of the Vietnam War. We aimed and shot at one another, imagining sticks or fingers as weapons. We hid behind bushes, around corners, and crawled on bellies. My best friend's father was a marine stationed in this conflict. We didn't begin to grasp the reality of what went on, but we admired his patriotism as we imagined defending our fellow marines against the enemy.

Dad was watching and called out to one of the guys holding part of a broom handle. We all hesitated as we thought he would stop our play, but instead he asked if there were other broom handles available. Along with some scrap wood, he proceeded to make the coolest rubber band rifles we'd ever seen. Dad raided every mop and broom Mom had in the house as other kids absconded with their own booty from hall closets from home. Wide eyes gleamed as every kid on the block left the garage with a rifle.

"Who's that one for, Dad?" I'd ask as one by one he handed a little marine a rifle. Soon the last of the guys left.

With no more handles available, I realized I wouldn't be getting one. I was a girl. What did I expect? Dad picked up the remaining six-inch piece of what was left of Mom's broom. I slumped down on a stool as he went to the woodpile, picking up a scrap.

"What's that?" I asked.

"Mom's been asking for some shelves, this looks kinda like a bracket. Whatcha think?"

"Yeah," my hope gone.

I watched as he began to shape the wood into what looked like a shelf bracket. I went into the house to hide my disappointment. I couldn't stay away long. Dad would never hurt me intentionally. Checking on his progress, I saw Dad attach the remaining broom handle to the top of the "bracket" and position a clothespin. Painting it black, I couldn't help but think Mom wasn't going to like this bracket much. Then he turned and handed it to me. It was the most beautiful rubber band pistol ever made. I hugged him hard before I ran out demanding "I can too be a marine!"

That evening, moms all over the neighborhood found hall closets emptied of mops and brooms and kids ate every bite of vegetables on their plate, never revealing the "black-op" my dad initiated that day.

My pistol has been on a shelf next to his picture the last forty years.

Gail M. Murray

Macaroni Sunday

It was the fifties when television was still in its infancy and sitting around the living room watching TV as a family actually brought people together unlike today's technological world of personal devices.

Dad would prepare Sunday dinner casserole—a scrumptious and flavourful mix of elbow macaroni, stewed tomatoes, Bravo tomato sauce, and aged cheddar cheese. No store-bought tomatoes for us. Mom had grown them in our large vegetable garden, and then spent painstaking hours simmering, peeling, and canning them in Mason jars to store in the root cellar.

"Bill, what are you doing with my canned tomatoes?" my mother shrieked.

"They'll add flavour to the macaroni casserole. What are you saving them for?" he said with a wink.

It was true. Rows of canned peaches, pears, tomatoes lined the shelves in the coolest and driest part of our basement, being saved for that rainy day.

Dad had special touches with cooking, like adding an egg and milk to our mashed potatoes as he whipped them into a bowl of deliciousness. No stranger to cooking, as the eldest child in his family at age twelve he was expected to have dinner on the table when his parents arrived home from their gruelling factory jobs at Stelco in Swansea. Dad had learned to make apple pie, beef stew, poached eggs, and the piece de resistance—roast beef with roast potatoes and Yorkshire pudding. As my parents shared the cooking, we were in many ways quite modern for the fifties.

My mother re-entered the workforce when my younger sister started school, making me responsible for dinner at age twelve. This interfered with watching

Dick Clark's "American Bandstand" and learning the latest dances. Once, while watching a dance contest, I saw flames leaping from the frying pan. I rushed in just in time to save the day. After that I learned to stay with the cooking. I would get dinner started by setting the table, peeling the potatoes, chopping the vegetables. Dad would arrive home from his electrical job and give me pointers, teaching me how to cook. Of medium height, wearing his flannel shirt and cotton pants held up by suspenders, he would peer out from his dark-rimmed glasses at the pots and frying pans, making adjustments, frying or simmering. He had big blue eyes, an open smile, and a kind heart. To a girl who did not take naturally to domesticity, he was patient and kind and never scolded, unlike my mother.

Though we worked as a team, I left the real cooking to him. He knew his way around a kitchen and took pride in his fast and easy macaroni and cheese that we fussy eaters simply devoured.

Completing the casserole, Dad popped it in the oven to merge the flavours. The cheddar made a crunchy, gooey top crust.

Then we all gathered in front of the box to watch our much anticipated Tarzan movie. The station ran these action adventure films every Sunday. No question it was family fare with Cheetah, the precocious chimp, adding humour with his zany antics and Boy (Tarzan's adopted son) played by Johnny Sheffield, rounding out the jungle family. Though many actors played the Edgar Rice Burroughs' hero, it was Olympic gold medal swimmer Johnny Weissmuller who was the quintessential ape-man.

Each film had swimming sequences and battles with crocodiles but the greatest battle Tarzan fought was with encroaching Europeans trying to ruin the harmony of the jungle by illegally capturing wildlife or harassing local tribes. Each film had Tarzan emitting his distinctive, ululating yodelling yell as he swung through the vines on a rescue mission. "Tarzan's New York Adventure" (1942) was my favourite with Tarzan looking uncomfortable in a suit then discovering the "hotel waterfalls" (really a shower) and standing under it wearing his suit. Soft-spoken Jane was there to bridge the gap.

During the commercial we would all dash to the kitchen to fill our plates as Dad served us, breaking through the crusty cheese topping. As tomato flavours escaped, he spooned the gooey mixture onto our plates. We would sit our dinner on the coffee table or on special TV trays—metal trays with legs—so our knees fit nicely underneath. Imagine creating furniture for this purpose?

Dessert was served as we segued into "Walt's Disney's Wonderful World of Colour." Earlier in the afternoon, Mom had cut up bananas and oranges into a large glass bowl. Typical kids we craved ice cream, Oreos, chocolate chip cookies, butter tarts, and Twinkies. Luckily for us Mom limited sugar consumption. I can thank her today for my love of fruit and my trim waistline.

The crowning glory of Sunday night television was "The Ed Sullivan Show." This strange-wizened-up, stone-faced emcee, a former New York entertainment columnist, had an eye for talent. His was the longest running variety show in the history of television. To appear on his show was a hallmark of success. If you could sit through the plate spinners, juggling acts, and smarmy crooners, you could see "live and on our stage" the greats of rock and roll: Elvis Presley, the Beatles, the Doors, and the Rolling Stones. Ed was the first host to break racial barriers and have African-American greats like Harry Belafonte and Nat King Cole perform.

When Elvis performed "Hound Dog" in 1956 with his reckless gyrations, the teen-age girls in the audience screamed and swooned. My three-year-old sister, Wendy, mimicked them squealing and hurling her little body against the back of the soft sofa in mock faint. My parents got more laughs out of her that night than the stand-up comedians.

When I think of comfort food, it takes me back to those early times with my nuclear family. Grilled cheese sandwiches, hot chocolate, and macaroni and cheese lovingly prepared by my dad.

Sunday Macaroni and Cheese

elbow macaroni
butter or lard
can of stewed tomatoes
can of tomato sauce
1¼ cups of grated cheddar (half cheddar/half mozzarella)

– Add dry macaroni to boiling water and cook for 8-10 minutes. Drain macaroni and place in greased baking or Corningware dish.
– Add stewed tomatoes and tomato sauce and sprinkle in cup of cheese. Stir to mix. Sprinkle remainder of cheese on top.
– Cover and bake in oven at 350 F for 25 minutes.

Bea Purcell

Papa

Papa's favorite saying was *En el pais de los ciegos, el tuerto es el rey*: "In the land of the blind, the one-eyed man is king."

After graduation from high school, my father studied bookkeeping at Cebu Trade School in Cebu, Philippines. He worked for two companies during his adult working life. At eighteen years old, he started as bookkeeper for Tabacalera, a Spanish tobacco exporting company, where he learned fluent Spanish. Later at Corominas, a shipping and copra exporting company, he reported to the general manager who was American, and learned to speak very good English.

Papa rode his bike to and from work every day. The commute from our house took an hour each way. I could not remember a day when he stayed home and did not go to work.

During WWII, my parents evacuated to the mountains for safety from the Japanese. Here Papa joined other Filipinos in the guerilla movement to help the American military. The group's main responsibility was to warn the community of approaching enemy, with the use of sounds and signals.

During this time, three older siblings—a brother and two sisters—were born. Medical help was not available, and all died a few days after birth. When I asked about this time in their lives, my parents would only say it was a difficult period. The memories brought deep sadness to their faces. They did not want to talk about it. Papa's mouth would set into a thin hard line and he would shake his head. I did not go further than knowing the names of my siblings.

The middle child and oldest of the boys in a family of five, Papa was true to his name, Pacifico—peaceful in character. He never raised his voice; his was the calm and reason in family and community disputes. But he enjoyed dancing;

whenever there was music, Papa danced. My parents instilled in me the spirit of independence. My father and mother sacrificed, so I could have the education necessary for a bright future. They used to say, "Wherever you go with your life, you will always have your education with you. We will not leave you with material things."

From Papa, I learned the value of hard work, integrity, and appreciation of life. He also instilled in me independence of thought. He used to remind me, "Don't readily believe what you hear from others; think for yourself. Remember the one-eyed man."

Vivekanand Jha

A Banyan Tree

that you planted with your erudite hands,
in the dirt barren like the sands of a seashore
has blossomed into an insignia of immortality.

Its every leaf—large, gristly, glossy green,
inherits your benign wisdom, resplendent
like a beam of the rising sun.

Swaying in harmony like a sea of poppies,
giving a breeze to every ambler,
roasted, scorched in sizzling summer.

Standing on its rhinocerous root,
adding and multiplying into a knot
of branches, roots, trunks, leaves, and fruits
symbolizing a true meaning of life
teeming with a cascade of complexities.

Forming a shelter and shadow like a cloud
even travellers, needing no respite
from heat wave, heaving and parched
have to check their egos for a moment,
stopping by the tree, mutters in marvel:
Which hands have sown its seeds?

Cynthia Mendenhall

Chef Daddy

My father was a welder by trade, but a cook at heart, seizing every opportunity to assist in the kitchen. He held two main pleasures: creating recipes for restaurant foods he liked and planning menus for special occasions.

A local diner's hamburger sauce caught Dad's taste buds and for a period of time, burgers became a weekly meal while he refined his version of their Sumburger® Sauce. Several festivals and summer fairs in a row, Dad ordered the Italian sausage sandwich, scrutinizing the process and ingredients of the short-order cook. In the end, it was a secret squirt of mustard that perfected the taste. This was all long before websites and shelves of cookbooks.

Dad often helped Mom plan and cook holiday meals with a twist. One Christmas, he replaced our traditional ham with prime rib, and one Easter we were served mutton. He cooked shish-kebabs for company on unfolded wire hangers, and often created a variety of round, toasted sandwiches over an open fire in summer.

With one eye always on crown roast pictures and recipes, he'd sigh, "Doesn't that just look impressive?" While grocery stores or kitchen appliances held no intimidation for him, recipes never kept his attention. My dad followed recipes about like he drove, always looking for shortcuts and a speedy end.

A whistled tune often signaled Dad was in the kitchen on weekend mornings. Breakfast was probably his favorite—to cook and to eat. We would sometimes gather early for the show. He flipped pancakes with abandon, winked before clicking bread down into the toaster, and continued whistling as he cracked eggs into the skillet.

Even today, my brothers and I eat our fried eggs over medium with mustard.

That was Dad's trick to help us as small children get the whole egg down. On special days, our eggs were served with a side of "little pigs." Most people call them sausage links.

This past Christmas, Mom gathered everyone in the kitchen for breakfast with our traditional side of "little pigs." The young adult grandchildren scrunched their faces and in unison said "Links!" with exaggerated smiles. They never met him.

It's cool that I can recall my dad easily through one of his recipes, or by seeing a jar of Spin Blend® at the supermarket. I call him to mind while measuring coffee into the filter with a teaspoon like he taught me. I ponder his patient lessons in the art of gravy making when he used to stop by on his way home from work to help me stir. The click of a toaster reminds me of his goofy grin. But the sad thing about associating your father so much with food is that special times can seem less special without him.

And yet, I accept the challenge to hand these stories and memories—his recipes—down to my daughters, niece, and nephews. I do that most often by getting out his old metal meat grinder and making one of his best and most-loved recipes: Baloney Salad.

It's an event that happens only two or three times a year. But when it does, we buy a couple of loaves of sliced white bread and call it a family party.

Dad's Baloney Salad

3 pounds bologna
1 dozen hard-boiled eggs
1 pint sweet pickle relish, undrained
1 quart of Miracle Whip®, or less
1 pint of mayonnaise

Grind the first two ingredients. Add relish. Work in the dressing and mayo with your hands.

Corinne D. Furtney

Everything But the Kitchen Sink

My grandmother had three sons, of which my dad was the oldest. In raising her three boys, there were certain things she wanted them to know and learn how to do that would help them later in life. It was important to her that they learn how to cook, how to do laundry, and how to iron their own clothes. She wanted to make sure that if and when they got married, they would be able to help out around the house and not just expect their wife to do everything.

My dad can cook. I remember him helping to peel potatoes and carrots and put all the necessary things in the roasting pan on a Sunday morning so that when we got home from church, lunch was ready. He cooked the turkey for Thanksgiving or Christmas and was great at carving it. He was really good at barbequing and enjoyed making spaghetti. He also had a way of making the best popcorn for us to eat while watching Hockey Night in Canada.

When it came to making things he liked to eat, he was quite creative. Some of his most interesting creations were apple juice rice; bacon, lettuce, and relish sandwich; and, of course, peanut butter, lettuce, and mayonnaise sandwich. He enjoyed all of the creations he made, even if no one else did. The one I think he enjoys the most is chili. He makes it his way and will eat it for days in a row if he can. There is no exact recipe but he starts with a few simple items and then adds to it, depending on what items he can find in the pantry and in the fridge. Think of it more like a guideline and then add to it, to make it your own!

Dad's Everything But the Kitchen Sink Chili

1 lb. lean ground beef
2 potatoes, peeled and chopped
2 carrots, sliced
1 can whole tomatoes
1 can kidney beans
1 can brown beans
2 stalks celery, chopped
some mushrooms, chopped
1 onion, chopped
chili powder (optional)

Brown lean ground beef in big pot. Drain off any grease. Add to cooked ground beef, potatoes, carrots, can of whole tomatoes, kidney beans, and brown beans. Add in chopped celery, mushrooms, and onion. Let simmer in pot for several hours.

Note: This is only the start of the recipe. Check the vegetable crisper in your fridge to see what other vegetables you have and might want to add or substitute. If the chili seems too dry, then try adding some spaghetti sauce or tomato sauce.

Sue Hardesty

Dad's Reassurance

Mid October of 1958, I was ten and looking forward to Halloween and trick-or-treating with my friends. Bonnie, Linda, and I were going to a sleepover at another friend's Kathy's house. Her mom would take us around the neighborhood for candy. When we returned, Mrs. Sims would make hot chocolate and serve us various treats. Later we would gather in Kathy's bedroom and tell ghost stories.

However, two weeks before Halloween, my hopes and dreams were shattered. As we sat around the kitchen table devouring Mom's awesome fried chicken and mashed potatoes, Dad dropped the bomb.

"Kids, this weekend we are moving to sunny Florida. Isn't that exciting?"

The spoonful of potatoes I had just stuck in my mouth turned to paste. How could he do this? I can't leave my friends. We have so many plans.

"What do you think about that, kids?" Mom smiled brightly.

"Warm weather all winter sounds great to me," my older brother said. "Besides, I don't like my teacher much this year."

I dropped my chicken leg back on the plate and sat there in stunned silence for a short time, as a tear squeezed past my lashes and slid down my cheek.

"Suzy, you're being awfully quiet. Don't you think it will be fun to visit the beach, while everyone here in Illinois is scooping snow?" Dad asked.

"But, I don't want to leave my friends! We are going to have a Halloween party."

"I want to go swimming," my younger sister squealed, ignoring my protests.

"Me too, me too!" Timmy, my youngest brother, said.

"How can you be so happy about this? My world is coming to an end," I whined, as a couple more tears rolled down my cheeks.

"Now, Suzy, everything will be okay. You'll make new friends and I'm sure there will be parties you can attend in Florida." Dad wrapped his arm around my shoulder.

Tensing up, I said, "But it won't be with Kathy, Bonnie, and Linda. We do everything together. I can't make new friends in a week."

"Let's finish supper and make our plans for packing," Mom said, patting my arm.

That night as I lay in bed crying my heart out and dreading the task of telling my friends about the horrors of leaving them, and how life would never be the same again, my dad slipped into my room, and sat on the edge of the bed pulling me into his arms. "Suzy, I'm sorry you're so upset about this move, but I don't have a choice, I have to go where my work is."

"I know, Daddy, but it's going to be so lonely there without my friends," I said, sniffling.

"Girl, you will make new friends real quick. You are a great kid and all the girls at your new school will love you." Dad gave me a big hug and kissed my cheek. "Now try to get some sleep and have sweet dreams."

"Okay, Daddy. I'll try." I hugged him back.

The following Saturday Mom and Dad loaded us five kids into the van and we started our long trek from Illinois to Florida.

Several weeks later, I had adjusted to my new school and made some friends.

Sandy invited me to a sleepover on Christmas break, along with Janie and Sheila. We were having a swimming party. Imagine that, a pool party at Christmas time. I couldn't wait to write to the girls back in Illinois and tell them about this.

I loved it when Daddy would take us kids to the orange groves and show us how to tell if the fruit was ripe. He would pick an orange from the tree and then let us eat the fresh juicy citrus.

Most Saturdays we would all pile into Dad's work panel truck and head to town. Sometimes he would take us to the beach, where we floated on the waves in inner tubes, made sand castles on the shore, hunted seashells, and watched the seagulls swoop down for a morsel that someone had dropped.

Other times we would go to the strawberry fields and pick the biggest red berries. Mom told us not to eat any until they were washed, but occasionally I couldn't resist and slipped a sweet delectable one into my mouth.

After our adventure for the day, we would stop at the local grocery store so Mom could buy the food we needed for the week. She would take the baby with her into the store, but the other four of us would usually hang out in the back of the van, playing games, bickering, or just talking.

Dad would tell us, "If you kids behave, I'll bring you a treat when I come back from the feed store." He always bought our dog's food at the supply store.

Sometimes he would bring us a sack of candy or chips, but my favorite treat was when he would open the back of the van and lay a stalk of sweet smelling, bright yellow, mini bananas amongst us. "You can have one," he'd say. "You older kids help the younger ones peel theirs."

Timmy would clap his hands and sing, "Nana tree, nana tree. I love nana trees."

After helping him open his banana, I would look for the brightest yellow one and pull it from the stalk. Then I would hold it up to my nose and sniff the sweet aroma. Next I would slowly break open the peel and slide it down the fruit, then lift it to my mouth and take a mouthful, savoring every bite.

When I had delighted in every morsel, I would ask, "Daddy, can I please, please have another one?"

"I don't want you to spoil your supper," he would say with a chuckle.

We would all chime in with, "Just one more."

"They are little," I'd protest, adding, "I promise if you'll let us, I'll help Mom with dishes and not complain."

He would laugh and say, "Well, I guess if you will help without grumbling, you all can have one more."

Once home and the groceries were put away, Mom would tell my older brother to get a few oranges from the crate, and have me pull several bananas from the stalk and peel them. Then she would take the box of strawberries from the refrigerator. "Oh, goody, are we having fruit salad for dinner?" I would ask.

"Yes, we are. Now slice the bananas, James can peel the oranges and dice them, while I cut up the berries."

"I love living in Florida." I clapped my hands.

Now as an adult, I remember how my dad's wisdom, love, and reassurance carried me through that—and later other—difficult situations.

Sue Chenette

Rules of the Road

Make a plan, follow it, Dad likes to say.
He is studying the county plat book
while my sister and I slather mayo on whole wheat.
Coffee percolating, Mom's philodendron draped
green around the window—this

is where our expeditions are launched—
hikes to Morgan Falls, canoe trips on the Namekagon—
in the morning's sense of sunny order,
ham and relish from the fridge,
bird book, binoculars.

There is a right way to do things: canoe secured
to the roof rack with taut ropes, life preservers in the trunk.
Three parts to any job: Assemble your tools. Do it. Clean up.
Another of Dad's maxims, though he never pronounces
in ringing tones, only seems to let us overhear.

***

The summer my sister and I set out to wander Europe
he jotted down, along with family addresses,
Rules of the Road: Drive under control. Get the big picture.
After the last one, a jaunty exclamation point:
Keep your wits and windshield clear!

We tucked them away in a backpack,
forgotten metaphors (Aim high. Leave yourself an out.)
as we pitched a tent, left Tivoli at midnight
for a weekend with strangers, thumbed rides
in our short skirts—

still,
they'd fold in with the maps, a kind
of protection, as if
they could see us safe home.

Joyce Gero

My Champion—My Dad

He was a giant among men in his time, his rawboned six-and-a-half-foot frame towering head and shoulders above his peers. The skin of his back and chest, unexposed to direct sunlight, was as smooth and white as a baby's, while below the brim of the straw hat he wore in summer, a farmer's tan permanently bronzed his face and throat in a shade that was repeated from the base of his rolled-up sleeves to his fingertips.

By the time I came along—the afterthought among five children when he was almost half a century old—those fingers were swollen with arthritis, reminding me of the thick, stubby carrots we used to pull from barrels of sand stored in the cellar for winter vegetable preservation. I remember a heavy head of salt-and-pepper hair that, no matter how often he combed it, never lost the cowlick and the unruly shock, reminiscent of *The Star Weekly* comic's Dennis the Menace character, that constantly fell over his right eye. I also recall the glasses that, no matter how often they were cleaned, always bore a smudged film that made me wonder how he could see at all. I can still feel the warmth of a huge hand as he pulled me to his side, a normally undemonstrative man showing in his own way that he was especially proud of some accomplishment. I have no memory of him shouting in anger, but can hear his voice clearly in a crowded room, along with the respectful silence of those around him.

I carry early memories like snapshots—being plucked from my crib and put in bed with Mom before Dad headed to the barn for morning milking, "helping" him thresh burlap bagsful of dried beans on the barn brow, tagging along as he tapped sugar maple trees on our property beside the lake, watching as he sharpened farm implements on a whirling grindstone wheel, occasionally accompanying him when he drove the school bus to pick up my brothers, my sister, and neighbouring children, listening as he imparted bits of wisdom and knowledge into my sponge-like brain.

I was probably five or six when we got our first television. In a farming community on Canada's East Coast in the 50s and 60s, viewing was limited to the two channels we could pick up with rabbit ears, and I grew up watching the programs my father watched, cheering the six original teams on "Hockey Night in Canada," developing a musical taste from "Don Messer's Jubilee," a weekly folk music variety show, and learning about the world through the evening news and "The 20th Century," a series of documentaries hosted by Walter Cronkite and sponsored by Prudential Insurance, which I remember being advertised as "solid as the Rock of Gibraltar."

Because of my father's influence, as a child I had far greater knowledge about our country's geography and leadership, world events, and politics, than I could ever hope to have today. I vividly recall the names Dag Hammarskjöld and U Thant, but have no idea who came after them as Secretary-Generals of the United Nations. I was familiar with NATO, NORAD, and the Warsaw Pact. At seven, I followed national coverage of the case of Steven Truscott, a 14-year-old boy wrongfully convicted of the murder of a young girl. Because Dad listened, I did too.

Unfortunately, there were other things I paid less attention to. Mental arithmetic tips, distant family and community relationships, shorter routes from here to there on a Sunday drive—these are some of the things my father shared that I wish I could recall today.

Ours was a home filled with reference books, novels, and magazines, with puzzles and games, with a thirst for knowledge and learning. There was an implicit understanding that we were a little brighter, a little more literate, a little more refined than our contemporaries, and we strove to live up to our parents' expectations. We were encouraged to earn the respect of our neighbours, a respect that our father had earned before us, albeit couched with a bit of good-humoured ridicule.

There is a story I heard years later about an encounter with a former neighbour, who enquired after Dad's health. Another neighbour had told him that Dad had been hospitalized briefly "with a rupture. Of course, he called it a hernia, but you and I know it was a rupture."

On another occasion, he became the brunt of long-term teasing in our own home. Always, we had a cot in the kitchen, and it was here that Dad would settle for a nap after the morning barn chores were done. One Christmas, as Mom prepared our noon holiday feast, a carrot pudding steaming on the stove exploded. Bits of hot battered fruit rained down on Dad, only to be plucked up by him as he lay still sleeping, and popped, warm and spicy, into his mouth. Dad, of course, with high expectations of both himself and his family, did not share our amusement.

While expecting much, he took pleasure and pride in our simplest accomplishments. I remember "performing" for guests at his command when I was four or five, lying on my tummy and lifting to touch the back of my head with my toes. Or accompanying him to threshing parties the fall I was eight, driving tractors belonging to every farmer in our community as we gathered oats. He may not have been as pleased with my driving skills in later years, when I accidentally dumped him off a hay wagon during a sudden stop, or when he abandoned his post on the verandah steps to avoid being crushed by my sister's car as she bravely coached me in driving.

For us, a treat was a Sunday drive in summer, with a stop for a soft ice-cream cone along the way. We seldom had Dad participate in our play, but during those drives we sang along to hymns and standards, delighted in his recitations of long poems, such as "The Cremation of Sam McGee," and played word games, inspired by the sights along our route. Perhaps he mellowed over the years, for later, when grandchildren came along he was much more open to physical play. I remember him lying supine on the floor as one of my nephews fell on him over and over again from a standing position, yelling "Timber!" on his way down.

I remember my father as someone who knew everything and could do anything. A schoolteacher when he met my mother, he settled for a life of farming, supplementing his income as school bus driver, census enumerator, and other seasonal or short-term ventures. In 1959, when I was seven, we moved to a larger farm half an hour away in another county, leaving the beautiful lake of my early childhood behind. In 1963, the year my elder brother took sole charge of the farm and my older sister left home for university, my father resumed his teaching career. Six years later, when one-room schools in our district amalgamated into a regional elementary school, he was forced to find new work, and at sixty-three, began a weekly commute to an Irving mill in Saint John where he had been hired to scale pulp. Eventually, his work moved closer to home and he was able to return each evening, until in his early seventies he retired to enjoy travelling and relaxation with our mom, going so far as to help with the cleanup after a meal.

Roles in our home were always clearly defined. Dad handled most of the outside chores, finances, and bill payment while Mom took care of cooking, cleaning, sewing, laundry, and tending the vegetable and flower gardens. Mom, who did not drive and had not worked outside the home since her marriage, depended on neighbours to chauffeur her to Women's Institute meetings, and on Dad to take her grocery shopping in town, a distance of ten miles. Despite their comfort with traditional roles for themselves, both encouraged their daughters to pursue post-secondary educations and careers. Dad, especially, would speak about the future in terms of continued advancement and opportunities.

In 1967, as we celebrated Canada's Centennial, Dad and I talked about the changes we could anticipate in the decades ahead. He spoke about how different the world and our lives would be by the time we reached the twenty-first century.

"I'll be gone by then," he told me, "but you should still be around."

I was fifteen at the time, and it seemed so far away as to be unimaginable. Today, at the age he was then, I look back at the intervening years and the progress that not even he could have predicted, and sometimes, in the midst of doubts and uncertainty, twenty-nine years after his death, I find myself thinking, "I wish Dad were here. He'd know what to do."

Tammy Pfaff

The Adventurer

Dad and I woke early one summer morning, anchored in the Elk River in Maryland on our 19-foot runabout. I was about six years old. After gathering together a box of cereal, milk, and sugar stored in Tupperware containers, we rowed to shore in a dinghy, leaving Mom and my two older sisters behind to sleep in. We settled up in a woodsy area just above the beach. Dad handed over to me the cereal he so lovingly prepared. The first bite tasted kind of strange. "Dad, I think there is something wrong with my cereal."

"There's nothing the matter with that, you eat it," he said.

I tried another bite. "Dad, it tastes salty."

He dipped his fingers in the unmarked container, took a taste, and chuckled. "I must have grabbed the salt instead of the sugar."

I was thankful he handed me a new bowl of Corn Pops, even if it was minus the sugar. I am even more thankful that he didn't force me to eat coffee soup, consisting of a plate of homemade bread, coffee, milk, and sugar. Dad was raised on coffee soup at his grandmother's house and actually enjoyed it.

My father, Ronald Thomas Stewart, grew up in Western Pennsylvania during the forties. His parents moved around quite often as his father served in the navy during World War II. For many years, my dad lived with his grandmother, a widow running a boardinghouse near a brick factory in St. Charles. Before Dad reached kindergarten, he nearly died of scarlet fever, and was quarantined in his grandmother's home for a month. Medication wasn't like it is today. Finally his fever broke. No one could enter the home until all the linens and the mattress were burned.

I believe while growing up with his grandmother, she instilled in him the value of working hard to earn a good day's pay. Dad held a job as janitor at his local church from the time he was twelve. When he graduated from high school, he took a risk coming from the rural community to find work near the city of Philadelphia. His uncle arranged an interview at Gulf Oil, but it didn't pan out. He worked odd jobs, commuting back home on the weekends to spend time with his fiancé. He was determined not to quit and head back home where work was scarce. Shortly after he married my mother, he was hired at Scott Paper. Through seniority, he was eligible to train as a machine adjustor for the plant. Throughout his career, he worked shift work. Every week his shift changed.

It was nothing for Dad to drive us to the marina in Maryland after his midnight shift, to spend the weekend boating. As a boater, he worked his way up from sharing a 19-foot runabout with his cousin, to owning a 25-foot cabin cruiser. He achieved the ultimate dream when he purchased a 1968 32-foot Luhrs with a flying bridge in 1972. It was a big step for Dad, but it helped that his best friend encouraged him along the way. He took our family on many boating trips, acquiring lifelong memories.

As soon as spring burst through, Dad would work many weekends preparing the boat for the water. My sisters and I were encouraged to help out. We scraped barnacles, sanded varnish, and added coats of paint each year. Dad usually tended to the engine maintenance.

The big day finally came when I turned twelve years old, and Dad taught me how to dock the 32-footer. I sat proudly behind the steering wheel way high up on the flying bridge. It took great skill to maneuver such a large boat between two docks in reverse into what appeared to be a very small slip. Dad did it with ease, it seemed, even in the wind.

Dad learned how to chart the waters, through boating school and his cousin who was in the coast guard. He was unsure of himself the first time out in the bay with no sight of land. His confidence only grew after the first trip. Dad was never afraid to venture out to sea.

One dark night we were heading out to Veasey's Cove. Mom and I were tending to the bow lines. As she reached to place the rope on the hook of the piling, she lost her footing and slipped over the rail. Knowing that Mom couldn't swim without a life jacket, I yelled up to Dad who quickly hit reverse. A little shaken and a little wet, we fished her out to safety.

One of Dad's fondest and longest trips by boat was to Crisfield, Tangier, and Smith's Island off the eastern shore of Virginia. I walked the five-mile stretch of

Tangier one quiet evening, an island that only supported about 1,500 people. Warm and friendly, the community made their living through fishing and crabbing.

Dad's most fearful trip was to Rehoboth Beach in Delaware. Along the way we were coming out of Delaware Bay at the breakwater into the Atlantic Ocean. The waves quickly went from an average choppy to thirty-foot swells. The waves were so high, Dad was afraid to turn the boat around. But at his instinct, he got us up on top of a wave and managed to turn around and head toward Indian River to get us to our destination. I always referred to those waves as the roly-poly waves, not knowing until recently how afraid Dad was.

I consider myself the luckiest girl to have grown up in the spring and summer months on the water—not an average childhood opportunity. I could always find something to do, whether it was skiing, fishing, crabbing, or just sunbathing on the bow of the boat. There was nothing like the spray of water brushing my legs as I dangled my feet over the bow during a boat ride. I can still remember sitting on the dock in the early evening, looking out onto the still quiet river, and seeing the sunsets varied with colours of pink and yellow. We made many great friends at the marina. Dad made all these memories possible.

My father instilled in me the value of working hard and being a responsible adult. He led me back to church to give my children a Christian upbringing. I believe I am finding adventure through Christ because of the examples my father set before me. Just like being out in the middle of the bay with no land in sight, my dad—the adventurer—taught me that when I can't see what's ahead, to take a chance and step out in faith.

Mansoor Behnam

Sunday Afternoon

It's Sunday afternoon. And geese are just
Another passerby waving hi and bye to everyone
Including Jesus on his next cross.
The sun whispers her secrets over page 38
Of a collection of Wordsworth's poetry that Grandma
Is reading, on a sofa that looks like a pregnant seal.

It's Sunday afternoon. The chimney's caught cold,
Sneezing, drawing abstract lines over the sunset.
Here, Lucy the cat is purring incessantly on my lap,
Waiting for Mom's footsteps to go to the fridge
And pour her a bowl of milk.

It's Sunday afternoon. Grandpa is telling his story
For the 836th time and I pretend that I have never heard it.
It's different again. This time it happens in Budapest.

It's Sunday afternoon. Jimmy the usual streetwalker
Ties his shoelace on the steps of our backdoor
And taps on the head of the neighbour's dog.
I see his cigarette's smoke following him
Like a flag over his head.

It's Sunday afternoon. And it feels like I'm wandering
In a recently discovered painting by van Gogh.
It smells like wine. Perhaps he sipped his wine while
Painting, or used vinegar to make a natural gold colour.

It's Sunday afternoon and I feel old-fashioned enough

To write this poem about it, while Vivaldi's melodies
Dance the leaves outside my window.

It's Sunday afternoon as I turn the page of Don Quixote
of La Mancha. The windmill turns on my page
And like him, I try to fight it
with my pen;
And out of the corner of my eye the TV's showing an ad
about chiffon cake like Grandma used to make
And have with Grandpa in 1959
Next to the chimney. In a dream,
Flavoured by fresh brewed coffee,
As he was following the lines
On the pages of "Teach Me How To Cry"
With his trembling finger.

Kristi Lewis

Irrigation Pipes Like Chimes

He walks alone in the field out there
and he stares at the mountain sometimes
and he drives around in the tractor
irrigation pipes like chimes

He helps the mothers bear their calves
and builds a better fence
He defends his fields from choker weeds
He walks in silence

He rumbles down the gravel roads
Built a swimming pool for us
echoes of our laughter
filled his heart, replacing dust

He's put rooves o'er all our heads
He's helped bread be on our tables
Sometimes when I was little
I'd watch him cleaning up the stables

We all say he works too hard
but his eyes still sparkle true
He says it's all been worth it
He says these things to you

He plays cello and recorder,
Oma at piano keys
They sing praises to the Lord
Together making memories.

When the cows went it was hard for him
to know just what to do
but he keeps it all still trucking
for his beloved few

So he's built this sacred kingdom
says he could die tomorrow
'neath the breast of the Beaufort Mountain
that he'd not be plagued by sorrow

He walks alone in the field out there
and he stares at the mountain sometimes
and he drives around in the tractor
irrigation pipes like chimes

Sonja Grgar

The Man with a Typewriter

For my father Milenko, with love

The man with a typewriter
Is a chronicler of the world;
He is as old as the universe,
And as innocent as an embryo.

He whirls molecules, quarks, and stardust
Into elegant lines,
Etches them into
The forgiving blank
Of a page on his typewriter.

That page is where he is most alive,
Where he paints the unforgiving
World
Into a stylized order,

Airs all his grievances,
Failures, successes,
And all his obsessions.

It is where he reassembles me
Daily,
And always inaccurately.

He says that all of his letters
And journals
Are for me,
To have as a memory
Once he is gone,

But I am afraid
To take a peek
Into his universe,
Afraid I will lose myself in it,
Or find myself
With painful
Clarity.

Andrea Arthur Owan

My Father's Shoes

My father was dying, and we wouldn't admit it. Even the doctors seemed lost in making a proper diagnosis and rendering care.

Evidently my dad had an unusually difficult case of Parkinson's, and a small stroke complicated matters. When he confessed to his general practitioner that one day while driving he had to lift his right leg up manually to move it from the accelerator to the break, Dr. S first stared aghast at him, then told him his driving days were over. I knew it would be downhill from there: If my dad couldn't drive and travel, then—as far as he was concerned—life would become stagnant. He often said, "Once you've traveled, it sort of gets into your blood."

Soon after his stroke, my youngest son and I went to my mom and dad's apartment on Saturday mornings. My son would help my mom with cleaning and vacuuming while I'd roust my dad out of bed for some water therapy in their pool.

I looked forward to that Saturday morning ritual—time my dad and I had alone, to relax, to talk, to reminisce. He'd don his black walking shoes, swim trunks, and polo shirt, and off we'd go. One day, however, as he dressed to return to the apartment, he couldn't get his black shoes on without my help. From that time forward it became a ritual: I'd take his shoes off and put them back on. The table had finally turned. Although frustrating for him, helping my dad was a blessing to me.

Within several months, and just a week following his eighty-eighth birthday, my dad died. And that's when I really started thinking about those shoes and the places my dad's feet traveled—the places he'd seen and things he'd done that affected his life, and, consequently, affected mine.

It seemed my dad had lived an entire lifetime by the time I was born. Those feet of his took him across the world, and I loved hearing his life stories.

In high school in Waterloo, Iowa, during the depression, he hopped a moving train like a hobo. That almost got him killed, so he never attempted that risky trick again. He walked around town selling baked goods, wanting to earn just enough money to buy a bicycle, which he did. He must have tired of riding a bike though, because he eventually traded the bike for a horse and cart. He obviously loved that horse, Woody, because he spoke endearingly of him. Unfortunately, they had to put Woody down after he stepped on a rusty nail and developed lockjaw.

When the United States entered World War II, my dad hotfooted it down to the recruiting office to enlist as a pilot. They rejected him—something to do with his eyes—so he entered the army and drove supply trucks across North Africa, France, and into Germany under Patton and as part of the Big Red 1 unit. While growing up I'd rummage through his memorabilia, imploring him, "Tell me about the war, Dad," but he avoided discussing it. My mom said he went away one man and came back another, and—like so many other men who returned—was never really the same again.

Only later in his life did he offer more detail. When telling my husband and boys about it, he'd get animated and descriptive: popping the supply truck hood to heat coffee and rations on the hot manifold; trading cigarettes for fresh farm eggs in France; spending what he described as "the worst three weeks of my life" in a pup tent because of torrential, relentless rain. And he'd often shake his head in sadness and wonder aloud, "How can people do that kind of thing to one another?" (He'd witnessed the aftermath of a concentration camp following Germany's surrender.)

Following WWII, he again pursued the Air Force and was once again rejected. So he obtained his private pilot's license and joined the Civil Air Patrol. Then he joined American Airlines and eventually moved from ticket counter agent to personnel manager. In that position he flew around the United States hiring new college graduates. When American wanted him to advance to corporate headquarters in New York City, he said "no, thanks," he didn't want to live that lifestyle. So, his feet took him to another job, which eventually landed us in Hawaii, where I grew up. That lifestyle suited us just fine.

One of my earliest memories of my dad was when we lived in Dallas, Texas. He was a handy guy and liked to work in the yard. At the age of two or three, I got to "supervise" and ride around in the wheelbarrow, which I considered a very boss-like thing to do.

After Dallas we moved to Las Vegas, where my mom and dad bought a small apartment complex. Everywhere he lived, my dad engaged in a little real estate investing. (I have that in my blood too.) Every spring, swamp cooler pads needed replacing and early summer saw us draining, scrubbing, and refilling the pool. I helped with both jobs.

We also harvested an almond tree growing next to the main house. It was a yearly ritual: I held the bags while he climbed into the tree and dropped almonds into them. Then he'd shell and roast them, always peering frequently into the oven to make sure they didn't burn. We'd feast on those delicious almonds for days.

His feet also took him golfing and fishing. On one deep-sea, Pacific Ocean, excursion, he won the award for the biggest catch. He received a monstrous (to me) trophy, along with a substantial cash prize, and took enormous delight in sneaking unseen into the kitchen throughout the day to wedge wads of large bills in the fish ornament adorning the trophy's top. His eyes lit up, and he giggled every time my mom squealed in delight with her discovery. I was so proud of him and that trophy.

It was his feet that ran alongside me as I learned to ride a bike. They took me to the North Shore of Oahu to go shell hunting, and strolled miles on Waikiki Beach and across the Hawaiian Islands and Johnston Atoll. On weekends, they'd take me to coin shows, where I learned to search bags of change for rare coins to snap into blue coin collection books. Even at the time of his death, my dad had coins he wanted catalogued.

He started a gymnastics school in Hawaii and opened a free class to disabled students. My dad rejoiced in watching the thrill those kids experienced when they performed something they—or their parents—never thought they'd be able to do.

Another place his shoes took him was out onto our apartment window ledge in Hawaii—fourteen stories above the ground, without railing or harness—to wash the sliding glass windows. I always thought I'd have a nervous breakdown watching him, so I'd retreat to my room to busy my hands and head until he finished.

He toured the U.S.; cruised twice—once on the Queen Mary when they used that vessel to return Europe-stationed troops to the U.S. following WWII;

waterskied in Mexico (where he managed to flip upside down and almost drown); and traveled through Europe—this time as a tourist—nine times. He was happiest when he traveled and learned about new places and people. He instilled that love in me too, and I've passed it on to my husband and sons.

He walked me down the aisle to give me away in marriage, but not before taking my arm in the church narthex, looking me squarely in the eyes, and saying, "If you want to change your mind, we can keep walking right down the aisle without stopping and right on out the back door." We stopped at the altar, I got married, and then he had my mom call me the second day into my honeymoon to see if I was all right.

The most important things to my dad were loyalty and family. He quietly helped others and once told a newspaper reporter, "No matter where you live, you should be of service to your community in some way."

Soon after my dad died, my mom called us over to clean out his side of the closet. She couldn't look at his clothes, hanging there vacant and ownerless. We bagged everything, promising to give them away or see what might fit my husband or our boys.

But I couldn't bear to part with the black shoes—reminders of my dad's rich, full, complex life; reminders of the last, tender moments we'd enjoyed together. Every so often I pull them out of my closet, run my hands along their creased leather, and thank God for the earthly father who blessed me with so much opportunity, joy, laughter, and love.

Oh, how I miss the man who walked in those shoes.

Jenne Acevedo

Wedding Trusses

Memories of wedding plans do not usually include steel beams, but mine do. As I remember those magical (and expensive) days of caterers, flowers, and finding the perfect songs for every moment, I think of cutting beams of steel, welding, and Daddy.

I did not always call him Daddy. Even as a young girl, I called him Dad. But as I grew up and learned more about life, I saw how God had blessed me with this incredible father. Our relationship began to change, and I began to call him Daddy. This name was not only a term of endearment, but a term of respect. As an only girl growing up with three brothers, I was always close to my mom, but Daddy has a special place in my heart.

I admired his dedication to our family and his love and protection of my mom. I knew I wanted a husband like that some day. His commitment to our church as a founding family also was something he took very seriously, serving in leadership for as long as I can remember. Although I was not exactly a pastor's kid, everyone knew us by our parents and watched us as though we were.

Daddy cherished me. He understood the significance of being a daddy and the role he played in my growing spirit. I knew I had to find a man to cherish me like that. Anything less would simply not do. I was blessed with this amazing man of God to protect me, guide me, teach me, and love me as I blossomed from a little girl into a woman. The basis of his love, grace, and integrity gave me a solid foundation to understand my heavenly Father. I knew this was a gift not many were given.

When I was old enough to date, Daddy made it clear that every date was an interview with him first. If the initial handshake did not go well, the first impression was shot. Dates came and went until the right one came into my life. This man had big shoes to fill and my parents spent lots of time in prayer. Through five years of ups and downs with one young man, Daddy trusted in the Lord for the right husband.

Once engaged, we started planning the big wedding, an expensive event for 450 guests. The groom's family was huge, while my church family was even larger. They all had to be invited to share in this special day. As Mom and I researched and planned, Daddy looked at the bottom line. He wanted to give me everything I ever dreamed of and took an extra job on the side to pay for the expenses. This project, building trusses for a commercial building, became lovingly known as the "wedding trusses." After working all day in his general contracting company, he spent evenings outside in his shop working with beams of steel. I never heard him complain or ask why I needed such an expensive day. He just built.

I would go outside to his shop to share the latest wedding plans or issues as he welded and worked hard to pay for our special event. Between cuts and welds, he listened to my excitement with a smile and told me how much fun it would be. Although he was not into all the specifics, he knew how important every little detail was to me and listened intently.

The wedding took longer for us to plan than it took Daddy to build the trusses. In just under five weeks, Daddy purchased the steel, cut it down to the exact size, and welded it. This custom-built project was installed in the ritzy gallery after each of the six steel web trusses were sandblasted and painted beautifully to display gold-plated chandeliers and large, heavy artwork. Although that building is no longer a gallery today, the wedding trusses still hang overhead.

About a month before our big day, Daddy took me on a fun daddy/daughter trip to Washington, DC for five days. Both of us soaked in the culture and history as we visited the Smithsonian, various galleries, and national memorials. We had a special time together and I will always remember going to our nation's capital for the first time with him.

One of my favorite wedding pictures is of Daddy and me before we made our memorable walk down the aisle. Just before getting into position, the photographer snapped a precious picture of us from behind, looking back. As Daddy gave me away to the man of my dreams, we both knew it was the defining moment that would change our relationship forever. No longer would I look to Daddy for guidance and protection, but I would look to this new man. Daddy took this ceremonial act very seriously and gladly gave me away, confident in God's choice.

My daddy has given so much to those around him. He is loved, respected, and admired by many, especially by his children and ten grandchildren. "The godly walk with integrity; blessed are their children who follow them" (Proverbs 20:7 NLT). I have been truly blessed by my heavenly Father who gave me such a special daddy.

Bonnie Nish

On His Own Terms

Everyone loved my dad. From his quirky sense of humour to his open kind heart, he was a determined man who loved life and all those he came in contact with. Every Sunday night when I was a child, we would order in food—often Chinese, and then after dinner when our stomachs were full, we would sit around in the living room watching "The Wild Kingdom," "The Wonderful World of Disney," and "The Ed Sullivan Show." Dad would lie across the sofa and I would lie across the top right above him. I remember feeling so safe and protected and comforted there. That is how my dad always made me feel.

Years later, when Dad was sick and I was finding it hard being across the country, I went out and bought some Chinese food, sat down on the sofa with my youngest daughter, and watched a Disney movie. Recapturing this childhood memory gave me the strength and courage to go on. I could once again feel wrapped in the love I felt whenever my dad hugged me or put me on his shoulders to carry me as a young child or simply just lay beside me on the sofa on a Sunday evening. These simple gifts are the ones we cherish, save, and pass on.

My dad passed on so many wonderful things to me, which I am proud to have. They are not the material possessions that so easily come and go over our lifetime but rather the incidentals; the things no one talks about because they are the everyday things. The things we take for granted that we all should have and the momentous things that only certain people can give us. These are the things my father gave to me.

My dad gave me my words. Whether it was through a poem he recited over and over again through the evening drives we took when I was a teen when he made his business calls, or the rhymes he made up to make us laugh, he was full of poetry. On our drives I also learnt to think critically, to question everything, and to believe in the power of love because my father so loved me. And while that may seem like a simple statement, it isn't. Working on a day-to-day basis with children who don't always have a safe place or anyone who makes them feel loved or special, I know it is the most important statement we can make about one another and the greatest gift we can give our children.

My father taught me that you receive the greatest joys through compassion and giving. I know because he was so proud of the fact that he knew each one of my friends not by name but by their street address as he insisted on driving us everywhere. This was his joy and also his way to stay connected. Even as a teen I was honored to have him in my life in this way. Near the end when my dear friend Sue went to visit him, he at first didn't recognize her. When she told him she lived on Clinton Avenue, he knew right away who she was. All my friends adored him. But Dad did this for everyone whether they were family or friends. He was truly generous with his time and made sure that if someone was in need he could be there to help him or her. That was who he was.

My father taught me by example. He was strict because he had a sense of justice and what was right and wrong and was determined to pass this along to us. But he also had a sense of adventure and curiosity. He taught me to skate, took me fishing, and showed me that it was never too late in life to switch careers or go back to school. He was always pushing himself to be more and find out what was just around that next corner. At eighty he was still playing tennis three times a week. He never stopped until he eventually couldn't walk any more. At eighty-seven when he wanted to stay in touch with family he had a volunteer in his nursing home teach him how to Skype. He could do this before I had even figured it out.

When I was little and we would be fishing, he made a huge deal every time I caught a sunfish even though he then made me throw them back. Dad made me feel that what I did was worthwhile even in the smallest thing and that he was proud of me. He made me appreciate my accomplishments because he helped me to work hard to achieve. He knew that some things didn't come easily for me like spelling or math and yet he never gave up on me. He pushed me to keep trying. I never did become good at math or spelling despite his best efforts, yet because he kept an open mind he gave me the ability to think freely and to create myself. Through it all, my dad gave me one of the greatest gifts I could ever ask for, ultimately the ability to live life on my own terms as I saw him do every day of his own.

Bonnie Nish

Eulogy

It is in the skies
that our eyes meet,
memories washed against
a backdrop of scarlet
flood around us and as you remember
I remember too.
You are pulling
the string to roller blinds
their yellow tinged stained bottoms
block our view of the world
when drawn.
You release the darkness back
out to earth while robins
and blue jays
swirl near lilac trees.
The cool morning breeze blows
through windows usually shut tight.
We eat scrambled eggs in silence
you read the paper, I look at comics,
we can talk tomorrow or next year
it doesn't matter I think,
after all when you are seven
you believe there is the rest of your life
to catch up.

But you, you realize that each morning
is another day past being,
a pearl you tuck in your pocket for later
along with the frail pages
of love letters you wrote now forgotten
and poems lost you always remember.
These are the treasures you gather for the days
when you come home and don't leave
the ones that sustain you when the darkness returns
and the blinds are closing.
I hold your hand
feel your heartbeat slowing.
"Can you see the blue jays?" I ask.
You nod, look beyond me to where
the lilacs have dropped their leaves.
The robin's nest is empty
the garden silent.
Your stillness fills the room
your eyes no longer search the skies,
but I know every time a cloud moves
I will feel you once again.

Linda Grace Cousins

The Bounty

It was a particularly beautiful autumn day, the colours a grand mix of bright yellow and red glorious hues. Pulling into the drive, I got out and took a slight detour, walking to the shore of Lake Ontario. The lake was active, frothy, and the sun danced on the steel blue surface. I sat on a large boulder, feeling heavy, unsure of what I was going to say to this once vibrant, animated, funny man. Today I was here to see my dying father on what would be his last Thanksgiving. Dad had an insatiable love of nature and language. As children we were often enlisted to help care for wayward animals that somehow made their way to our yard. Dad nursed a wounded snow owl back to health in our shed one winter. And on another occasion, we became the caretakers of six tiny wild bunnies who had been abandoned by their mother. Dad placed them on a heating blanket and patiently fed the little rabbits a mixture of English custard and water through a little dropper.

His delight in the idiocies of the English language was also a constant source of amusement to him. While visiting London one year, he saw a subway, or rather a Tube doorway, with a sign that read: "This door is alarmed." Dad pointed at the adjoining door and said, "This door is asleep."

Pulling my sweater close as the wind from the lake picked up, I glanced over at a huge maple tree in full red glory. I recalled a time, as a small asthmatic child hospitalized at Toronto's Crippled Children's Centre, when I phoned my dad, little fingers excitedly dialing the number.

"Daddy, Daddy!" I recall saying excitedly through the phone. "I just read Dylan Thomas' 'A Child's Christmas in Wales'."

"That's wonderful, sweetheart," he said with encouragement. "What grabbed you?"

"Well...there was this moment in the book…this funny moment!"

"What was it, love?"

"A little boy 'mittened' at the door Daddy…'mittened'!"

My dad's delight was obvious.

"How clever of him…that Dylan Thomas," he said.

"I know!" I replied enthusiastically. "That's what I do! In the winter, I 'mitten' at the door!"

"Yes, love, you do."

"Okay, well, I have to go now, Daddy."

"All right love, keep reading!"

"Ok...bah bye."

* * *

Dad loved Thanksgiving and would always throw himself into the preparations, never one to let Mum do it all. I looked down at my basket full of carefully labeled Tupperware containers of traditional fare I would be feeding him this year. My brothers and mother had already been by, as we made it a point to never leave him alone for a minute.

We were helping him pass, in the most beautiful, familial way as the tentacles of his tenacious brain tumour wrapped around his brain stem, stifling forever the very thing he valued most in life—his mind.

Suddenly I was brought back to reality and flinched as a large wave hit the break wall where an old man and a small boy sat fishing. I looked away toward the water and suddenly heard a loud thump! It was far too close for my comfort. Turning to look, my stomach tightened as a very large fish lay writhing on the rock beside me. Startled, I jumped up in shock. The man was cheering and the little boy was running toward the three-foot fish laying on the rock with a large hook in its fin. The man excitedly pointed at the fish saying, "Feesh! Feesh!"

My face reddened as I said softly, "Yes. Wonderful. Good for you. Bad for fish." The man looked at me quizzically. I smiled at him, eyes filled with tears. He suddenly looked very uncomfortable, quickly looked away, picked up the fish, and left, the little boy following quickly behind. "Best to move along," I thought picking up my old worn, picnic basket.

* * *

I sat beside my father, his body limp, unable to move. He smiled a wide smile and I kissed him on his lukewarm cheek. "Dad," I said smiling, "it's Thanksgiving! I made you a turkey!" Without missing a beat, he glanced up at me with a twinkle in his lovely blue eyes and said wearily, "That must have been some trick.

"Poor bloody turkeys," he said smiling as I reached for the basket. I opened the dish of ground-up bounty and waved it under his nose. He tightened his lips and said, "Uuuummm…smells deliceeous!"

Together, we laughed lightly, as I fed him his ground-up turkey, gravy, mashed potatoes, and beloved mushy peas. My dear dad squeezed my hand, his eyes squinted shut, his mouth smiling widely, and I looked at him through a lens full of tears, love, adoration, and appreciation for this, our last Thanksgiving.

George W. Frey

Proud to Be His Son

My daddy was so smart. I thought he knew how to do everything—hunt, fish, camp, cook, milk a cow, whittle, plow a field with a team of mules, raise the best garden in the town, build a house, do electric and plumbing tasks, and he was a good preacher too. His name was Samuel, from the Bible, though everybody called him Sammy except my mother who called him Sam.

My three older siblings graduated high school before I ever started to school. Growing up as an only child was not only lonely but gave me a chance to invent my entertainment. I spent a lot of time with my daddy who taught me how to feed the chickens, rob the beehives of honey, milk the cow, and slop the hogs. During wintertime, everyone in the house woke up to a deafening noise that sounded like a freight train coming through the house as Daddy removed the clinkers and ashes from the stove before he lit a new fire.

Daddy had a good job at DuPont in Old Hickory where he worked forty hours a week, providing a living for his wife and four children in the home he built, but he struggled with a higher calling. At age thirty-five, standing at a crossroads in his life, he finally gave up the struggle and answered God's call to be a preacher.

His decision was a difficult one. He was shy, and thought his education was insufficient, but he knew how to read Scripture, share his own personal witness to the gospel, and pray with people in prayer meetings.

Daddy shared his faith with Richard, a neighbor and coworker, who eventually also felt called to preach. They reminded me of Moses and his brother Aaron. God had a pair of preachers whom He called to tell the world about Jesus, but they had no idea how to do it. With a charisma and passion to witness to anyone, anywhere, and everywhere, these two young men set out to spread the Good News.

After prayer and brainstorming, a notion emerged to become a team and together take the gospel to the world. One could preach one night and the other the next night. They would become evangelists for Christ. They would go into the highways and the hedges and compel folks to come in, just like the Scripture said.

This germ in the leavening began to ferment and bubble—changing forever the lives of these two young zealots for Christ. With more prayer, they trusted the Lord and came up with the name "The Highways and Hedges Evangelistic Party."

Sixty years later, I visited Richard and watched the tears roll down his cheeks when he spoke of Daddy. He told me I would never know how much my daddy meant to him. But, I could imagine because I knew how much he meant to me.

My visit with Richard, fifty years after Daddy died, were precious moments. Being a small lad of seven when their ministry began, excitement filled me to hear him tell his memorable experiences. They preached everywhere there was an invitation and some places where there was not. Their church became the hospitals, prisons, the forgotten parts of the city, and the countryside. Invitations included sites with no church. They improvised, met in tobacco barns, someone's living room, or even built brush arbors. People gathered, Sam and Richard showed up, shared the gospel, and saw many changed lives.

They shared their dream with other people to take the gospel to their world, as they knew it, and soon the contributions made it possible to acquire a tent and all the trappings. Their equipment included a three-pole tent, 100 chairs, piano, songbooks, and a trailer to haul it. They built a shed to store it all, bought a public address system, mounted it on the car to advertise their meeting to the community, and sometimes held impromptu street services.

As a child, I remember how much fun it was when we drove up to an empty lot with a trailer full of equipment. The attention was enormous. Kids emerged to watch and men volunteered to help. Watching the men drive the stakes with a sledgehammer, raise the tent on those long sixteen-foot poles, and tie the ropes to the stakes, was awesome.

According to Richard, with a full tent every night, overflow people stood around outside. For two weeks, Daddy preached one night and Richard preached the other. Repentance and salvation came to as many as fifty souls in the two weeks, with baptism taking place afterward in the local creek.

A tight schedule prevailed because when the service ended each night, they would rush home, change clothes, and leave to go work the graveyard shift at their job. One evening while coming home from a service, we had a flat tire. Daddy was changing the tire when his carpool showed up on their way to work. They stopped, helped change the tire, and then took him on to work.

Richard wanted me to tell him about the children's chorus Daddy always directed each night before the main service began. This was the best part of the evening for me because I loved to sing. All the children came to the front before the service began, sang choruses, and recited Bible verses from memory. Soon the children learned that the most popular and shortest verse in the Bible was "Jesus wept." When we sang the last song, we placed our hands together like a cathedral under our chin, closed our eyes, and sang, "Come into My Heart, Lord Jesus." While humming the second time through, Daddy or I would say a short prayer.

Just before his sermon, he would invite me to sing a solo. I could do that very well and always looked forward to singing for my daddy and the Lord. Sometimes it was embarrassing when he referred to me as his sugarbox.

With pride, Daddy told Richard that I would go to college to study music and become an evangelistic singer some day. I did go to college, but during my last year, a call came to me in the wee hours of the morning of an unforgettable tragic occurrence. Daddy had suffered a massive heart attack. Successful heart surgery was decades away and his demise was certain, but my regular and timely visits for the last ten days of his life were not deterred. I had been married for less than two years, our first baby was on the way, and in four months I would graduate with a degree in music. Daddy's short life denied him the opportunity to see me graduate from college, know any of my children, or hear me give a concert.

His fifty-eight years was a full life. He preached many sermons, saw many people come to Christ, and baptized hundreds. Daddy was young in years, but his body was as tired and worn as someone much older.

My grief over his loss lasted one solid year, waking up at night in tears of disbelief that he was really gone. Daddy wasn't supposed to die; he was my role model. A long way from being perfect, he was an honest, upright, decent father, husband, and dedicated Christian. I miss him to this day and wish many times I could sit down and tell him things—like how proud I was when he called me son. I know one day he and I will meet again on the other side of this life.

Richard conducted his funeral and I proudly sang that great old gospel song "The Love of God" one more time for Daddy.

George W. Frey

My Daddy

My daddy was a gentle man
Who filled his life with fun.
He always liked it when I laughed,
What joy when he called me son.

I'm thrilled to call him Daddy.
While looking back I see
An honest upright man of faith—
The best that he could be.

He taught me values for my life,
And thought I never heard.
With life so short, he never knew,
That I got every word.

Someday in heaven, we'll meet again.
We'll no longer be apart,
But until that time, my daddy
Will have a special place in my heart.

Leila Mason

The Back Porch

The back porch on a summer's night held a magical lure for my father and me. I would creep out of my bed, tiptoe past Mother, and quietly go out the back door to where I knew he would be sitting. Silently, I would sit beside him and we would smell the sweet odors that drifted across the distant meadows. There would be no words spoken. It was enough that my father knew I was present, someone to share the beauty of the night and hear the crickets sing—crickets that he knew were singing, but that he could no longer hear. What little hearing he had was dependent on a hearing aid, the size of a deck of cards—huge by today's standards. The aid was kept in his shirt pocket, and a wire ran from it to where it plugged into his ear. It malfunctioned regularly.

Sometimes the deep croak of the bullfrogs would join the melody of the crickets. I asked, "Dad, can you hear the bullfrogs?" He replied, "Yes." Somehow, I didn't believe him. Perhaps he heard them through my ears as he held my tiny hand.

On one occasion, a skunk, that was a resident under our barn, marched up the porch steps. She looked briefly in our direction, proceeded towards the empty garbage can, then turned in a huff, tail held high. I remember the excitement of having a skunk that close to us. Would we get sprayed? My father sat quietly, as he always did, but he had a smile on his face that the light from the kitchen window illuminated. I felt his calm and by staying still I saw the skunk's true colours. Silken black contrasted with white and a nonchalance that gave her as much right to be there as we had. She silently stomped away on padded feet. I was left awestruck, heart pounding with the excitement of a little girl, which I knew my father could hear.

Benjamin Creighton

Everything Will Be Okay

Nothing can really prepare you to have a family member who is an addict, especially when that family member is a parent. When you first find out, there's a part of you—how large a part depends on the individual—that wants to hate them, simply because of the choices that they've made. That part is probably also indignant about how those choices have affected you personally. That part was always there in me, but it was muted, overshadowed by a more powerful feeling: No matter what mistakes my dad had made, I couldn't hate him for it. He was one of my heroes, and I was smart enough at the time to realize that heroes make mistakes and this particular mistake was complicated enough that I couldn't just blame him outright. Chemical imbalances and a physiological need for a substance are not things that are easily controlled; I already knew that, ironically because Dad had taught me about it.

When my parents told me in high school they were separating, my response was surprisingly calm. I didn't know this at the time, but it was so calm it terrified my dad, since it seemed I didn't care he would be moving out. The truth was—aside from a moderate case of shock—I was sure that our family would face this issue like we had every other and come out intact. Both of my parents, but especially Dad, instilled in me the idea that "everything will be okay." So when I learned Dad would be leaving, it never occurred to me that I wouldn't see him regularly, or that things between my parents wouldn't remain amicable, or that my family would be caught up in a difficult period for a very long time.

Everything would definitely be "okay." It would just take a long time to get there.

The first time I saw Dad for any considerable amount of time after the separation, my brother and I went to spend an afternoon with him at my uncle's apartment where he was staying. The plan was to just hang out and watch a movie, like we used to. I had mixed feelings about the visit, partly because of life at my mom's, and partly because I didn't like the idea that a visit with my dad could come to an end and that going "home" meant leaving him somewhere else. And also because of the additional knowledge about him I had picked up by then. A little voice in the back of my head reminded me to look for dilated pupils and odd behavior; in my mind's eye, I could see the jagged shape of broken crack pipes at the bottom of Dad's old desk, which I never wanted to stumble upon again.

Overtop of that, though, was a more powerful feeling of excitement at just hanging out with my dad. I'm willing to accept that my almost unconditional acceptance and forgiveness of his addiction and what it had caused probably makes me an outlier. Everyone else affected by Dad's addiction—my mom, my brother, my relatives—didn't seem as quick to forgive. When people asked me things like "He hasn't asked you for money, has he?" or insinuated that what he had done was horrible and unforgivable, I'd get angry and defend him. How dare anyone criticize my dad for faults that were, to a degree, out of his control? Based on everyone else's attitude during this time, and what I've heard from other families dealing with addiction, this behavior on my part is definitely uncommon. And that's okay. As Dad (and George Carlin) would say, everyone has their "stuff," and we're all free to deal with it differently.

* * *

So the mixed feelings I had on that first long visit were more complicated than anyone my age should have to endure. The worst part of it, I think, is that the person I wanted to talk to the most about it was the one person I couldn't confide in. There was too much anger, too much hurt, and too much of Dad's negative self around for us to have the calm, logical conversation I needed. So when Dad went to his bedroom halfway through our movie and passed out—whether out of fatigue or something else, I never did know—and I was having trouble waking him up, all I could do was sit next to him on the bed and cry. I cried because I needed Dad the way I had always had him before. I cried because all I wanted was to spend time with him, and it didn't matter what we were doing, even if he was asleep. I cried because I was afraid that all the things my mom and my later-to-be stepdad said about him were true, and that I was the only one in the world ready to forgive him for all of it, just because he was my dad.

The hardest part of the entire situation came later, when Dad headed north to finally get clean. I understood why he had to go, and that it was the best way for him to truly fix himself—as much as one can with an addiction—but it didn't really make it any easier. Now I was going from seeing Dad semi-regularly to hardly seeing him at all. This arrangement was especially complicated because I was heading to university, and we were both pretty poor, so we would have to rely on us both happening to be back home at the same time in order to hang out.

Things only got harder during the first year or so of Dad's recovery, when he was at his lowest and struggling the most, and I was trying to support him while not "enabling" the behavior he was working to correct. It didn't help that others kept telling me I had to sever ties with him in order to help him, so that he would have a purpose for getting clean: to be able to talk to his family again. But I refused to accept that, since I knew if I were going through the same process, the only thing that would get me through it would be the knowledge that my immediate family still supported me. And so, as hard as it was sometimes, we kept in touch throughout the process.

Contrary to what some people might have expected, I think that choice helped—and it actually strengthened our relationship. Dad has always been an open person, and now that his one secret from me was finally revealed, he wasn't afraid to give me the details about his recovery. I learned about the actual root of his addiction—alcohol—and his steps to avoid the need to drink. I listened to his favorite speaker from AA, Earl, and a surprisingly serious talk by Craig Ferguson, who shares my dad's condition. I became aware of the different steps Dad would need to take to fully recover and even gave him advice on how to move forward with them.

Looking back on it all now, I know how lucky I am. Throughout my life, there are countless occasions where I could have lost my dad forever, for a number of different reasons. Somehow both of us made it through with our relationship intact; today, Dad would probably say it was God's plan at work, which I'm not sure I buy into. But if there is a plan at work, I'm grateful for it, since it meant I was able to congratulate Dad on his five-year medallion, and then celebrate his fiftieth birthday—two events we were both worried might never happen, and he was able to stand with me when I received my Bachelor of Education.

Most importantly, when I need to talk to someone about something serious, my dad is always there.

Which is how I know that, no matter what, everything will be okay.

K.V. Skene

Our Dad

A quiet man whose fences never fell,
he built too well. With gentle hands,
he fixed dolls and bikes, tied laces extra tight
and every single night
locked out the dark.

A stubborn man whose tides were certainties,
Father/Mother to us all. Holding his hand,
a child felt snugly harboured
and he was always there
when it grew dark.

A solid man whose life was the rock
we all built on, His steady hands
held us up until we grow old
and bold enough
to face the dark.

Gillian Harding-Russell

What My Father Brought

home from the war was reticence
and a well-made watch whose leather
cracked and had to be replaced
with nylon navy against dark hairs
bronzed by sun as he bent an arm
out the car window and explained
that he had to strip a German prisoner
of war, poor devil (at least he'd given
him cigarettes and two cans of bully
beef when the next soldier in line
might have given him nothing)

What my father brought home
from the war was passing mention
of a Harley Davidson he rode
as part of his job in Intelligence
the speed and concussions (were
there three?) How he gave it up
after the war for my mother
who wouldn't ride behind

What my father brought home
from the war was a voluminous silence
details adrift as stray memories in the wind
of a strange dream while the clouds
passed by—or was that himself
in flux—two friends out of
three killed in action, disoriented
if he tried to place events
too securely, anchor things

as we sat in the car in front of the Richelieu River
watched ruffled waves on a cold summer day, no one
around, sun between clouds when my father, cheery
in his matter of fact answered a few random child
questions, leaving more blank spots in my mind
than before he had spoken

deciding we should go for that swim
we'd come for, the water warmer when the air
was cool and the skies were grey
he said

Liz Barton

Covered Chocolate

If frost appeared within fifty miles, my mother routinely made hot chocolate as a morning ritual. She would leave the sweet brew on the stove in a covered pan for us as she went about her other chores. If the last person to dip a cup of hot chocolate failed to replace the lid, allowing the mixture to cool, my father would glance into the pot, grab the skin between his fingers, and slide it down his throat as we children shuddered in horror. He is the only one I ever knew that actually liked the hot chocolate skin, but I wonder now if maybe he just enjoyed our prickly reaction.

Hot chocolate was our mother's weekday treat for us, but sometimes, our father would take over on a lazy weekend morning. On these rare occasions, he would rise before any of us, don one of my mother's aprons, pull out half her kitchen equipment, and begin frying an entire pound or more of bacon, testing several strips to make sure all were crunchy-crisp. If any pork sausage was in the refrigerator, that was fried too. Then using the inch or so of grease left sizzling in the skillet, he would fry over-easy eggs for all of us. He added buttered toast and hot coffee, and that was the extent of his cooking skills.

As the welcome smells of breakfast woke us, Momma would set out her eighteen jars of jam, and we would gather round the table. Daddy would laugh freely and eat enthusiastically. The usual tension that filled our home was temporarily hidden during these breakfasts, perhaps under those layers of grease. But before the last bite was eaten, the golden spell would be broken. Maybe one of us children might break it with a snarly remark, but more often our father would snap an unwelcome announcement or make another caustic criticism. All too soon, the anxiety and distress would again invade our kitchen, biting us like a swarm of mosquitoes till the next drought of tranquility ended.

Possibly, some of Daddy's misery was left over from his childhood. His parents uprooted the family often, sometimes several times during one school year, to follow the construction sites my grandfather worked, denying my father a place of geographical belonging, long-term peer friendships, and the security of living among extended family. According to my aunt, if any extra money existed after the essentials, my grandfather frequently wasted it on alcohol. My father told us how he stole coal and wood during this Great Depression era to help heat his family's home. Once, after I asked, he explained how his index finger became caught between a tree and a truck that caused it to be permanently bent. Other than these two events, he never alluded to anything else about his boyhood, keeping all other stories carefully covered.

While still a teenager, my father joined thousands of his generation to serve in World War II. Later, he joined the National Guard, the extra income helping pay the bills for his young, increasing family. Soon the Korean War erupted and he was shipped across the country to Washington State and then on to Korea. He returned home safely, or so it appeared, to my mother, my two brothers, and me. Any anecdotes that happened during this time that may have influenced my father's life and mine were never mentioned, more of his past forever lost.

Again, like thousands of men of his age, my father earned his college degree with the GI bill while working full-time, attending night classes, and studying whenever, often with the sounds of children playing or arguing or a baby crying in the background.

Things went well for a period. With his college degree, my father accepted a well-paying job, and we acquired all the necessities and many luxuries. Just as he was winning the Monopoly game of life, mental illness landed, demanding a ransom. His tremendous intelligence and work ethic could not lift him from this pit of unexpected bankruptcy. Whatever pain, terror, or panic he experienced internally—either from the wars, his childhood, or some unknown medical cause—could no longer be wiped away with a lucky roll of the dice. My father lost the ability to be a loving parent and unwittingly dumped on his children debts of heartache that took years to forgive and mend.

For decades, like my father, I kept wretched childhood memories wedged under forgotten boxes of incidents in the dusty attic of my mind. I learned as a child and teenager to navigate without my father's assistance, and like most survivors, developed independence and determination. I pushed unpleasant thoughts away and listened to happy events from friends' childhoods, but carefully sifted my own collection of anecdotes, only retrieving isolated, random tales that revealed nothing of my anguish.

I learned to forgive my father the wrongs he committed, but my focus had been on my hurts, my sorrows. I never wanted to know anything about him. I just wished to keep my distance from him and prayed he caused no more harm to anyone. His role as a painful parent influenced me to fear and distrust most authority and to overcompensate when I raised my family. I overprotected my children as long as they allowed me and gave too freely when sometimes I should have demanded more. They thrived, despite my inadequacies. Only now, fifteen years after his death, have I wondered about my father's life before his demons destroyed him.

Whatever each generation heaps on the next, each one must forgive the other for mistakes, appreciate the good, and teach lessons learned. When I search, I discover our family had traditions—those things that offer security and a sense of belonging. To these I must cling and attempt to pass to the next generations.

I no longer indulge in eating bacon, sausage, and greasy eggs, but any chilly morning is reason enough for hot chocolate. As I stir the mixture and guard against the unwanted skin, I also guard the few happy moments I shared with my father and cherish the sweetness that can come from the most bitter of circumstances. When from my carelessness a skin forms on hot chocolate, I no longer recoil, but smile, remembering the joy my father experienced as he swallowed a blob and listened to his children howl.

Hot Chocolate Recipe

Bring ½ cup sugar, 1 tablespoon cocoa, 2 cups water to a rolling boil. Stir in 1 can (12 oz.) evaporated milk and 1 cup milk. Remove from heat and IMMEDIATELY cover with lid or pour into cups. Marshmallows are optional, but certainly add a nice touch.

Patricia Kirby

Owed to Dad

Now that you're gone so many things
remind me of you: my brothers' faces,
my cousin's laughter, newspapers, tools,
crosswords, costs, savings, and stocks.
You worked wood for fun; now tools are
talismans and woods cathedrals.
Always an alpha, you also worked numbers—
never my inclination but instead, my inheritance,
along with an abiding sense of impermanence
and a permanent remembrance of you.

Patricia Kirby

Lessons Learned from Dad

Many people have my father to thank for most of the lessons they learned, in or out of school, for their escape from a tight spot, or their success at a job. Or like me, all of the above.

– one horsey ride around the living room is all you get from an adult who worked all day;

– if you shine those shoes properly, you can earn five cents a pair;

– it is possible to slice a cake evenly into fourteen pieces;

– work is what counts most;

– if you wipe up promptly, your house will stay clean with almost no effort;

– pay cash whenever you can;

– pay your bills even when you can't;

– work is the lion's share of what counts;

– if you loan money to family members, you may never see it again;

– things can be repaired;

– sometimes people can be repaired, sometimes you can employ what's not broken;

– work is really what counts;

– fire back when someone's shooting at you;

– it doesn't help to get upset in a crisis—cool heads will keep your plane in the air;

– if someone freezes in fear, take over for them, or else you'll all go down in a fiery crash;

– work is pretty much all that counts;

– a stiff drink eases some problems and a little cash eases others;

– get a day job first, then you can play all you want after hours;

– it doesn't matter what the neighbours have or do or think of you;

– if someone attacks you personally, agree with them and then go one further (i.e., you're not just mean, but the meanest S.O.B. this side of the border);

– Work is really all that counts in life: not what you do but how you do it. That includes how you think things through, what kind of creativity you apply to getting the job done, what the results are, and most importantly, how you treat your fellow workers. Work is life and life is work.

Jane Jimenez

Remembering Dad

My father has been gone for over twenty years. It seems like yesterday…I miss him still.

He was a father from the "old school," an outdoorsman who took me out one freezing morning on a duck hunting trip. At twelve years of age, I felt honored that he trusted me enough to know I would be quiet and still along the river bank.

As Father's Day nears each year, memories build of little things with big consequences. Daddy loved order and strategy. An electrical engineer, he had a system for ordering 1000 pieces by their bumps and slots, an assembly-line method for putting puzzles together. Today, my colour-coded filing system owes everything to Dad.

Perfectionists to a fault, both of us, we had our fair share of rows. Particularly vivid is one battle where we locked in an argument over how to slice Mother's homemade bread without leaving any bread crumbs on the wooden board. The battle turned into a war, complete with slamming doors and morning apologies. Funny, today…fiercely serious, back then.

Poor Daddy. He often joked about being the only man in the house surrounded by women. When my mother took a college class on semantics and discovered an additional set of connotations and denotations for every word in the English language, she tripled the words at her disposal for overwhelming him in conversation. It was the ultimate Mars/Venus communication gap before John Gray was around to explain it.

Remembering Dad, I wish every kid had a father close at hand to create good memories.

Today, statisticians are explaining why we need fathers. The value of dads is computed in statistics of crime, risky adolescent behaviors, and economic well-being. Researchers are trying to appeal to our logic, arguing that families benefit from fathers…dads.

Why? What do numbers have to do with explaining the longing of the human spirit? The value of my dad is more personal than that, impossible to quantify as a statistic.

Today psychologists and educators create classroom lessons teaching children how to be nice to each other. They are working to teach the very things my father taught me in the everyday details of living together as family for over twenty years.

Therapists help women develop self-confidence in their abilities to problem-solve and be self-reliant. I learned this from a father who let me watch and help him fix my sewing machine.

Spiritual leaders preach forgiveness. I learned this from a father who knocked quietly on my bedroom door and entered to tell me he was sorry. He wanted to show me his technique for slicing bread without crumbs…but it wasn't worth fighting. And we forgave each other.

Special funding for special programs is directed to the promotion of careers in science for women. My father showed me how to shape a wooden peg on the lathe, he taught me his system for tracking the prices of stocks and bonds, and he let me show him what I learned in an auto mechanics class…how to change the rotor and adjust the timing on my VW bug.

Self-help gurus write books and appear on Dr. Phil, preaching the techniques for building healthy marriages. I saw this in the daily highs and lows of married life between my parents where words spoken in anger were covered over with apologies, forgiveness, and tenderness.

If I have had any success in being a parent, I can look to my dad and the sacrifices he made to be a husband and father. When family life is tough, I hang in there because my dad gave me a vision of tenacity and hope. When I look for strength inside, I find it because my father put it there through his affirmation of me as his daughter…worthy, capable, and loved.

Dad's encouragement…his example…his love can never be replicated by social programs and tax dollars. No number of psychologists, teachers, or federally funded initiatives would ever have filled the shoes of the man who loved my mother and spent a lifetime building a picture of that love in the daily details of life.

I need no research to prove the value of fathers for raising daughters and sons. The proof is written on my heart. It is honored in passing on the gift of marriage to our own children.

He's been gone all these many years. But he's never left me. My dad.

Effie-Alean Gross

He Just Kept Going

Born in 1906, my dad lived until America's bicentennial year, 1976. One of my last memories of Richard Elmer Valentine Groves involved a commemorative silver dollar. He had lost it somewhere in my house, and when I searched everywhere until I found it, he was elated. "You take this and keep it," he insisted. Reluctantly, I put it in an envelope and dated it with a memo about its significance. Dad was quite a guy.

He was rarely without his fedora dress hat. As soon as he stepped into someone's house, he removed it from his head of gray-white hair combed straight back with no part. I didn't realize it at the time, but Dad was showing respect by this gesture of baring his head when entering a church or any other structure. Sometimes he would kid visitors and say, "Here's your hat, now what's your hurry?" This was taken to mean, "I think you've stayed long enough," but Dad would never discourage anyone by a serious remark. His sense of humor coloured his personality.

Besides wearing the hat, Dad was always "dressed to the nines" in a starched and ironed shirt, long trousers, silk stockings, and polished shoes. No one would guess by looking at him or at any of our family members (three older brothers, one older sister, Mom, and the baby—me) that we were poor. Living through the Great Depression of 1929, getting married a year after, having five children by 1944, and struggling through WWII, poverty came easy. Yet, Dad just kept going. One of the qualities I admire most about my dad is the ability to persevere in hard times. I hope I picked up his tenacity in light of the unpredictable future and considering our massive global problems.

Energy is high on the list of the world's concerns now, as it was back when my dad worked in the coal mines of Iowa. His father, Stacy Grove, had also gone into underground shafts on small rail carts with dangerous working conditions and long shifts. I'm told how Dad used to carry peanut butter sandwiches in his lunch pail, actually a recycled lard tin with a lid and a wire handle. My dad and grandfather did whatever was necessary to make a living and provide the bare necessities for their families. Consequently, they both ended up with lung disease: Grandpa Grove died of pneumonia and Dad died of lung cancer, Black Lung.

Dad was an excellent example of how to honor parents. He took Mom and all five of his children to visit his mother and father often. We never called ahead, because we didn't have a telephone, not even the old-fashioned "party line" where several families shared a switchboard service. Neighbors could listen in on other people's conversations. By not having a phone, I guess we were insulated, so to speak, from gossip.

When we arrived, unannounced, at the grandparents' house, they stopped everything and visited with us. We talked to each other. During such times, I learned that my dad was of Irish, Scottish, and Cherokee Indian descent. Before we left our grandparents' house, Grandma had wrung a chicken's neck, boiled the hen, plucked the smelly feathers, cut it up, and fried it for our dinner, along with making mashed potatoes and homemade biscuits. Hospitality was as common as the corn in the Iowa farmers' fields.

"Come here, Scalawag," Dad would say when it was time to leave. "Scalawag" was his pet name for me, being interpreted: "rascal." I didn't even know what the term meant until I got older, but I knew it was a good name…so much for innocence. I trusted Dad. He said that he only teased people he really liked. He loved me. He loved his wife, his children, his grandchildren, and his great-grandchildren…his family.

Around nine o'clock at night, he would lift me up to his shoulder with his strong arms. I could smell the Old Spice aftershave he'd splashed on, and I felt secure in his tanned, hairy arms.

Dad and Mom disagreed on more than a few things, but the one thing they really couldn't agree on was the number of children they wanted. If Dad had had his way, Mom would have given birth to a dozen babies. They stopped with me, number five. Dad always called me his baby, and until the day he died, he carried a picture of me as a little girl in his wallet. He used to pull it out and say, "Here's my baby." Don't think I haven't had to live that one down!

Prior to digital clocks, one of Dad's favorite antics was sticking out his left arm and looking at his wristwatch, winding the stem, and listening to the rhythmic ticking sound. Then he'd call over one of the grandchildren, put the watch up to the child's ear, and say, "Hear the horses? They're eating hay." Now what child isn't enthralled by listening to horses graze? Dad knew how to entertain youngsters with his storytelling ability. Actually, with a friendly smile and animated gestures, he could talk to anyone, strangers included.

Dad had a list of pleasurable activities he could discuss or—better yet—get someone to join in with him. He liked drive-in movies, picnics, and the outdoor sports of competitive horseshoe tossing and swimming. Indoor activities included checkers, billiards, square dancing, and attending auctions and movie theatres. Of course, we were constantly visiting relatives, both his family and Mom's family.

Occasionally we traveled across America to some destination having to do with joining up with family. Once we went from Iowa to California in an old car with no radio, no air-conditioning, and no spare tire. We kids didn't have road games to play, but we read comic books and squabbled over them. Like most kids jammed together in a space smaller than a jail cell, we found ways to entertain ourselves. When a tire would blow out, Dad pumped up the jack from the trunk, removed the tire, and rolled it down the highway until some Good Samaritan picked him up, while Mom and the kids waited on the side of the highway for what seemed like hours. Finally we saw Dad return with yet another used tire. On the road again, the car climbed mountains and crossed the desert, until another tire blew or until we reached Los Angeles, whichever came first.

Dad was driven by love for his family. How else could anyone explain why he'd take the Greyhound bus from Iowa to Baltimore, Maryland, in order to see his U.S. Army son being deployed to France? After the full-dress ceremony on the parade grounds, Dad bid farewell and then drove his son's 1952 Hudson back home, over 1,000 miles. He did things like that for all of his children. When I got married and moved to New Mexico and later to Texas, Dad drove for days to see me. He didn't have any relief, either, as Mom never learned to drive. By then, his cars were more reliable, with a radio and without fussing kids in the backseat.

No matter where I relocated, Dad either came to see me or wrote to me. His handwriting was what he called "chicken scratches." I didn't care that he used lower case for the first person noun "I." His penmanship was a result of only going through fourth grade. I didn't care. When I got a letter from Dad, I couldn't wait to read it…savor it…and save it. Better yet, when Dad's car came up my driveway, I put on the coffeepot, adding "a few more beans." Dad liked his java strong, just the way he lived.

Through all of his trials, Dad never seemed to worry. Like his Timex® watch, he just kept going.

Carolyn Hei-Kyoung You

Letters and Numbers

A keen observer
of birds, baseball, markets, weather
His stories hidden
in line scores, stock tickers, temperatures, wind speeds

He reads me a bedtime story
And I fly to sleep
Under his watchful eye

My stories hidden
in dreams
I wake and watch
My days unfold
in pages, letters, words, phrases

Who can decipher
Our stories?

Terri Elders

The Choosing Shoes Blues

My big sister, Patti, and I rarely agreed on anything in our adolescence, but when it came time to shop for back-to-school shoes, we sang the same tune. And it was the blues.

Back in 1951, the high school set considered black patent leather Mary Janes or Capezio-type instep strap shells as good as it gets, so of course we longed to step into them ourselves. But Daddy believed in function, not fashion, plus he moonlighted as a shoe salesman at Sears Roebuck department store where he enjoyed an employee discount.

Even though World War II was behind us, and the economy was good, these were still conservative days, and Daddy, who well remembered the Depression years, worked two jobs to provide for a wife and three kids, and to send a few dollars monthly to his aging mother.

For weeks Patti and I had been showing Mama the ads in the daily *Los Angeles Herald-Express*, and pleading our case. But though she'd been sympathetic about our entreaties for straight skirts, pullover sweaters, and Peter Pan collars, when it came to shoes, she agreed with Daddy. Shoes were costly, and a single pair each would have to last the entire school year.

We pouted, we sulked, we sighed, but all to no avail. One inevitable September Saturday morning we piled into the backseat of the family Chevy, and Daddy drove to the Sears store that anchored the shopping strip at Slauson and Vermont.

* * *

"Meet me in the shoe department in about half an hour," he said, pulling into the rear parking lot.

Patti and I exchanged gleeful glances. While Daddy punched in at the time clock and got his cash register set up for the day, we could browse Lerner's, Mode O'Day, and some of the other dress shops that lined Vermont Avenue. And we could peer into the windows of Buster Brown, Kinney's, and Bakers, and admire the latest trends in footwear and accessories.

That half hour sped by, and we finally had to drag ourselves back to Sears. In those days, shoe salesmen still used a shoe-fitting x-ray unit called a fluoroscope to determine proper size. Patti stepped up first to have Daddy measure her feet.

Patti's feet had grown into a size seven, so she grinned and gave me a quick wink. She now wore the same size shoe as Cousin Patricia, and would benefit when Aunt Betty, Daddy's sister, came over with her annual armload of hand-me-downs.

Aunt Betty lived in a large house in Altadena with a swimming pool. When her daughter, Patricia, a few years our senior, purchased new school clothes each fall, we got the cast-offs. We looked forward to trying on the discards, and some of the sweaters and jackets were very welcome. Mama would discreetly set aside most of the dresses and blouses for Goodwill, though, since she considered them far too mature or worldly for us. But Patricia's shoes were to die for…ballet flats, moccasins, even some Cuban heels.

But I still measured my same old size six, so this meant that whatever shoes I…or rather, Daddy…chose would be the ones I'd trudge to school in every day all year long, unless I could double or triple my babysitting business, which paid a quarter an hour.

I'd edged over to the shelf that held the rounded-toe Mary Jane look-alikes, and brandished a pair under Daddy's nose. "These look really nice," I cooed.

"Nonsense. They'd fall apart in a week." Daddy knew shoes, so there was no debating.

My heart sank when he plucked up a pair of black objects that I could only describe as indescribable. They looked like squat, stocky, clunky Mary Janes…but without the strap, dumpy, stubby loafers…but without the slot for the penny. But to Daddy they simply looked…sturdy. I knew I was doomed.

"These are shoes made to last!" Daddy declared.

"Why, they look just fine," Patti said, feigning delight. I grimaced but nodded.

The first few weeks of school I skulked about, hoping nobody would notice my footwear. I caught a few girls glancing downwards and hiding grins. I pretended not to notice, but determined to find a way to get some other shoes. Patti, of course, left the house each day light-footed in a variety of secondhand but fashionable shoes.

So I landed a soda fountain job at Owl Drug Store, right across from Sears. I'd be working Mondays and Fridays, 5 to 9 p.m., and all day Saturday, earning the munificent minimum wage of sixty cents an hour. I'd fry up hamburgers and toss together root beer floats, and at the end of Saturday afternoon, Lucky, the fountain boss, would hand me a paycheck.

The first thing I bought, of course, was a pair of Capezio-style strapped shells. In about six weeks I'd worn holes in the soles. When I took them to the shoe repair shop I learned that they were too fragile to resole, so I had to make do with liners I cut from an old cardboard box. They lasted another week until I had to slog home from the drugstore one night in a downpour and the sodden straps fell off.

Reluctantly, I dragged out Daddy's nondescript clunkers and wore them for the rest of the year. I could be fashionable…or I could be warm and dry. Why did those two alternatives have to be so incompatible? Once I even caught Lucky smirking at my feet when he thought I wasn't looking,

Fortunately the following autumn black and white saddles came into vogue, so when we took our annual trek to the Sears shoe department, I eyed those stalwart oxfords with genuine appreciation and even expressed gratitude for Daddy's discount. Now I could save my paycheck for brand new angora sweaters and matching angora socks, and leave the latest batch of Cousin Patricia's leftovers, mostly out-of-style tweed sheathes, to Patti, along with the outdated size seven Mary Janes.

Somehow that early experience killed my lust for stylish but flimsy shoes. Over the years I've tended towards loafers, sports shoes, and pumps. And recently I've come to realize that the Hush Puppies I favor today look suspiciously like descendents of those stouthearted shoes I once blushed to be seen in.

That, of course, was in those distant days before I came to share Daddy's practical philosophy of good value for money…and learned that utility should trump fashion.

Sue Chenette

Expedition

It's the Sunday of my grandparents' visit.
They came on Friday, in their gleaming green Nash.
At dinner my father carves the roast
brought from Minneapolis, wrapped
in white paper and brown tape, a standing rib roast
greeted with exclamations: "Oh! from Johnson's!"

"Would you like the end piece, Mother?"
My father, his fine brown hair combed smooth,
stands at the head of our dining table,
which used to be Grandma and Grandpa's.
He's smiling, the lines that crowd
above his eyes in his quiet times
so faint they've disappeared.
All of us know Grandma prefers the end piece.

Grandpa's hair is white, unruly.
"When one is served, all may eat," he says
with the hearty professor's cheer he kept
after he retired. He lifts his napkin,
a great white flag. "Well Susie"—
a ringing voice as if I might not hear—
"what did you learn in Sunday School?"
My father always asks me too:
What did you notice? What did you learn?

In the afternoon we drive to the cranberry marsh—
Largest Single Low-Bush Cranberry Bog in the World—
a place we've been before, with other visitors.
We walk the low dike road between flooded beds.
On either side bright berries
ripple among the floating branches.

Grandpa wears his Sunday best,
trousers loose, creased, cuffed. His felt hat
almost makes him tall. Crossing his arms,
he stops to survey. "How many acres?"

My father, in his khaki Conservation Service pants,
boots he wears to tramp the farmers' fields,
explains ditches, floodgates,
how water keeps the berries from freezing.

Wind blows across the marsh, blows our hair
out straight, bunches the water into fine waves.
I am cold and bored. But I can tell
from the way he stops and points,
explaining a wheel that turns to lift a sluice gate,
that this is important to my father—
his answer to a question—
What did you learn today?

Daniela Elza

What Makes a Man Tell a Story

what makes a man tell a story over?

the orders crackled through: my great grandfather
was to hold the mountain ridge.
buy time with his infantry.

saw his men die— one after
the other. including his best friend.

he ordered the living to line up the dead just so—
their helmets on guns pointing and ready.

every few meters propped on rocks trees
—a death chain.

bullets mortars shells begin again.
a few men flee. behind them— fireworks

of flesh and bone.

at the dinner table :wide eyed: my dad listens.
the story always ends:

my best friend saved my life.

what makes a man

tell a story over and over? as if
there is still something in it for him
to grasp.

Grandfather Memories

More and more,
when I single out the person
who inspired me most,
I go back to my grandfather.

James Earl Jones

Raymond Fenech

The Swing in My Grandfather's Garden

The swing hangs dangerously on the broken chain
screeching loudly in excruciating pain,
dribbling rusty-red, bloody and hanging lame
on winded years, day in day out the same.

How many a child has sat and played
how many on its wooden bucket swayed
before with age its outer skin was flayed;
time flew, the child grew; all to rest were laid.

Just memory of all that time remains
like photos shot in some special frame,
sparked from an urge or mania to maintain
immortalize this life we live in vain.

The swing hangs creaking on the broken chain
as the summer breeze wistfully speaks in pain,
whispering emotionally about our joy and strain
like conscience when hard it pokes us in vain.

The swing squeals contemplating on the rain
joining chorus with time's tick tock refrain,
of life that's been: will never be again,
like dreams escaping on a choo choo train.

Connie Kinnell McKinney

The Scotsman

As the legend goes, Scottish people are so frugal, that one day, a Scotsman dropped a quarter and dug until he found it and that is how the Grand Canyon was formed. Now, perhaps, that story is just a wee bit exaggerated, but it wouldn't surprise me if my grandfather had a hand in digging just a corner of it!

My grandfather was born in Kirkaldy, Scotland, in 1892 and immigrated to America in 1922 in the company of four other Scottish lads. He soon found work at Vail Ballou, a book printing and binding company in Binghamton, New York. He would continue working there until his retirement, forty-eight years later, at the young age of seventy-five!

Thomas Kinnell (pronounced kĭn-nel') descended from the MacDonald clan, but as yet, I haven't seen any inheritance of Happy Meals coming my way. Still, Grandpa Kinnell left a far greater inheritance to his young and impressionable granddaughters, Holly, Connie, and Valerie or, as he would write our names, Halley, Connie, and Valaria.

My earliest memories of Grandpa Kinnell were of watching him dance a little Scottish jig, then letting us take turns standing on his feet, while he tried repeating the same little jig. We held on for dear life and laughed until the tears flowed. As we got older, he just held our hands and we danced that little dance together (though Grandpa's feet could no longer kick quite so high). Grandpa was also able to make what I thought sounded like a little "squirrel" sound coming from the back of his throat. This feat was mesmerizing to little ones. Later, I was able to figure out how he did it (but I never told him I had mastered the squirrel sound too). Then again, there were times when he would bring us marshmallow chickens or amazing Mexican jumping beans, the latter of which proved to be the best baby sitters (now remember, these were the days long before the arrival of the Xbox and iPods!).

Yes, Grandpa knew how to kick up his heels and have some good, wholesome fun, but his part in the American legacy was bringing a bit of his homeland and weaving it, like a Scottish plaid, into the whole of the American dream. As with so many like him, Grandpa found his spot, worked and saved, worked and saved some more. He never became wealthy, at least as some would count being so. But, Grandpa was rich in generosity and of a life lived honorably and nobly—day in and day out. By this, he dug his "canyon," wide and deep, into the hearts of others and his granddaughters.

It was not uncommon for Grandpa to come for a visit, take us shopping for groceries or other needed items, and pay the entire bill. For a young family starting out, this was a greatly appreciated kindness. Grandpa saved to give away. Even as a young child, I noticed his charitable heart and learned from his generosity. It took me awhile to realize it, but the change Grandpa dropped from the "hole in his pocket" for his granddaughters to find by "accident" was probably just another game he enjoyed playing with us. My first clue was when I tried to return his change one day. He just grinned and, with a wink and little twinkle in his eye, told me to just keep it.

Grandpa Kinnell passed from this life on Christmas Eve, 1979, but my childhood memories of that dear Scotsman live on. Was he thrifty? Yes. Was he generous? Yes, even more so, and from time to time, I think about the Scotsman and his little jig and wonder if he ever knew…what a treasure he had invested into the hearts of Halley, Connie, and Valaria over a "quarter" of a century ago.

Martha E. Link

Bluebottle

"Ya better stand away back while I crank this old geezer up. This beast has a mighty kick to it, Martha, but I plan on getting this cantankerous critter running even if she kills me."

"Maybe we should wait for Daddy to come home, Grandpa." I was genuinely worried. They almost always drove Uncle Ralph's fancy International with the silver horns on the roof.

I backed away, my ears buzzing, as my dad's words of warning echoed inside my skull. "This is one mean machine I wish I'd never paid a penny for. Must have been invented by the devil himself. Good-for-nothing contraption seems intent on breaking my arm every single time I try to start it up." I could tell that Dad was afraid of the old red truck. "If it weren't for divine intervention, I'm sure that red devil would just as soon kill me."

From the safety of the other side of Stadacona Street, I thought I'd best speak up a little more strongly about my concern. "Daddy only uses this truck for emergencies. Grandpa, is this an emergency?"

His tall muscular frame bent forward in front of the grill, Grandpa had finally anchored the crank in the crankcase. Straightening up, he looked heavenward, then turned and looked at me. "Unfortunately, dear child, I'm afraid it is." He dusted the rust from his hands. "I don't think the Good Lord is done with me yet, but if this beast kills me, run and get your grandmother. Until then, you'd best hold your peace so I can concentrate on what I'm doing."

My elbows pinned to my chest, I glued both hands over my mouth to stifle the terrified squeal that wanted desperately to erupt, and watched my grandpa's powerful arm yank downward on the crank handle. I exhaled, as he stood back unscathed. The old truck screeched and the antique engine coughed to life. Leaping into the gyrating cab, he did something to the choke and the red devil settled down somewhat. He retrieved the crank, threw it into the truck bed, and then got back in.

Grandpa leaned across the cab and the passenger door creaked open on rusty hinges. Above the racket, he hollered out, "Hop in. You might as well come along for the ride."

I looked at my grandpa with open admiration. "You sure are strong, Grandpa. Daddy has to crank and crank and crank to make this thing go. You got it going on the first try." I was surprised he even knew how to drive as I'd never seen him do it before.

The truck rolled out of the driveway and turned right. "The Good Book says, 'Ask and ye shall receive.' All my strength and all my help come from the Good Lord. And, I expect I'll be needing it quite a bit more before this day is through, little girl." We passed old McCormick's house at the end of the block, and headed down the dirt road that snaked across the prairie, out of town. I joined in, as Grandpa started singing, "Count your blessings; Name them one by one." We kept the windows down so God could hear us better.

When we finished the hymn, we rolled the windows back up so we could talk. "So, Grandpa, what is your emergency?" I was a curious child.

"Well, awhile ago, my palate was growing tired of eating all that fish your father ordered from that fella down East. So, I told the Good Lord that we were in dire need of some meat. Well, sometimes, not too often, mind ya, He says 'no.'

"I had pretty much come to accept the fact that this was one of those times, when this fella I'd never set eyes on before approached me on the street corner. 'Mr. Booth,' he says, 'I hear you're quite the gardener. I was wondering if you'd be willing to strike up a fair deal with an old chicken farmer.' Then he winked at me and introduced himself, told me where he lived, and said he'd like some potatoes and carrots and corn and would I be interested in some chickens?"

"I bet you made a good deal, Grandpa," I said, confident in his bargaining skills, but wondering if getting chickens was a real emergency. I asked him as much, in a half-teasing tone, as we lumbered along the trail, kicking up the dust.

"I sure hope it was an answer to my prayer, and not my own appetite leading me down the garden path, so to speak, child." He sounded as though he might be having doubts.

"What do you mean?" I asked.

"Well, it's kind of difficult to explain to a youngster like yourself." We came to the top of a rise and could see that the trail ended below us, at a ramshackle cluster of weathered grey buildings. He continued the story as we headed down, the truck rocking over the ruts. "This fella seemed a little rough around the edges, if you get my meaning." He glanced at me.

I nodded vehemently, to make sure he didn't think it was the bouncing of the truck, hoping for more details than that. "I read lots of books, Grandpa."

We pulled up in front of a curtainless two-story house with rickety steps. Grandpa pulled on the emergency brake, but didn't get out right away. Staring around at the shambles that was the man's farm, he blinked back tears and took my small hand in both of his big ones.

"Martha, my dear, I fear I may have made a gross error in judgment in bringing you with me on this fool's errand. What I mean to say is, this fella's language was a bit ripe for your tender ears, and by the look of this place, the whiskey I smelt on his breath might be more of a problem than I gave it credit for at the time."

Deep in thought, he looked around, seeing no sign of anyone home. Taking out his pocket watch, he studied it and put it away. "Well, I'm here on time, right when he told me to be here. I have a strong feeling that if it was the Good Lord who sent me here, it was for something else besides chickens." He shook his head and looked up where heaven would be if there was no roof in the truck. "Sure would appreciate some kind of a sign."

So low, that I wouldn't have caught it if I hadn't been watching his lips move, he mouthed, "I pray, dear God, this fella doesn't have a loaded gun."

I gasped, my heart thundering out my own silent prayer. I was terrified of guns.

"I think it would be best if you stay in the truck."

I was glad he didn't turn off the engine. It was a long way back to get Grandma if the cranky old truck or the stranger decided to kill my grandpa.

Still shaking his head, he pushed on the handle and the door creaked as he leaned it open. Standing on the running board, he bent to retrieve the Good Book (which he went nowhere without) from beneath the driver's seat. He gave a quick start when something quite big and blue whizzed past his head and darted into the cab. We both watched open-mouthed with awe as it hovered a second, then settled on the dashboard.

It kind of resembled a dragonfly that the camp councillor at Long Lake Bible Camp had called a dragonelle, except this creature was beautiful. There had been hordes of the small, ugly, brown flyers hovering over the lake. I had been afraid to go near the water, until I found out they didn't bite.

"What is it, Grandpa?" Its body was about the size of a brand new crayon, its colour as blue and transparent as bottled sky. Gossamer wings resembled the fairy wings in the storybooks that had come with the encyclopaedia set my dad had bought to enhance my education when I was five.

"I think it is called a 'bluebottle,' " my grandpa replied, adding, "And I believe this is the sign from the Good Lord, that I just asked him for."

"He's so pretty! Do you think he'd make a good pet?"

"No. I don't think God would like that, Martha. They are a very rare type of dragonfly. He ought to be free to find a mate. I doubt if God would mind, though, if he stays in here to keep you company until I get back." Grandpa hugged the Bible close to his heart. "If I'm reading the message in the bottle rightly, I may be awhile."

And, knowing my grandpa, I believed him!

Daniela Elza

Learning to Read

everyday my grandfather walked to his print shop.
sometimes   hand in hand   with my mother.

at five   she knew how to read and write.
to set the letters   neatly
with blackened fingers.   to nest them

        as if   eggs   about to hatch.

                                (I did not know this
                                until I cared.)

at forty
I sent my mother a photo of an old printing press
asked: was this the type   my grandfather had?
(the one that made him   the printer of his town.)

the moment I saw it   she said   I smelled the ink.

then told me   how
                this spring
                        she watched
                                        the crows
                                    build a nest
                in the linden tree
below our balcony
        as if setting letters
                        for a text
                                we could learn
                                            to read.

Faye Adams

Grandfather's Way

"Cona Faye," Grandfather would say to me with that certain tone in his voice, "you have to do what's right." Then he would be silent for long moments. It was hard to wait for his next words, but I knew there would always be a story.

My grandfather was not one to talk in a crowd. Whenever the family gathered, he sat quietly with an amused look on his face, listening to the chatter flowing around him. Occasionally he would inject a "harrumph" to one of Grandmother's comments, the grin on his face widening slightly.

But when we were alone I was fortunate enough to be the recipient of his considerable wisdom. I suppose he borrowed his method of teaching from Jesus, because his stories were a little like the parables in the New Testament. Every story had a point, a lesson to be learned about life.

"If you want to milk a cow," he would say, "you have to learn about cows. And, you must get to know this cow. What does she like? Is she a good mother? Does she give lots of milk? Is she docile, or does she wait until the bucket is almost full and kick it over?" Then he would tell another story, driving home his point that I must learn to think of others and get to know the people in my life if I wanted to grow up to be a responsible person.

Grandfather's way was to use everyday things as object lessons. One evening as we sat on the porch swing, he pointed out one of my grandmother's rose bushes. "Look at this," he said. "Do you see how delicate the petals are, how vibrant the colour? Would you have imagined such beauty springing from those brown thorny limbs last winter? It takes great care to bring that beauty to life come spring. First, your grandmother must loosen the soil, then add fertilizer and mulch, water it faithfully, and check often for insects.

“People are like that rosebush. It takes effort to bring out the best in another person.” He talked on about the necessity of pruning and said that if you didn’t prune it properly, the bush would grow too large for its space, and if you pruned too much, it would die.

Then he looked up at the sky and said, “God has done his part. He made this world for us and furnished it with good things. Some are good to eat, some are beautiful to look at, and some bring us pleasure, like those creeks you love to splash around in. Think about how good it is to take that dipper off the hook and take a long, cold drink from the spring. Think how good those eggs you just gathered from the henhouse will taste tomorrow for breakfast. Think about the softness of the grass when you lie on it and gaze up at those puffy white clouds, and how the sun feels warming your skin. But it isn’t ours just for the taking, without giving something back. He’s given us a job to do. Our work is to take care of those things in our world. It would be unfair of us to misuse the land and the animals who give so much to us.”

Grandfather fell silent as he pushed the swing gently back and forth with his long legs and I knew he was thinking of his son, Neil, who had gone off to serve in the navy and had never come home. I wondered if he was remembering some conflict with my uncle or regretting something he forgot to say to him. I wondered if he thought about their lost daughter, Vernell, lying in her tiny grave in Wells Cemetery, and how he felt about those Sunday afternoon visits Grandmother insisted on which always made her cry.

With my father married and farming his own place, one son living in Idaho, another in St. Louis and two more still in the navy, Grandfather was farming alone. Sometimes when Grandmother rang the dinner bell, he came in looking stooped and weary. But his prayer of thanks always prefaced the first bite, after which he would pick up a biscuit, slice and butter it with his knife, and hand the first half to me. It became a routine with us at every meal. No biscuit has ever tasted as good since.

* * *

Grandfather’s way of teaching me to share was by his own example. I watched him harvest produce from his garden or corn from the field and load up the wagon, hitch the team, and deliver to a neighbor whose crop had been ruined by hail. I saw him spend a week cutting, raking, and piling hay, only to offer it to the widow Jackson to winter her milk cow.

* * *

I was proud of my grandfather. I felt important walking beside him in town. In most families, only the boys went to town with their dads or granddads but he seemed proud of me and introduced me to his friends. He made me feel safe and loved. He made me see the world and all its riches as being worthy of my respect. He taught me that I could make a difference by doing good deeds and showing kindness to others. That was my grandfather's way.

Sylvia Adams

Listening for the Dead

My father's death surprised him as much as anyone.
A stroke they said, like his mother before him.
No warning except for an aching neck
the day before. Didn't know what a headache was,
said my mother, who suffered from migraines.
Preparing for bed one night, thinking perhaps
of Hallowe'en candy, in case the grandchildren came.
Or planning, at last, a Florida winter.
My mother heard him fall.

By the time I arrived, there was my father,
who'd vowed to leave this world
a tidy place, debt-free, being carried
out in a blanket, a doctor as old as himself
struggling to keep those cold, pale feet
from bumping the stairs.
Toward morning, we tried to sleep—
my mother, her mother, both sobbing, upstairs,
I on the couch in the living room.
I kept listening for him
but the shadows were shocked into silence.

That winter, in dreams, his slippers whispered
across the carpet, the way they did when, at four,
I lay on my stomach, shading Rapunzel's hair
with my favourite jumbo pink crayon.
I glimpsed him once at the kitchen phone,
receiver to ear in voiceless dialogue.
Perhaps in repeating daily rituals
he would discover that nothing had changed.

Early in May, in the last dream, he sat at a banquet table,
eating cake with strangers. I called to him,
but he rose, walked away into dazzling air.
He turned when I called, and held out his hand—
Not yet—The light an ovation of white beyond him
searing my throat as I woke,
his hand still nudging mine: Wait.

My mother takes flowers to the cemetery
in containers she knows won't get stolen.
Is she thinking how the lilacs she brings
brush her cheek like fingertips of the dead,
how my grandmother's mouth opens like a bird's,
waiting for ice cream?

Heide Brown

Me and John Brown

John Brown's body lies a mouldering in his grave
But his soul goes marching on.

Martyr?
Or traitor?

My great, great, great grandfather.

The man who gave his life
To free the slaves.
The man who precipitated the civil war,
Which freed the slaves.

Unspoken expectations
Coloured my ideals, my beliefs, my actions.

I grew up questioning the status quo, the powers that be.
I unconsciously assimilated unspoken rules.
I imprinted that what is most important is:
Fighting for freedom;
Standing up for what I believe in;
Making a difference;
Being stoic;
Focusing on the Greater Good;
Following my heart—

Wait a minute.
Following my heart?
My heart wants to rest.
My heart wants to write,
To paint,
To focus on peace
And beauty.

I don't want to be a martyr.
I want to walk my dog;
To sit in my garden
with my journal and a cup of tea.

Many rough years
Of internal Odysseys
And then
The stubborn determination
Of my famous ancestor
Re-emerged in me
Giving me the strength
To allow myself to evolve
To go beyond the struggle;
To take back my life;
To banish the guilt, and
To enjoy—
Walking my dog, and
Sitting in my garden
with my journal and a cup of tea.

Joanne Culley

Harry Culley —Pianist Extraordinaire (1895–1968)

Every week after school, I walked down the street to my grandparents' house for my piano lesson. I had started taking lessons from my grandfather when I was eight years old and loved it, even though I found it hard sometimes to coordinate my right and left hands together.

Turning the corner, I came around the hedges and went through the rose-covered arbour. Going in the back, I knocked on the inside door before walking in. My grandparents lived on the main floor of their triplex, where they rented out the basement, as well as the upper apartment.

As I entered the large, bright yellow kitchen, my grandmother, putting down her tea cup, would greet me and tell me to go into the living room where my grandfather would be sitting in the wing chair in the corner, smoking his pipe and reading the *New Yorker* magazine. To me, he was the epitome of class and sophistication with his wavy grey hair, wire-rimmed spectacles, and leather slippers. Even though he was relaxing at home, he wore a white shirt, wool cardigan, and tie.

Upon seeing me, he'd smile, and make his way over to the piano, while I slid onto the seat. He'd ask me how my week went, and then listen to what I had practised. I'd start with scales, arpeggios, and chords in every key. Then I'd plough through the study, and finally the piece he'd assigned to me. Occasionally, he'd demonstrate how it should go, and I'd be dazzled by his fingers flying deftly over the keys, evidence of years of practice.

Harry Culley had spent his whole life as a professional musician. He played piano for the silent movies in Toronto around 1912, when there was a need for a live soundtrack to enhance the action on screen. It was while playing in a theatre close by that he met my grandmother, also a pianist, and they married. They later performed together as a piano duo, in two-pianos-four-hands-style, playing on stage, on the radio, and on a tour of England and South Africa, accompanying silent movie stars-turned-stage actors Bebe and Ben Daniels. Upon their return, he played piano and was conductor of the dance orchestras at the Royal York and the Embassy Hotels.

After World War II, Harry became the musical director for the Royal Alexandra Theatre on King Street in Toronto, a plum position, where he conducted the orchestra and played piano for the international stars that came through town, such as comedian and singer Tessie O'Shea. He and my grandmother also toured across Canada playing accompaniment for British film star George Formby and appeared as guest artists on Kate Smith's CBS variety radio show in New York.

My grandfather was pretty much retired by the time he was giving me lessons, although I remember going to the Ice Capades at Maple Leaf Gardens one time when he played accompaniment for the figure skaters.

I started out in Grade 1 of the Royal Conservatory of Music program. Every couple of grades my grandfather would book an exam at the conservatory on Bloor Street. He would wait outside, while I, terrified, went into a cavernous room that was dominated by a large grand piano. A grim, officious adjudicator sat offside at a table, pen in hand. I was so nervous that I made mistakes in pieces I knew by heart and had practised for months. But by some miracle, I passed each time.

After my lesson, Grandma would have supper ready for us in the kitchen, not the dining room, which was reserved for special occasions such as Christmas and Easter. My favourite supper was mashed potatoes, mashed carrots, meat loaf, and custard. Sometimes as a special treat I would have a ginger ale ice cream float.

Then we would play cards. I loved playing casino, gin rummy, and cribbage. Grandpa usually won with glee and didn't spare a thought to letting me win because of my age. We would often have to consult Hoyle's if I protested a play he made. When it came time to leave, I would walk the four blocks back home, crossing Mount Pleasant Road on the way.

One time after my lesson, I asked Grandpa about our family history. That was all he needed—a willing ear! He told me about his grandfather James, a shoemaker with a shop on Shoe Lane in London, England. Deciding to give his children a better life, he and his wife Sarah immigrated to Canada in 1867, settling in Toronto. One of their twelve children, their son Teck, Grandpa's father, became a flutist in the Toronto Symphony, then taught at the Royal Conservatory of Music. Teck and his wife Kate raised seven children in a three-story home on Dufferin Street near Dundas. Harry was the eldest.

I asked Grandpa for a piece of paper, and started writing down names and drawing in the lines of the family tree, to keep track of who was who. Then he brought out some old photos of ancestors looking very dour and formal, standing beside potted plants. He gave everything to me, including his old books, some of which dated back to the 1700s. I dragged it all home and carefully put it away in boxes in my closet.

Even though my grandfather liked living in Toronto, he was always hankering after another life, a more illustrious career in a larger, more cultured city such as New York or London. One of his favourite quotes was from Samuel Johnson, "When a man is tired of London he is tired of life: for there is in London all that life can afford." He envied his two younger brothers who had become famous, wealthy musicians in New York.

He kept up-to-date on world affairs and, reluctantly, with the contemporary music scene. I remember when the Beatles first appeared on "The Ed Sullivan Show," and I was almost hysterical with excitement, his comment was, "You call that music?" But the next week at my lesson, he asked if I wanted to play some of their tunes, and I took a break from my classical studies to learn their songs, as well as others such as "Downtown" by Petula Clark and "Moon River" from the movie "Breakfast at Tiffany's."

Shortly after my Grade 8 piano exam, when he was seventy-three, my grandfather died of lung cancer. After that, I lost interest in the piano for a long time. Now that I am older, I value his legacy to me and have returned to the piano, learning to play jazz. And I find myself remembering the knowledge he imparted to me all those years ago.

Raymond Fenech

My Fishing Trip with Granddad, Danger and a Maltese Fish Recipe

What great fun and excitement! My granddad's boat was green and red and only 11 feet long. I loved rowing it out to sea and in those days, we couldn't afford an outboard motor. Still I found it a great challenge because we used to row our way out to sea and sometimes had to struggle over the waves caused by other larger boats. But in my mind there is one particular night fishing excursion, which remains indelible in my memory.

It was in midst summer, August. The sea was extremely calm and there was no moon. We were about five miles out from the Grand Harbour of Valletta and the only available light source were the paraffin lamps, which served to warn other bigger sea crafts of our presence, and made it possible to be able to fix our baits on the hooks. The weather and the darkness had been very rewarding and we had caught quite a lot of big fish that night. But suddenly the fish were not biting any more.

My granddad seemed worried, something that wasn't really part of his nature because he was a big natural joker, a man full of fun who loved to be with his grandchildren. That night had been my turn to go fishing with him and I simply loved it.

"Granddad, why aren't the fish biting anymore?" was my obvious question. I was twelve then and my granddad always treated me like an adult. He used to say that children needed to learn to be tough to survive in this jungle, in which eventually they will inevitably find themselves on their own to deal with.

"There is only one reason why fish would suddenly stop to bite in such ideal weather: There must be a huge predator fish around and small fish can sense that immediately and run away."

I can't say I was afraid. I simply felt a surge of excitement and shivers went down my spine causing goose pimples. I realized the danger but I couldn't help feeling this was the type of adventure any boy of my age would die for. As I said, the boat was very small and the surface of the sea was very close. Now come to think of it and knowing the danger, it seemed much, much closer. Granddad moved to the middle part of the boat for better balance.

"Son, turn off the paraffin lamps quickly. Large fish are attracted by light and we cannot afford to let it see the light. Hopefully no other big boats will come around because there would be the danger that they won't see us in the dark. Best is to wait, don't move the oars so as not to agitate the water. That can also attract whatever is beneath the surface."

We sat in silence for about twenty minutes. Then I heard a faint splash in the distance. Then came another and another. Granddad and I scanned the calm sea for a ripple or a splash. Having much better eyesight than Granddad, I was the one to spot the movement first and it came in the shape of a huge dark gray fin that sliced the water as it rose to the surface and dived again in an almost rhythmic motion. I could tell it wasn't a shark because it was spouting water through its blowhole. I was elated and almost shouted the news to Granddad who was quick enough to shush me to silence.

"Granddad, I think there is a school of dolphins and they are coming in our direction," I hissed, unable to contain my excitement. "They must have followed one of the larger vessels we saw coming earlier through the harbour."

Dolphins often used to come inside the harbour, but we were usually quite a distance from them, closer to land and in much shallower waters. This time things were different because we were far away from shore and in the darkness and distance, without a compass, it was probable we would be swimming blindly for hours, possibly in the opposite direction to where we should be going. I also remembered that white sharks were not uncommon visitors in this area and company like that were far from playful. Granddad was in his late seventies and had suffered a stroke a year before. "Surely," I thought, "he would drown, even if by some remote miracle I could manage to swim long enough until help arrived." All these awful and frightening thoughts started to go through my mind and the previous feeling of excitement suddenly started to turn into fear.

Granddad was quick to explain that although dolphins were very friendly creatures by nature, they were also very playful, huge, and clumsy and sometimes didn't realize their own strength.

"Son, the last thing we want is to be capsized in the middle of the sea and have to swim back five miles. Keep quiet and don't breathe, not unless you have to. Keep your head down and let's hope they'll pass us by without deciding to use our boat as a toy for their joyful entertainment."

The dolphins came closer and I could hear them puffing water as they came up to the surface for oxygen. There must have been about twenty of them and some were over twenty-five foot long. They came so close to our boat that I could feel their fins gently brushing against the bottom. One of them decided to take a jump near our boat, rocking it dangerously. For a moment I thought I was going to lose Granddad but he managed to hold his balance. We were wet through, but that was the maximum damage. Before we knew it, the dolphins vanished and all was quiet again.

My grandma never allowed granddad to go fishing again after that incident. One thing I learnt that day was that panic in the face of danger brings fear and confusion and both ingredients together can spell disaster. Granddad remained calm and knew what he was doing all the way. That probably saved the day.

To celebrate our narrow escape and somehow not having to swim back home, my grandma cooked us her special Maltese traditional Aljotta (fish soup). Although the ingredients of this soup are changed often according to the tastes of the individual who cooks it, the basic materials remain the same. Here is the recipe as my grandma used to make it and I hope that you will enjoy it as much as I do. I simply love fish to this day and I would exchange it for meat any time.

The Traditional Maltese Aljotta (Fish Soup) Recipe

2 lg. onions
10 cloves of garlic
3 spoonfuls of fresh capers (*rinse well with water if using the preserved ones in vinegar)*
3 tomatoes (*peeled and chopped*)
fresh mint
1 tbsp. tomato paste
olive oil
1 lemon peel
half cup of rice
head, tail, and fins of large fish (*e.g. grouper*)
or about 6 whole small fish (*e.g. damsel fish or scorpion fish*)
marjoram salt
pepper
You may also add giant prawns and even shell fish.

Chop onions and fry slowly in oil until golden brown. Add garlic, fresh mint, and marjoram, tomatoes, and tomato paste diluted in four cups warm water. Add capers, making sure they are well rinsed. Add half lemon peel chopped or grated and cook slowly for 10 minutes.

Boil fish in separate container and leave until it has cooked well. Then place it in sieve netting and use potato masher to squeeze juice out of fish. Pour boiling water repeatedly, squeezing several times until most of juice has been taken out. NB: If fish is a steak fish and has no bones, you can simply boil without squeezing it. In that case, place in the other container when it has cooked properly. Same applies to shell fish and prawns.

Add cooked fish juice/and or steak fish with the other container and mix well. Simmer for at least 30 minutes.

Towards the end of cooking time, you can also add a half cup of rice (optional).

Serve fish soup with lemon wedges.

That's all it takes to make Aljotta. Hopefully, you will experience a little piece of Malta and the Mediterranean Sea and try this delicious fish soup for yourself.

Sonja Grgar

Emil

For my grandfather.

His quiet smile
Undoes the darkness;

Weakened lungs
Inhale smog and despair
Into incorrigible goodness.

His eyes swallow
The sea,
Which he saw only in his dreams.

But even those dreams
were not for himself,

He lived his life only for us…

And when the sun breaks
Through the clouds
Shyly,
Tirelessly,

And nectar divine
Quietly takes over
Like intrepid tide,

I know that he lives on
Here, somewhere,
By my side.

Gay Ingram

Pépè Played the Fiddle Sundays

Legend has it my grandfather rescued the violin after it was used in a barroom brawl. The black tape holding together the case's several splits certainly gives evidence to the tale. Pépè's early years, so I've been told, speak of him being a heavy drinker until God got a hold of him.

By the time I came along, he came across as a gentle, peace-loving family man. His musical talent was God-given; he'd self-taught himself to play both the harmonica and the fiddle by ear.

Sundays growing up meant that sons and daughters, along with a passel of grandchildren, would all come from their scattered homes and gather for the day. Everyone brought something for the dinner but Mémè provided the pies for dessert. When finished, she would place them on the warming shelf on the coal-burning stove, and uncles would glance over in that direction upon entering the kitchen, checking to see if their favorite was there.

Daughters took over the chore of setting the table and serving the food while Mémè supervised from her rocking chair. Extra leaves were inserted in the round oak table and chairs crowded close to fit as many as possible.

Once the meal was over, we kids were sent outside to amuse ourselves and some of the uncles strolled down to the VFW to toss down a beer or two. Late afternoon found us all crammed into the living room; sleeping babies on the bed nearby while kids took up floor space at their parents' feet.

That's when Pépè put harmonica to mouth and began to play. When one tune ended, someone called out the name of another. He worked that harmonica until there was no more breath to play. He then took up the fiddle and continued to play requested songs.

Mémè's constant request would be for "Amazing Grace" and Pépè acted like he didn't hear her as he played one tune after another. Finally, as if he knew she'd reached the end of her patience, he'd begin those familiar notes. He always kept the best for last.

Lengthening shadows signaled packing-up time. Sleeping babies were carried out to waiting cars; washed bowls collected for kids to tote with them. We who shared the three-family house my grandparents lived in stood along the porch railing, waving as each car pulled out of the driveway.

Already we were looking forward to next Sunday's gathering.

Brett Johnston

Dear Grandpa...with Love

I was driving by Burger King the other day and it reminded me of the many times you and I patronized the one on Indian School Road down from the shop. You would drive halfway across town, pick me up bright and early Saturday morning, and sometimes (more often than not, probably) you would have to wake me up because I slept through my alarm. Then, of course, we made our way to the Dunkin Donut shop and I would get the cinnamon roll and you would get a donut and a cup of coffee.

We finally made it to the shop to begin the day's work. Sometimes my job was to strip the fabric off furniture and then the old finish. I'd always watch you cutting fabric or sewing the fabric or putting the fabric on an old piece of furniture. That was my favorite because you used to throw a bunch of tacks in your mouth and use your magnetic hammer to pull them out of your mouth and pound them into the furniture. I used to wonder if you ever swallowed them or cut the inside of your mouth, but you never did. You were a master craftsman.

Other Saturdays, my job was to cut all the weeds down around the shop, clean the sidewalks, or fix the windows on the Quonset hut. Then, on special weekends, I got to go to the house to do the lawn work. I say special because those were the days I got to visit both you and Grandma. Some weekends I would spend the night and share a bed with you and that was always a treat. The most fun work I got to do was price the million different fabric samples once a year. Well, maybe fun is too strong a word...It was definitely a challenge. It was fun to find that rare piece of fabric that was priced $130 per yard (I think it was salamander or something like that). I wonder how much that would cost now.

Almost without fail, we would go to Burger King for lunch. I always looked forward to that. You would give me twenty dollars and your order (always a double cheeseburger, large fries, and a hot apple pie) and I would walk to the counter and get all the food. Sometimes we would get food for your worker Frank too. Then we would all sit down in the shop and eat our lunch. Often you would tell stories of when you were young, working for your father back in Kansas City. When we were driving around picking up or delivering furniture, you would also tell stories. I always liked those stories; I learned a lot.

After a hard day at the shop, we would hop in the truck and head back across town. Some days you would write me a check and other days give me a twenty dollar bill. Who would have thought I could spend the entire day with my grandpa and be given twenty dollars to do it? Talk about the best of both worlds! I was very fortunate. I think back now and realize, I would have done it for free to get to spend time with you. I sure enjoyed the money back then, though.

And now, Grandpa, I spend a lot of time working with wood. Whether I'm refinishing an old antique or building new furniture, I love every minute of it and I learned many of the techniques I use from you.

I think back and realize the weekends spent with you were some of the best weekends of my life. You taught me a lot and I'll always be grateful. I learned what it was like to work hard. I learned, by watching you, that it was right to do good work and to satisfy and respect people, whether they were customers or not. I learned how much you loved my sister and me, and Mom and Grandma, and how great a man you really are. You are my hero, Grandpa, and I love you very much.

Love always,

Brett

Deb Kemper

PawPaw

Paw's gray felt hat's on a hook behind the door
smelling of Brylcream, Old Spice, and sweat.
He sat in a straight-back chair on the porch
come evening, hat low on his wrinkled brow.
He lit his pipe, crossed his long legs and watched
night fall over the mist shrouded pond
to a chorus of bullfrogs and cicadas.
He shared anecdotes of his people, come from England,
rich heritage, proud, a worthy legacy.

After the first stroke he cursed like a sailor,
good-natured, laughing all the while.
His mind flew, leaving the husk of his body
and his care to a family who loved him.
Sixty years a carpenter developed his long, lean frame
into wiry muscle, difficult to subdue.
He understood we belonged to him
though he'd forgotten our names.
Years later I watched, in a cold gray hospital
room, as his serene body relented.
No more evening pipes, tall tales,
or fishing yarns.
But, PawPaw, finally, perfect peace!

Honey Novick

Gershon, the Grandfather I Never Knew

"…at first we love the illusion of perfection. Later on we come to love imperfections, because they signal vulnerability: and what we love, we yearn to protect…" Clifford Irving

"Where did she come from?" That question was always asked when people didn't understand me, something that first started when I was a little girl. It seemed to be the portent of things to come. I am a nontraditional free-spirited person who loves music and language. I didn't have the little girl fantasy of getting married and being a mom. I'm different, unique, with personality traits like being a vegetarian, opinionated, somewhat articulate, artistic, sensitive, "a dreamer"—eventually attributed to Gershon, my grandfather. His name comes from the Yiddish and means "stranger in exile," a Jewish or Hebrew name of uncertain origin. It may mean "an exile," but it could also be interpreted as "a sojourner," from Hebrew *ger sham* meaning "a stranger there" (from the *Concise Omega English Dictionary*). My understanding of Jewish history is that the people were nomadic travellers and were considered strangers wherever they rested. This entomology is full of imaginative meaning for me in reference to my grandfather.

My cousin Sarah, who lives in Chicago and is a little older than I am, remembers…

> I was seven years old when Gershon died in Chicago. And for those seven years I had no idea I had a living grandfather. Chicago was really not that far, geographically; I could have met him. My mother told me he died. My father resented his father for several reasons including:

a) his not filling out the American immigration papers properly*, forcing my father to seek refuge, alone, in the British colony of Canada;

(b) for abandoning him as a child, leaving his mother and handicapped sibling; and

(c) just for not being there.

* I also heard that in 1929, the year my father went to Chicago, beside the stock market crash, there was a quota on Jews or Eastern Europeans and my father couldn't get into the USA because of that.

I paid the price in that I wasn't given a chance to know him. It was a loss.

In 1961 I went to Chicago for the first time alone at age twelve on the Canadian National Railway line. It was a brave and possibly risky thing to do. I'm grateful, however, that my parents allowed me to do that and that the world was a little different then.

In Chicago, my cousin Faye showed me many books belonging to my grandfather. She asked me to take them but I didn't want the extra weight in my baggage. I remember meeting the work of H.G. Wells, Laurence Durell, and Anne Frank. That meeting was like inheriting a certain legacy. H.G. Wells' *The Time Machine* gave me a chance to imagine time and space differently, and Anne Frank inspired me to keep a diary, which I did faithfully, consistently for nine years, even getting certain items published in *File Magazine* many years later.

* * *

From my grandfather, I feel a certain kinship to being an American. I express that kinship in a certain rhythm of scat singing or American language inflection and syntax, clipped or elongated sounds and modulations. That part of American culture, I think, is part of my blood memory DNA.

"Where did she come from?" Accent on "did"! That question, rhetorical, wistful, was repeated again and again when I, as a child, did something my mother couldn't understand. For instance, my mother was noted for her cooking, but I wouldn't eat much of it, preferring to eat raw fruit or vegetables or just plain dairy products. That seemed unusual for a very little girl. It was a time before eating disorders was part of the lexicon. By age nine, it was discovered that I loved music and languages and taught myself French and Italian. Finally, it was declared that my behaviour could be attributed to my grandfather who was a vegetarian and language tutor. Since my mother and I never met him, who could argue? That "stigma" stayed with me my whole life. If I couldn't earn an acceptable living though music, it was noted that "she's like her grandfather, not being able to make enough money."

When I think of blood memory connections, I strongly think of my grandfather as I see him. Once, I found a photo of him—very dapper with a fringed, bald head and moustache. Dapper is never an adjective used to describe me but when the word handicapped—as in the current vernacular, people living with disabilities—is used, we are connected. I work as a music facilitator with people living with disabilities. How this connects to my grandfather, I can only speculate as he abandoned a handicapped child and a brilliant child. Maybe in the realm of reincarnation, it can be answered. When I started to work with differently-abled people, I remember my grandfather and uncle. Am I atoning? I don't think so; I just feel a certain indescribable understanding like that blood memory, or it could be karmic retribution. I heard my father's sibling was "retarded," yet my grandfather—a vegetarian who wouldn't harm a living being—rejected his family. This contradiction becomes part of the human's multifaceted character, like a diamond, manifesting and creating in my development.

I often wondered if Gershon drank sacramental wine on the Friday Sabbath dinner or at Passover. My mother would buy concord grapes by the crate, and we would squeeze the seeds out of EACH one of them by hand, putting the grape in a bottle and letting it ferment. Would my grandfather have dipped his pinky finger in the wine and put it on my lips to taste?

Would my nattily-dressed grandfather have eaten "nothing"? Nothings are the flour and butter delicacies cut in a rectangle and then twisted into a bow or bird-shaped cookie. They are deep fried, and finally sprinkled with icing sugar that falls everywhere making a mess. Nothings are loved by sweet teeth, everywhere. Maybe he would have been too "fussy" or fastidious to eat nothings, or even like little kids.

I know very little of my grandfather. He was an intellectual who was part of the Jewish Mosaic from Eastern Europe to Palestine to the United States. He wasn't much loved, yet in his heart he believed in doing no harm. Maybe he avoided children and wouldn't have liked me. He was controversial, yet ate a healthy diet. He was a reader, a teacher, a lover of ideas. All of these speculative things about a person only make me wonder that if it weren't for the family dinners, there may not be any story about him. It is food and a plant-based diet that connects me to an unknown grandfather. My grandfather would not eat an egg or tuna. I savour the memory of those delicacies. Without ever having met the man, I inherited a daily legacy that instills in me a sense of connection, of family, of association, of character, and of continuity.

Nora Peacock

A Treasure... Hidden No Longer

Grandpa entered heaven's gates when I was fourteen. I had overheard snippets from Mama about her dad—enough that I longed to know him. When he died, my secret dream of somehow meeting my Grandpa Hughes also died. But as long as Mama still lived, I consoled myself that she would one day tell me about her father.

Typical of a teenager, time spread ahead of me in endless supply; I would eventually ask Mama my questions—or so I thought. I married at eighteen and by age twenty-four, with a combination of birth and foster children, five little ones demanded my attention. Busy beyond belief with parenting, I would someday get around to talking to my mother about my desire to know her dad. But, someday never came.

All too soon, my world came crashing down when the unthinkable happened. Mama died during a routine surgical procedure. At the age of thirty-four, I felt more like a four-year-old child crying, "I want my mommy!" In addition to grieving her death, I soon mourned the opportunities I'd never taken to learn more about my grandfather.

I did know that Grandpa and Grammy divorced when my mother was fourteen. From that time forward, Grammy allowed no contact between her ex-husband, an itinerant preacher, and their daughter—my mother. In the early 1900s, Christians seldom uttered the "D" word. Divorce was almost unheard of for a minister and his wife.

As an adult, my mother began exchanging letters with her dad, a fact I discovered after she died. She never shared them with me, even after Grammy passed away. The hole in my heart remained. An unexplainable yearning for his embrace settled deep within me—deeper than I admitted to anyone.

The days, weeks, and months following my mother's death blurred while my family's needs forced me to put one foot in front of the other. My brother, Larry, agreed to take care of Mama's quilt box and the two metal trunks that stored all her belongings. My three sisters, my brother, and I decided that maybe a year down the road we might face the bittersweet process of sorting through her earthly possessions.

For whatever reason, Larry decided to go ahead and peek inside one of the trunks. A few weeks later, he handed me a small book, its orange cover frayed with age. My heart hammered when I saw the name on the cover: "E.G. Hughes." Tears burned my eyes as I read the title: "What Hath God Wrought—A Brief Biography—The Life And Ministry of E.G. Hughes." Later that night, I curled up in a recliner and devoured the priceless treasure I held in my hands—all 119 pages of it. The richest of jewels could hold no interest for me in comparison with the self-published book I clutched to my chest, when my tears made reading all but impossible. Minutes would pass while I struggled for composure enough to again focus on the printed pages. For the next two or three hours, I nestled on my grandpa's lap.

His words seemed written directly to me (spelling, capitalization, and punctuation from original text): "And now, beloved reader, who ever you may be, may I humbly intreat you to approach this narrative with open mind and heart, willing to receive whatever you may find therein that may prove a blessing and an inspiration to your own life."

Beloved reader.

Sitting in that chair, my grandfather's words of endearment enfolded me. I stepped back in history as he spoke of his own grandfather and grandmother: "They came to Texas with a colony and settled in what is now Hill Country, where my father was born in 1855. Because of the hostility of the Indians they returned to the eastern part of the state in 1857, settling in Tyler County."

My stomach knotted as Grandpa recounted my mother's birth. "The scourge of the flu that swept the nation struck our community...Our only daughter was due to arrive within a couple of months. It looked serious indeed...it seemed at the time that wife had felt no ill effects of it. However, the last day of december, when the time of her delivery came, trouble developed and three physicians declared it was hopeless."

Not only did my mother survive, so did her mother, despite the fact that she "lay unconscious with no hope held out for her life." I swallowed hard as I realized I owed my very existence to the miraculous survival of my mother and grandmother.

Grandpa's "narrative" revealed something of the reasons he and Grammy divorced: "The latter part of January 1914 I was married to a young lady of the community. She was a fine, clean, upright young woman, but unfortunately of another faith, and did not understand my Divine call to the ministry, and naturally was not in simpathy with it. I certainly do not attach the least blame to her for that."

His explanation continues for a paragraph, at no time placing blame. To this day, I feel a sense of loss for them.

I gasped when a few pages later Grandpa Hughes wrote of his love for Africa: "I read a large book that my father had, of the life and work of Livingston in opening up the dark land of Africa…It thrilled me, and some how there was planted deep within me an urge toward that land..." Shivers traveled down my spine as I discovered the intense love Grandpa and I shared in common for this country. He later wrote: "As previously stated, the very first response to our message, 'Loose Him and Let Him Go' came from Africa, and was a deciding factor in the launching of 'The Intercessory Prayer League'. Scores of prayer bands in South and west Africa were soon in operation. We have no idea how many there are in operation today."

I experienced mental whiplash as he next recounted a time in history when respect for the Sabbath Day was not only expected, but considered normal. Men gambling on a horse race put Grandpa's convictions to the test. "The race was to take place on the last saturday afternoon before the meeting was to close on Sunday night…It was causing quite a stir and was definite hinderance to the meeting." Grandpa told the sheriff and men: "Brethren, we are going to put this thing in the hands of God right now and let Him handle it…but if I should be the hinderance rather than the men who are gambling on this thing, and it takes my death to remove the hinderance, let it be so…" The drama ends with, "Before sunset that day both those horses had been shipped out and there was no race."

On another occasion, my grandfather prayed for his own need. "For years I had suffered with an affected appendix, sometimes suffering with attacks that would confine me to my bed for days at a time…'Lord, right here I am putting this thing to the test. It is either YOU, or the hospital for me. I am asking that you prove yourself in undertaking for me right now.' Instantly every pain left my body. I was healed completely, for that has been over twenty seven years ago and I have never had another attack of it."

As an itinerant preacher, Grandpa traveled by car, and many times on horseback, all over Texas and as far as Kansas. Halfway through his book, I gave up keeping track of the many times he moved on as he followed God's call. Grandpa eventually remarried, spending 25 years with his second wife, stopping his journeys to take care of her until she died. During this painful time in his life, he wrote his autobiography.

Now, almost a century later, I feel a special connection with my grandfather who also longed to write for God's glory. Grandpa Hughes' words resonated deep within me: "Several other manuscripts have already been prepared and ready for publication which we trust by the grace of God to get into print in the future." His writings and contacts reached around the world.

When I feel discouraged and wonder what difference my life has made, Grandpa's admonishment comforts me: "Oh, I know it may appear that we have failed utterly, sometimes, and that our little place of service just does not amount to anything and that God just does not even take account of it, but, NOT SO! when it is dedicated to the cause of our Lord and Master."

Before closing the precious book I held in my hands, I read my grandfather's final thoughts: "...praise be to God, if we follow our greater leader, our glorious Lord and King, clad in the whole armour of God, we have nothing to fear. God bless you."

I closed my eyes and thanked my Lord for filling the grandpa-shaped hole in my heart.

God bless you, Grandpa.

Felicity Sidnell Reid

A Year with Grandfather

As I toiled up the stairs one morning in my grandparents' house, a rumbling angry voice broke the normal silence. I couldn't make out the words, but the emotion behind them couldn't be misread, even by an eight-year-old. I hesitated, but my need to pee before school made a visit to the lavatory imperative. Luckily the volcanic tirade, punctuated by the popping of the gas water heater, was coming from behind the closed bathroom door. I crept past and shut myself into the separate toilet. But then I had a new problem—if I pulled the chain and released the water in the tank, the noise would certainly alert my grandfather to my unwanted presence. And what about washing my hands? I chose secrecy over training and cleanliness and scurried away to the safety of downstairs and escape to school.

Born in 1875, Grandfather had grown up in the reign of Victoria and by the 1940s was elderly not only in the eyes of his grandchildren, but also in reality. Short and slight, he was very upright and precise in his movements and, in spite of his small size, had considerable presence. His black hair, hardly touched by gray, and probing dark eyes defined his face, giving him an acute expression which lasted through his old age until his death at eighty-seven.

My mother, two sisters, and I lived with my grandparents for a year after my youngest sister was born while my father was still away in Europe. My grandmother, the middle child of a large family, was a sociable, opinionated extrovert, always looking for a laugh, while my grandfather rarely ever smiled. He was serious, stern, and exceptionally fussy about his domestic arrangements. He suffered from nervous indigestion for which he ate two charcoal biscuits night and morning. These unappetising black lumps, which could have easily been mistaken for real coal, were neatly laid beside his place each day. His food was served on the dot and often he ate it in solitary splendour, as my grandmother, mother, sister, and I couldn't be relied on not to chatter through the meal. Only the new baby's babbling seemed to appeal to Grandpa; the rest of us had nothing of interest to contribute to civilised conversation. Every night my grandmother served him his Benger's—a soothing, healthful drink supposed to induce sleep. Such routines required no speech and, as the old saying goes, silence is golden; thus on the surface anyway, the household was a peaceful one.

Grandpa—who was a lawyer and the coroner for Swansea, in South Wales, for over twenty-five years—dressed very formally. His shirts were starched, his silk ties a sombre colour, and he wore black suits, sometimes enlivened by a gray stripe. When he left the house, he donned a homburg hat, a black coat, leather gloves, and wore grey spats over his shoes. Even on our Sunday promenades with him and the old terrier, Mike, in Cwmdonkin Park, decorum prevailed. My sister and I liked to run along the path around the reservoir, while he preferred the gravelled walks dissecting the dahlia and rose gardens. But all walks started and finished at the gate by the old fountain, made famous by Dylan Thomas in his poem, "The Hunchback in the Park." There was something magical in its Victorian curves and curlicues, its overflowing bowl, and the small brass cups on chains for the use of thirsty passersby. But for Grandpa, these seductive little bells were only the prompt for a lecture on the prevalence of germs. Life with Grandpa was filled with proscriptions of activities that children relish. My bicycle was banished to the coal shed and even running was looked on as an unnecessarily dangerous pastime.

Grandpa ruled autocratically. My mother, his favourite daughter, wrapped up in her new baby, never questioned his authority. My sister spent her time at home entirely with my grandmother and my encounters with my grandfather were of his choosing. He liked to play draughts (checkers) with me though I was a poor opponent who always lost. And sometimes he would tell me about books, a passion of his and of mine, but of course our tastes did not often coincide. When I read his obituary many years later, I found he had belonged to an "exclusive club whose members were interested in literature." My grandfather's particular interest was modern European and, on his bookshelves, he had a set of Proust, beautifully bound, as well as Meredith, Hardy, and many other avant-garde writers of his youth.

At the time, I found it uncomfortable to be the recipient of his "instruction." It was stressful to listen to a commentary which I rarely understood and to worry about what to say or ask at the end of it. I—like the rest of us, except perhaps for my grandmother—was afraid of him and his sarcastic tongue. But perhaps I am too hard on him for I also recall that he gave me a school story, *The Little Green School* by Angela Brazil and *Lorna Doone*, at Christmas, both thoughtful gifts.

Books were at a premium during my childhood, either printed on horrible brown, friable paper or warehoused from before the war. My mother's sister, our favourite aunt and the rebel of the family, sent us *The Welsh Fairy Book*, which Grandpa might have seen as a provocation, had books been freely available. He, in common with many of his generation if they were schooled, spoke English without an accent and never used the fluent Welsh he knew from childhood, except in the office and the courts. None of his children were taught Welsh and all went to university in England. Grandpa, however, had been born and raised in Carmarthen and lived all his life in South Wales, except for the years he spent in Bristol articling as a law student. He never mentioned his family or his Welsh upbringing and his children thought he'd been brought up by an aunt in England, after his mother died when he was ten. In fact, the aunt lived in Carmarthen and took in his two brothers as well as him.

It was my grandmother, an Englishwoman, who used to introduce Welsh phrases into her stories or reprimands, exclaiming loudly, "Ach-y-fi," when something displeased her. She fought against my grandfather's dominance in her subversive way all her life. Silently for the most part but sometimes savagely, as when she burned the pictures of their honeymoon and many others of their early life together, which she admitted cheerily when I asked if she had photographs from when she was young. She loved to tell us about the wild things she had got up to in her youth. Marriage never wholly tamed her.

Their relationship was solid; divorce would have been unthinkable for such respectable, middle-class folks. Besides their bond was strong and they were used to each other, though they were a mismatched pair. Perhaps my grandmother appreciated that her husband was a compulsive hard worker and he knew that she was a constant fighter for good causes and for life in general. But all the same, though they were married for fifty years, Grandfather's obituary didn't mention his wife, who had predeceased him, only that he had three children, ten grandchildren, and three great-grandchildren.

Maybe I shouldn't have been surprised and horrified to hear Grandfather indulging in a diatribe that morning long ago. He may even have been cursing in Welsh! My grandmother knew how to get under his skin, even if we children were unaware of this. I wonder now how they filled their years after we and all the other children and grandchildren had settled again on the other side of the British Isles. I hope that my grandmother renewed her social life and enjoyed the company of fellow volunteers and her circle of friends. My grandfather, of course, had his work. He only retired from his law practice at the age of eighty, after my grandmother died, when he "had the distinction of being one of the oldest practising solicitors in South Wales."

We very seldom saw our grandparents after that year we lived with them. How often our impressions of older relatives seem to be based on a few encounters, and many of those on special occasions—on memories and absence, rather than presence. If fortunate, they may have acquired some attributes of a white-haired, smiling Santa Claus, the bearer of presents and treats. Or at the other extreme, they may be remembered as monsters. We knew "Grandpa" too well for him to achieve either reputation and, therefore, he remains in my memory as a complicated human being—prickly but sometimes admirable—from a world that has long ago passed away.

Dorothy Cox-Rothwell

Holidays with My Grandfather

On holidays my grandfather
walked with us, warm and alive
enjoying life, pointing with humour
at people and things we might miss,
tending gay flowers with him
reading books or listening
to him talk and laugh with friends
over wine and music,
with the sounds of my cousins
and the women making home sounds,
teacups rattling, scoldings and hugs.
The parlour window banked
with my grandmother's red geraniums
everything hushed while my grandfather
was dying.
Then childhood ended,
standing in the cold rain
my feet wet, shivering and sobbing
hearing the sobering words
"dust to dust", "ashes to ashes"
the alpha and the omega.

Joanne Sandlin

A Renaissance Legacy

My grandfather, Henry Paul Morinini, took a long journey to eventually become the mayor of a small central coast community. He left his native Switzerland at age fifteen to join the many immigrants who passed through Ellis Island, New York. Traveling West by train he joined an uncle near San Luis Obispo, California, who had come earlier, establishing a home where Grandfather could help tend the farm animals.

Henry later met another young Swiss immigrant, Claudina Cadloni, who would become my grandmother. They must have traded stories of separate ocean voyages and the irony of coming so far and meeting in America.

Henry and Claudina married and purchased the General Store in Surf, California, the water stop for the Southern Pacific Railroad on the San Francisco to Los Angeles route. The store soon became the community gathering place for beachgoers stopping for snacks or gas, and especially the railroad workers as the word spread of the tasty salami, cheese, and crackers. Glasses of wine were often raised with a clink and a hearty "salute" as everyone was always welcome around the table or in the store. Family stories tell of hearty bowls of polenta and stew adding to my grandfather's popularity, as the family grew to include a son and two daughters. Thus, he became the mayor of Surf!

The tradition of always-room-for-one-more around the table continued as the family moved to Santa Barbara, California, when Surf became a part of Vandenberg Air Force Base. People would stop to visit if they were in the area. (I think the lure of good food, graciously offered, was a welcome treat.) Since Grandfather was quite the Renaissance man—having taught himself English as well as Spanish, French, German, and the fluent Italian he learned as a young man—he could sit and converse with just about anyone who shared his table. I learned not only to be a gracious hostess, but to learn everything I could all of my life to expand my knowledge, and to be open to all people. I spent my early years absorbing with wide-eyed interest the tales of the travelers who stopped by, as well as enjoying books, reading, language and travel all of which I have continued to appreciate throughout life.

Grandpa was a short stocky man, always sporting a full beard and carrying a walking stick which I thought was a remnant from his Swiss hiking days. We might think he was a modern-day hippie if we were to see him today.

Vegetable gardens were popular during that time, and Grandpa also tended a small vineyard as well as keeping chickens. I thought he had a small farm in the middle of the city. On a year with a good grape harvest he would produce some of his own wine. Working alongside him as we tended this small plot of land, I learned that hard work brings rich rewards.

One day he asked if I would like to watch him perform a Cesarean on a loudly bleating goat who could not deliver her baby. You couldn't have pried me away! I watched in awe, chin cupped on folded hands, as he skillfully brought a new baby goat into the world which he lovingly cradled and bottle-fed, saving its life. The goat then followed him around with his dog, Capitan, and they were quite the threesome. He shared how he learned to care for goats and other animals in Switzerland and I thought he was a real veterinarian, at least for that day! From that experience I learned to have confidence in my skills.

When he would speak briefly of his coming to America, which wasn't often, I was spellbound for details. I learned to cherish adventure and be open to new experiences which had served him well and I knew could also add to my life. In my own travels I thought about the seed he planted in a young girl to embrace adventure and its accompanying educational, life-enhancing opportunities.

When I look back on my grandfather's adventurous eighty-four years I am reminded never to waste a day, but to treasure each dawn, look for a lesson to learn, a pleasure to enjoy, a pleasant interaction with an old friend or make a new one.

Although the town of Surf is now just a speck on a map, the lessons my grandfather taught will never be lost. He left me with a legacy of embracing each new experience with his walking stick planted firmly in hand as he took each step ahead. Thank you, Grandpa!

Gloria I. Taylor

Grandpa's Fishing Pole

His old rod stands in the corner
With his fishing box
Abandoned…
Not by its owner, who has departed
To a far off shore,
But by his family
Who see him no more.
What happy times we dropped our lines
Into the shimmering Quinte waters
Patiently expecting a walleye or bass.
What wonderful memories come back to me.

K.V. Skene

Grandfather's Wild Rice

Black needles sift into silent canoes
guided by natives. Autumn-ripe
seeds of rich watergrass
gathered, sold
in tourist kiosks and gourmet shops.

Wash one full cup, soak overnight,
(This is wild food—uncultivated,
unprocessed, untamed)
boil for thirty minutes
in three cups of water. Drain.

Gregarious gossips in the local
damn new mechanical harvesters.
Don't spill enough seed
back into the lake—year by year
the crop diminishes.

Peel and stew six large vine-ripe tomatoes,
(a pinch of salt if desired)
grate a generous cup of sharp
Canadian Cheddar.

Technology will destroy
what has always been, what
could always be
wild.

Slice one large onion, several
fat mushrooms. Sauté in butter.

Imagine Rice Lake
without its long grass-tangled shores.
Naked.

Gently toss ingredients together.
Cover and bake for one hour
in a medium oven.
Serve.

Nature is incredibly giving,
amazingly forgiving—but Mother
always has the last word.
No.

Dorothy Cox-Rothwell

My Grandfather "Hod" Barnes*

If I am to begin at the beginning, it would be being born in the Salvation Army Hospital in Toronto to my parents who were on the "dole" (social assistance) at the time. I didn't thrive in the hot city climate, and at about seven or eight months old my mother packed me up when my Aunt Kit was visiting and sent me home to live with my grandmother in Georgetown. This going back and forth would become a pattern in my life.

Looking back I realize what an amazing part my grandparents played in my life. My Gran, Maude, was small, with coal black hair, Irish, and stone deaf from scarlet fever when she was a young woman. Her mother had died in childbirth. Later while working on a farm a cow broke her leg and a drunken doctor set it, leaving her crippled, but she never complained about life. My grandfather loved her, though he complained about her "fresh air" mania. She was forever airing the house and freezing people.

My grandfather, George Barnes, was a small man of 5'4" but very spiff and firm. He was born in London, England, August 26, 1883, a "Cockney" by birthplace. Immigrating to start a new life in Canada May 1, 1909, when he was twenty-six years old, because of the wonderful promises made to encourage people to come to that country, he was never able to return home. He first came to Winnipeg and the first winter he nearly froze to death. So he moved to Toronto where he worked as a chef and met and married my grandmother Maude. He always said she was plump and rosy-cheeked and beautiful. They then moved to Georgetown and bought a small house while working at McGibbons Hotel.

He loved music, reading, and history and would sit in the evenings by the small black potbellied stove in the living room. Red geraniums filled the windowsills and his doctor friend, Rasmussin, would visit and drink homemade raspberry wine with him and chat. I loved to sit and listen to them.

I remember the sunroom where we had breakfast on a white enamelled table. My grandfather would crack my egg open and cut my toast into "men" to dip in the yellow yolk, while kippers smoked on the coal stove in the background and the CBC from London played the news of the morning and the bombing in England, where his sister still lived.

I did go back to live with my parents when I was two or so and have vague memories of that time. Of my mother pushing my younger sister Katie in a large old pram, up a hill with a dog named Jim...of an apple tree I climbed often...of a nurse who took me to Sick Kids to have my tonsils removed, and of starting school.

How did I become a "court ward" at the age of six? I was standing at my neighbour's screen door waiting for her daughter Marge to come out to play and I heard her say, "The reason her mother is in the hospital is because of Dorothy. She was sick too much last year." I ran away in tears. Did I cause my mother's illness?

True, I had been very ill the year before, having had pneumonia and strep throat. Two doctors had come to the house and, after consulting, finally decided to give me the new "sulfa" drug which they felt saved my life. I had missed a year of school with earaches, etc.

However, what happened was that my father had been conscripted to the Italian front during World War II. On the night before he left, my mother had been depressed. The next morning she went away to a hospital for a year and my father left for the war in Europe. I remember thinking as he waved good-bye that I might never see him again. It was on that day that my sister and I became wards of the court and my grandparents officially took custody of us.

My sister, Katie, was a year younger than me, and cried a lot. Our grandparents were very good to us, though very firm people. We slept upstairs in a room of yellow paper with tiny pink roses and dormers, feeling very secure. I felt I had to take care of Katie as she missed my mother so much.

I feel it is because of my grandparents that I had a loving and firm foundation for life. I was loved and encouraged in school, the arts, and sports by my grandfather who lovingly took a great interest in my activities and schoolwork. On Sundays he took my sister, myself, and cousins on long walks through the woods and for ice cream. He loved music and books and taught me to love and appreciate them too. We would take his lunch to his work at the Lower Paper Mill on the Credit River and watch to see how paper was made. Later we would climb on stacks of books from the libraries and take home coverless books to read. What fun it was.

During the war my cousins, three boys, and my Aunt Kit also lived in my grandfather's house. It was a busy, noisy household with five children, my grandparents, and my aunt.

My grandfather also took me to baseball games and hockey. When I ran my first race and won, he was there to reward me with an ice-cream cone. And he was there at the fall fair to praise me for red ribbons and flowers and painting. My grandfather was the only father we knew at that time. He continued to support and love us until he passed away in my eighteenth year, and he will be remembered always.

Last year he came in a dream on the spirit plane, almost as to show me he would be there waiting for me when my time came.

*My grandfather was nicknamed "Hod" because he had been a hod carrier at one of his jobs.

Men of Influence

Blessed is the influence of one true,
loving human soul
on another.

George Eliot

Stephanie Bell-Boissonneault

Ern
1892–1962

His hands were broad and wide. Hands that knew manual labour well. The skin, cracked and calloused like worn old leather. He took my hand in his and told me not to be afraid, he wouldn't let anything hurt me. His weather-beaten palm felt rough against the back of my hand. He guided it forward and into the warm nest under the hen.

"Do you feel anything?" he asked.

My hand moved around in the nest, ruffling feathers and straw. Then, just in reach, there it was. I sighed, relieved and excited all at the same time.

"Yes. I feel it," I said.

I reached in a little farther and picked it up. It was warm from the mother hen's body. I had done as I was told and retrieved the perfect brown oval from its resting place.

"Look," I said as I placed it in the basket. "Can I get another one? But this time all alone?"

"Why certainly. You can go all along the nests here and gather eggs from all twelve chickens if you like."

The next time he guided my hand it was just as frightening, and had it been anyone else, I think I might have said no.

This time I was to hold my arm out straight, palm facing the sky. He placed an apple in my hand.

"Now keep your hand flat. You don't want Roy to nip it. Extend your arm over the stable gate."

As Ern lifted me up to enable me to reach the rail, Roy snorted and approached the stable door. The giant Clydesdale loomed above but when he took the apple it was gently and I let out a sigh of relief once again.

"Now pat him softly on the end of his nose," he said.

Slightly damp, I felt the velvety black muzzle, making me think of a plush toy that sat on my bed at home. Then he snorted again and I startled and pulled my hand away.

"He's just saying thanks for the snack," Ern said. As he lifted me down to the ground I detected a odour of tobacco and farm scents on his clothing and person, not unpleasant, but earthy.

My sister and I thanked him for the visit and headed up to the house to buy the bread and eggs my mother had sent us to fetch.

When we returned to the farm a week later, my mother came along. She wanted to get some fresh vegetables she knew would be available.

Mrs. Barry had a beautiful vegetable garden, well tended and productive considering the soil she had to deal with. Fresh peas climbed on the fence and a crop of yellow beans were abundant and fleshy.

Along with vegetables, she also had several flower varieties. My mother pointed out the sweet peas, their perfume so delicate and colour such a vibrant pink. While she chose the vegetables she needed, my sister and I headed off to the barn where Mrs. Barry told us we could find Ern.

"He's in with the cows. Go ahead, girls, I'm sure he'd love a visit."

Once in the barn we saw him at the far end. The smell of cows and manure stung the inside of our noses, but a visit with Mr. Barry was worth it.

"Well, hello girls. Come over here and I'll show you something."

As we approached, he stood up from his stool and asked who wanted to milk a cow.

My sister, who was older and braver, piped up first.

"Sit here on the stool and I'll show you what to do," he said. "Tess, you stand there and you'll be able to watch."

My sister sat down and her lesson was learned quickly and accurately. Next, it was my turn.

As I sat on the stool under the belly of this mammoth creature, Mr. Barry took my hand and showed me how to place my fingers on the teats of the cow. It took a few tries but I did get the hang of it eventually. I never did like that farm chore, however.

Back up at the house my mother was in the kitchen having a visit and a cup of tea with Mrs. Barry. We opened the screen door and entered the tiny kitchen.

The wood-burning stove was on, even though it was midday and the weather was hot and humid. With the smell of baking bread filling the kitchen, we knew we were in for a treat.

That little house never had electricity or running water. Constructed of chinked logs and a tin roof, it was extremely small, consisting of just three small rooms and a loft. This had been the home of Ern and Irene since 1929. They had raised three children in this tiny abode, even boarding the teacher of the one-room schoolhouse one year.

Modest, one might even say Spartan, it still felt warm and inviting. The kitchen table with the blue-and-yellow printed oilcloth tablecloth, the hand pump and rudimentary tools and furniture, stepped right out of the 1800s. Not a single modern convenience.

Over the years we learned so many lessons from that wonderful man. His orchard of heritage apples, of which I still remember some of the names: Snows, Wealthy, Tolman Sweets, Northern Spy.

I still keep a piece of amethyst quartz he gave me as a child when he found out my birthday was in February.

Summers in the country were never the same without Ern Barry. My sister and I never knew our grandfathers; they were long gone by the time we reached the world. If I had known one of them, I would have wished him to be like Mr. Barry. As city girls, he showed us the ways of a simple existence that remain with us today.

Last week an evaluator came to value the farm I now live on. When entering the barn, his first comment was, "Whew, smells like cows. I hate that smell."

My thoughts were of warm summer days and our times with Mr. Barry. Barns to me smell of warmth and good natures.

Maggie Brackley

A Very Pukka Fellow

Hmmm…surely must be six by now?" With those hopeful words my father-in-law, Eric, would "open up the bar" in his home and dispense the nightly cocktails to us all. Nothing too much trouble, he would bumble around, humming to himself, catering to our individual tastes, genially serving Jamaican rum punch, gin and tonic, a generous dose of single malt—whatever your pleasure.

Eric was the ultimate host, always good-natured, his huge enjoyment of food and drink shared with all who came to visit. His strict adherence to the "cocktails at six and not before rule" was developed after spending his working life as an expatriate in the tropics, mostly in colonial India, then later in the West Indies, finishing up with a stint in the Middle East before retirement took him back to his native England. The colonial British had some rule about not drinking alcohol until the sun was down over the yardarm—originally a naval term but apparently made popular by Rudyard Kipling in his chronicles of colonial life, and Eric still adhered to the rule in retirement.

His girth testified to his love of good food. Whenever we went on a family vacation, whether it was Europe, England, the West Indies, or Mexico, first order of the day for Eric was to study the local restaurants for the most enticing menus. He always managed to produce a sheaf of these while the rest of us were still unpacking our suitcases. He would read out his picks, almost licking his lips as he did so: "deep-fried conch served with a hibiscus sauce"; "chicken in mole sauce spiked with chilies, spices, and a hint of dark chocolate"; "wild boar stew, simmered in red wine for two days over a wood fire"; "Iberico ham from pigs fattened with acorns"; and Eric's hands-down favourite, "moist sticky toffee pudding, steamed to perfection, and bathed in a rich, toffee sauce." Eric would soon have a couple of weeks worth of restaurant crawls planned, the gourmet tour, and we happily gorged along. After each meal, Eric would give it his typical accolade, "Well, that was pukka!" I don't recall many meals he didn't like. He was a talented cook himself. Rarely using a recipe, he simply cooked by instinct, the results always a delight.

Although hardly handsome by anyone's standards, women loved Eric. He was gallant, courteous, and considerate to all women who crossed his path—a "gentleman" of the old school. Married three times, and briefly engaged somewhere in between those marriages to a much younger, glamorous woman, he had a floating population of extended family who continued to visit and maintain good relations with him.

I possibly owe my marriage to Eric. After first meeting me, he apparently told my husband, "She's the best one yet." Never having met any of my predecessors, I have no idea whether this was a compliment or I was merely the best of a bad bunch, or perhaps a safe bet in a wide field, but the observation was heeded and here we are, still married forty years later.

Eric had a wide repertoire of jokes and anecdotes and never tired of telling these over and over. We all knew the punch lines but, of course, played along and laughed at the end as if we'd never heard the old, old stories before.

He had a quiet entertaining way with children, even the shy ones, intriguing them with a series of conjuring tricks, his standard being a sleight of hand with coins, which would magically slip out of a child's ear, or from Eric's sleeve, or just appear through his wiggling fingers. At card tricks, he appeared to be a mind reader.

With a huge love of England and the beautiful countryside where he had retired, Eric was a knowledgeable tour guide for his visitors. He knew the ideal riverside spot for a picnic, the perfect perspective for a photograph, hidden villages, and picturesque country churches. And, of course, his route invariably ended up at some quaint country pub with a distinguished menu.

Eric's working life had been remarkably full, working in several countries with intriguing cultures. In retirement, he hated to be idle and kept himself busy with small home improvement projects. These were done in his own inimitable style, involving numerous bits of wood salvaged from other projects and mismatched screws and brackets, the end result being complex gadgets which performed relatively simple tasks, only functional in a manner of speaking.

When Eric passed away at the age of eighty-nine, on seeing the beautiful oak and brass coffin at his funeral, his stepson remarked that Eric would probably have whipped off the brass handles and plaque and put them in a drawer for a future home improvement project!

Aside from his family, one of Eric's great loves was his pet mynah bird, Charles. Given to Eric as a crazy Christmas present by his mother-in-law, Charles faithfully repeated many overheard conversations between Eric and his third wife. These vignettes as presented by Charles would have us all falling around with laughter, the mynah bird being such a faithful mimic. The family suspected for the twenty years of Charles' life, the bird was really convinced he was the master and Eric simply repeated everything that Charles said to him.

When Charles passed away, he was buried under the camellia bush at the bottom of the garden. A year later, Eric himself died peacefully at home, sitting on his favourite chair by the window. In the week of his funeral in February, the camellia bush where Charles had been buried suddenly burst into bloom, unseasonably early. We weren't quite sure what to make of that, but we all agreed it was probably a good omen.

Sticky Toffee Pudding

1 cup plus 1 tbsp. all-purpose flour
1 tsp. baking powder
½ tsp grated nutmeg
½ tsp ground ginger
¾ cup chopped, pitted dates
1¼ cups water
1 tsp. baking soda
¼ cup unsalted butter, softened
¾ cup granulated sugar
2 large eggs, lightly beaten

Toffee Sauce

½ cup unsalted butter
½ cup heavy cream
1 cup packed light brown sugar

Preheat oven to 350 degrees. Butter 10-inch round or square baking dish. Sift flour, baking powder, and spices. Chop dates finely and place in small saucepan, add water, and bring to boil. Remove from heat and add baking soda. In electric mixer bowl beat butter and sugar until light and fluffy, then beat in eggs. Gradually beat in flour mixture. Add date mixture to batter and fold until blended with rubber spatula. Pour into prepared baking dish. Bake until pudding is set and firm on top, about 50 minutes. Remove from oven to wire rack.

Toffee Sauce: Combine butter, heavy cream, and brown sugar in small heavy saucepan; heat to boiling, stirring constantly. Boil gently over medium low heat until mixture is thickened, about 8 minutes. Prick pudding all over with fork, and spoon sauce over pudding. Can be served with whipped cream or ice cream.

Linda Jett

If Only We Had Met

Kids run away every day. In 1917, at age eight, Richard—the only surviving triplet born into the middle of a large family—ran away from the farm. He hitched a ride on a neighbor's hay wagon to the trolley line in Forest Grove, rode into Portland, and then made his way to the docks. There he signed on as a cabin boy on a merchant ship. The captain helped him write a letter to his parents, assuring them he was safe, but gone to sea. Over the next twenty years Richard faithfully sent money home in an effort to help save the family farm during the Great Depression. He ran away from the farm, but not from his responsibility to his family.

I never met this man, but I've developed a healthy respect for him over the thirty-three years that I've been married to his youngest son, Jim. Although Richard Elmer Jett died unexpectedly at age fifty-nine, he had already left an indelible mark on his then sixteen-year-old son. The more stories I hear about Richard, the more I think my husband's character was formed in his father's presence. Richard taught, just as he'd learned, from the classroom of life.

At the age of five, following in his father's footsteps, Jim ran away from home, pedaling down country roads on his tricycle. A mile and a half from home Richard drove up and asked, "Where are you going?"

"I'm running away," Jim said.

"Where?"

"I don't know."

"Why don't you get in the truck instead? I don't want you to run away."

Jim agreed. Richard put Jim's tricycle in the back of the pickup and drove home. Jim never tried it again. Clearly this man valued his son's independent spirit, choosing to redirect, rather than punish. Today Jim remains independently strong.

Souvenirs from Richard's many adventures, some known and some unknown, dot our house. A ship's bell from Jim's childhood home now rests on a post beside our deck. We don't know the story, but records indicate the ship, the M.S. Giulia, was abandoned and sank at sea in 1923. Richard would have been fourteen that year.

He participated in at least one Murmansk run and served in both the Atlantic and the Mediterranean before and during World War II. While in the Mediterranean he met his brother Dale, who tried to convince Richard to enlist in the U.S. Navy. (Dale didn't succeed.) We inherited carved ebony elephants with ivory tusks from Africa and a picture of Richard riding a camel to commemorate that chapter in his life.

When Richard decided he'd had it with war in the Atlantic, he transferred to the West Coast and signed on for ships in the Pacific. While serving there, the Japanese tried to bomb the ship he was on. In recounting that, he told Jim, "I wasn't nearly as smart as I thought I was."

Two silk kimonos hang in our closet. But more intriguing is the Arisaka type 97 sniper rifle. After the Japanese surrendered, Richard was on one of the first three merchant ships carrying food and first-aid supplies to enter Tokyo Harbor under destroyer escort. Armed Japanese soldiers met them at the pier. Not knowing what to expect, the crew was ordered off the ship and onto the dock. The Japanese soldiers lined up and handed over their rifles to these unarmed civilians. Richard knew these rifles would be considered "contraband" by the U.S. Navy, so he returned to the ship, dismantled the rifle, and hid its various parts among the pipes in the engine room. Later he reassembled it and brought it home.

Back home in 1945, while still a merchant marine, Richard allowed his sister to set him up with Mildred, the public health nurse who treated the sister's daughter during her bout with polio. At age thirty-six, after knowing her for only a short time, he married her, knowing she was independent enough to function during his long absences at sea.

Mildred gave birth to their first son Don while Richard was still in the merchant marine. Continuing as a public health nurse, two years later she gave birth to a second son, Bill. With both sons posing challenges, as they exhibited special needs, Richard felt the need for a job that allowed him to participate more closely in family life.

An intelligent man, he ended his thirty-five years in the merchant marine as a chief engineer, qualified for anything afloat at that time. However, he remained certified and active in the local merchant marine union hall. My husband treasures the memory of accompanying his dad to see the Savannah, the only nuclear-powered cargo ship, when it docked in Portland. (Years later Jim took our own son Michael to visit the naval vessels whenever they sailed into Portland for the Rose Festival. One navy man commented, "We've never had someone so young ask so many questions about classified information that I can't give out." The intellectually curious trait continues throughout the generations.)

After leaving the merchant marines, Richard took a job at Carnation. When his youngest son Jim was born, Richard moved into a night shift job as a watchman at a Portland brewery, maintaining the steam plant and systems. Mildred continued working. With one working days and the other nights, they often tag teamed at parenting.

The salt water never left Richard's veins. He often retreated to the Pacific Ocean to visit his sister and her family whenever he needed to recharge his spirit, taking his wife and three boys with him. We continue this tradition fueled by our own love for the Oregon Coast.

Jim remembers the time in the early sixties when Richard studied their old one-story, two-bedroom farmhouse, then decided it needed a basement. He proceeded to dig it out by hand! Not only did the new basement provide storage for canned goods, but it also housed a train set, complete with a mountain range and two tunnels. Only as an adult did Jim begin to understand the basement was really a bomb shelter in disguise.

Richard not only solved problems creatively, but also carefully calculated the risks. Following the Columbus Day storm in 1962, he took ten-year-old Jim out to the family farm to remove the fallen trees. He used this task as an opportunity to teach his young son how to handle dynamite carefully and with respect, just like he'd taught Jim to safely handle guns four years earlier.

Today, Richard would enjoy watching his thirty-two-year-old grandson, Michael, as he molds his own son, Danny, an energetic, curious, precocious five-year-old. Would he recognize some of Jim's own curious energy recycled into yet another generation? (However, Danny has not yet run away from home.)

How I wish I could have met this quiet, amazing man. But I suspect I encounter him every day as I walk through this journey called life next to a man who, like his dad, survived numerous adventures. The high school science rocket experiment that interfered with air traffic. The fifty-mile cross-country hike with his scout troop. Outward Bound in the Mt. Jefferson Wilderness. A navy ship's whistle's spewing feathers, conveniently after Jim had left the ship at the end of six long years.

Like Richard, Jim eventually settled into a career in order to support his family. However, Jim chose the computer field where he solved problems from a help desk, often outside the traditional box of engineering. Now in his semiretirement, much like his dad, Jim uses psychology on his bus's special needs riders in such subtle ways they have no idea they are being manipulated. They just know they feel safe riding with a driver they've learned to trust. Through it all my husband has exhibited a deep responsibility for, and loyalty to, our family.

Thank you for your example, Richard. What a precious gift.

Cherry Pedrick

Pop's Big Move

My family's first visit to the Vietnam Veterans Memorial in Washington, DC, was unusual. We were walking by the memorial when an elderly man ahead of us staggered and fell to the ground. He had a seizure and barely remained conscious.

Trained as a nurse, I rushed over to offer assistance while someone called for help. I sat at his side and reassured him, waiting to perform CPR if needed. My husband and son and the man's worried wife and relatives were standing nearby. Paramedics arrived, and he was taken away in an ambulance.

I have thought of that man and his family often since that day, wondering what was his story and what was the ending? Could he have been like Pop, my father-in-law? Pop served in the navy during World War II and was one of the survivors of the U.S.S. Quincy. I didn't know it then, but his home would eventually be in Washington, DC, and he would be buried at Arlington Cemetery.

When Pop announced his plans to move to the nation's capital, we were shocked. Why did he want to move to the Old Soldier's Home there in DC? That's what it was once called, an "asylum for the old and disabled." But it has now evolved into a thriving retirement community and is named the U.S. Soldier and Airmen's Home. My husband's father stayed in Florida for a year after his wife died, then surprised us all with his announcement. Jim and I invited him to live with us in Las Vegas. His granddaughter Candy invited him to live with her in Texas. But he refused our offers.

After his move, Pop lived four more years and we grew to understand his decision. When Jim traveled to Washington to visit him one year, he discovered that the Home is like a city within a city, with its own post office, chapels, a fitness center, restaurants, and even a bowling alley. Each day the Home's private bus takes residents to shopping centers, the Smithsonian, and other attractions. Pop had a private room with a bathroom down the hall. During his visit, Jim realized the biggest attraction for his dad was being surrounded by other soldiers his age. He and Pop went to the cafeteria for meals where Pop proudly introduced him and soon a conversation with other veterans would begin.

The accommodations seemed sparse, but Pop was happy. "Every morning they make a bed check. With over a thousand people here, they find a few guys don't wake up every week," he said nonchalantly.

With only his small room and no house to worry about, Pop felt more free to travel. He visited Candy in Texas and he visited us in Las Vegas. One day he wasn't feeling well. He wasn't sick, he said, just had a bit of an upset stomach. Could I make him some milk toast? Milk toast! My own dad had made this dish for himself when his stomach was upset. He'd been in the navy too; in fact he'd been a cook on a navy ship. Milk toast was simply warm milk with toast in it. My dad would put plenty of pepper on it (he loved pepper) while Pop would put a poached egg on top.

Milk toast was a popular comfort food in the late nineteenth and early twentieth centuries, fed to young children and the ailing. Although our dads never said so, Jim and I wonder if it could be requested onboard ship when you weren't feeling well.

From Las Vegas, Pop went on a tour of the western national parks. Another year he traveled to New Zealand. Pop was a survivor of the Battle of Savo Island in the Guadalcanal Campaign in 1942—a crewman on the heavy cruiser USS Quincy when it was sunk, with 370 men lost. During one visit we joined him when he went to a reunion of the Quincy which just happened to be held in Las Vegas that year. Jim listened to the survivors discuss their experiences aboard ship and after it sunk. It was like a floating city with over 800 men aboard, so it was no wonder that few men at the reunion knew each other. They all had a different story to tell and sharing their stories forged a powerful bond.

Pop has been gone almost two decades. Our WWII veterans are quickly vanishing. Jim proudly wears the Quincy hat he bought at the reunion, hoping to spark a conversation. He looks for similar hats and finds men under the hats always have a story to tell, but there are fewer hats today. More and more, it's up to us to keep the stories alive.

Milk Toast

butter
2 pieces white bread
1 cup milk
salt and pepper to taste
1 egg

Toast bread, butter lightly. Poach egg. Heat milk, add salt and pepper to taste. Put toast in bowl, and place egg on top of toast. Pour warm milk over both. Enjoy.

Be imaginative and add other ingredients to make it your own creation. Suggestions: cinnamon, sugar, paprika, raisons, dried fruit or nuts.

Cassandra Wessel

Like a Grandpa to Me

I was seven and a half when my mother invited her cousin Wilhelm Hedermann for the holidays. Father was none too thrilled, but although Mother rarely went against Dad, she said, "Honey, he's alone in the world and I promised Mother when he moved back East from Chicago that I would look after him." Reluctantly, Father caved to her wishes.

Off through the mail flew the invitation for Thanksgiving dinner at our one-story tract home in the New York suburbs. A week later Wilhelm's letter arrived from New Jersey. As Mom slit the envelope with her kitchen knife, sliding a thin sheet of onionskin paper out to read in the light pouring through our dinette windows, I peered wonderingly over her shoulder at his script. I'd never seen anything quite like it. What would the man be like who could write such beautiful calligraphy? When I asked Mother about him, she said he was her mother's second cousin. I asked if I should call him Cousin Bill, but she said to call him Uncle Bill since that would show more respect to an older person. I could have danced a jig over a visit from my very own Uncle Bill.

When the day arrived, Mother curled my hair, dressed me in my best hand-me-down frock from my Kansas cousins, put my ruffled socks on my small feet, and strapped on my best patent leather shoes with metal tacked heels. As I skipped down the hallway, shoes tapping and hands clapping, I was scarcely able to contain my joy. While Handel's "Hallelujah Chorus" played on the hi-fi, Dad told me to hush because my baby brother was asleep in his playpen in the corner. Then he rustled his newspaper as he went back to reading. Meanwhile my mother returned to her hot kitchen where she clattered around slaving over Thanksgiving dinner.

At that moment the doorbell musically chimed and I hopped for it. Somehow Father got there first, slipping me behind his back, but I peeked around his legs. He cracked the door and then swung it wide. On the other side of the storm door stood an older man, fedora pulled down over earmuffs, and overcoat collar pulled up against the cold. Muffled with a woolen scarf around his neck, he struggled with brown paper-wrapped bundles in his arms.

With his large grizzled moustache bobbing and blue-gray eyes sparkling, the stranger asked in heavily accented English if this were the Jackson residence. Daddy replied that it was. The stranger identified himself, removed a glove, and extended a hand toward my father, who had to unlatch the storm door to shake it. Uncle Bill grabbed Dad's hand, vigorously pumping it.

Mother bustled over from the kitchen, tossing her apron over a dinette chair as she came. When she attempted to hug her cousin, she found it nearly impossible due to the teetering packages in his arms. Dad rescued Bill's load as Mother relieved him of his overcoat, hat, and gloves, placing them in the closet. Then she gave this distant cousin, whom she'd not seen since her youth, a true welcome by kissing both cheeks which made them rosier than the cold had.

From behind my father, I jiggled my pleasure at seeing our only relative who lived near us. Dad eased me forward and said, "Bill, meet our daughter." When my uncle took my outstretched hand, instead of shaking it as I had expected, in European fashion he raised it to his whiskered lips, which tickled and caused me to giggle. Then he remarked how delighted my parents must be to have me for a daughter. I don't know if I blushed, but he certainly won my heart.

When he looked around for the packages, he found Dad had piled them upon the table. First he passed a large box to Mother, then a compact one to Father, next a box for me, and a flat one for baby. Mother took my brother's gift, opening it to find a delightfully hand-crocheted white layette trimmed with gold. She took the time to tenderly finger its softness, and then replaced each item back into the tissue paper and closed the box. Deliberately she folded the wrapping paper to reuse later while urging my father to open his gift. He pulled out a magnificent set of 18-carat gold cuff links replete with a tie bar. Dad's beaming face spoke volumes as he profusely thanked Uncle Bill for such a fine present.

Next Mother told me to open my gift, as if I needed urging for I had been pirouetting with impatience awaiting my turn. She cautioned me to be careful and save the paper. I slowly worked away the cellophane tape and laid back the wrapping, revealing a box imprinted with the likeness of a toy monkey holding cymbals. When I pulled it from the box, my uncle showed me the key and how to wind it up. Imagine my glee as the little furry monkey began to dance around, clapping its cymbals, making the most joyous racket, but my brother promptly whimpered his displeasure—which meant Mother never opened her gift until later. When she did, two matched boudoir lamps made from porcelain Chinese figurines peeked out at her from the tissue paper wrappings. She nearly wept at their beauty and said that her cousin should never have gone to such expense. But Uncle Bill, like most grandfathers, was not through giving yet.

Later, after Dad had blessed the food, we devoured apple-walnut salad, turkey, stuffing, mashed potatoes, and corn. While Mother cleared the remnants of dinner from the table and piled the dirty dishes in the sink, Uncle Bill rose to retrieve an unnamed parcel and proudly announced this one was for the whole family. He grandly opened a bakery box revealing the most lusciously decorated cake I had ever seen. On top stood an evergreen flanked log cabin and a pilgrim holding a blunderbuss standing beside his wife and a turkey in full plumage—all hand-sculpted from marzipan by my baker uncle. I fairly cheered from happiness, but Mother simply could not bring herself to cut into something so pretty. Instead she brought out her pumpkin pie and hand-whipped cream. For the remainder of that day the glorious cake held the place of honor on our dinette set. I could hardly restrain my fingers from dipping into the frosting until Mother cut into it for our bedtime snack, served with warm cups of cocoa.

Since we had a new sofa bed, Uncle Bill stayed for a couple of days. The next morning he got up with the birds and had our breakfast ready before we awoke. He set out such delicacies as I had never seen before—whipped cream-stuffed chocolate éclairs, cream puffs, iced muffins decorated with tiny icing turkeys, custard-filled donuts, scones, baklava, and light flakey turnovers. How I salivated gazing at the sticky delights!

To my disappointment, my ever-practical mother would not let anyone taste even one morsel. She insisted the baked goods were not a substantial meal, despite Uncle Bill's protestations that he had sold a great many for a quite satisfactory continental breakfast. Mother merely harrumphed and served her eggs, bacon, fried potatoes, and biscuits.

Dad had to work in Manhattan that day, but Uncle Bill was on a holiday and said he wanted to go for a walk. When he asked where he could buy a newspaper, Mother told him the name of a downtown store, but couldn't give him directions.

I piped up that I could show him the way, so Mother bundled me up, letting me tag along. He walked, but I fairly skipped beside him because my short legs couldn't keep up. It didn't take him long to slow his pace to a stroll. As we traveled along the slushy street, he pointed to all sorts of things I had never taken time to observe—a curving icicle, fluffs of snow tucked into an evergreen, gray clouds scudding across the sky, a pigeon pecking at sand and taking to wing as we approached. Then he asked me about myself.

What did I like to do? "Run."

What did I like to read? "Little Black Sambo."

Did I like school? "It's okay."

He said to study hard for that was the key to a good life, and then at the store, he bought me bubble gum and himself a newspaper. When we got home he read it, but I popped my gum as I looked at the funnies.

Years later he took sick and went into a nursing home in Los Angeles, but he still wrote beautiful calligraphic letters to us with an increasingly unsteady hand. When those ceased, Mother discovered he had passed away. I will never forget Uncle Bill, who proved to be like a grandfather to me, or a Thanksgiving that was really more like Christmas.

Richard M. Grove

My Uncle Gordon

For my dear cousin Paula

My Uncle Gordon
taught me to play chess
in the broad-beamed window sill
of my childhood bedroom
that looked out to the "black-witch branches",
as he called them, of a dying apple orchard.
"Strategy, it's all about thinking ahead" he would say.
I knew him as a generous soul.

My Uncle Gordon
asked me to build his idea of a flying train.
Balsa wood and glue were provided by him
with his engineered plans.
On his next visit we flew it outside his car window
as we ripped down the gravel road cheering
with excitement at its modest success despite
it careening, tether broken, crushed under wheel.
I knew him as a spirited inventor soul.

My Uncle Gordon
invented a word game,
WordSmith, he called it.
I helped to design it on my computer.
We played it visit after visit.
Like the flying train it crashed and burned,
lost under the wheels of the next invention.
I knew him as a creative soul.

My Uncle Gordon
made me think about God, bringing me citations
from *Science and Health with Key to the Scriptures*
by Mary Baker Eddy.
"Man is the reflection and expression of Love,
I know it's hard to believe" he told me,
"but we have to remember. It's important" he said.
I knew him as a spiritual soul.

What he was to you and you and you
I do not know
but I knew him as a generous, creative, spirited inventor,
a spiritual soul and much, much more.

In recognition of Gordon Frances Grove (1926 – 2012) *and his true spirituality.*

Deb Wuethrich

Dads for a Lifetime

Some people form solid, lifetime relationships with one man they call "Father." I've known the love of not just one, but several father figures. My biological father, Will Brown—who worked as a night watchman at the Kendall Oil Refinery in Bradford, Pennsylvania—taught me my earliest lessons about love and responsibility. Among my strongest memories is the smell of crude oil on his clothing, combined with the Vitalis in his hair and Beeman's gum, when he'd slip into our bedroom in the wee hours, just to be sure my sister and I were tucked in, and to plant a kiss on our cheeks. Sometimes I'd lie awake and wait for that moment.

We lived in a small house, which some today would call a shack. It had no indoor plumbing except for a cold water pipe into the kitchen sink. The house was perched atop Rock City Hill in New York State's Allegheny foothills, an area I later learned was considered the fringes of Appalachia. But I never felt poor back then. It was because of Daddy, I think. He took the time to push us on a swing he'd built on the forest's edge, and explained what he was doing when he had his head stuck under a car hood. He also taught me to identify trees by their leaves.

If Daddy had to go somewhere, he'd invite us to tag along. We attended stock car races with him and sat with his friend's wife as her mate was the driver of the car while Daddy worked in the pits. Once he borrowed an old truck to go pick up a new outhouse. I was allowed to go with him and we shared ice-cream cones on the bench seat of the truck cab on the way back.

Daddy wanted better things for his family and when he finally saved enough money, he bought a house with indoor plumbing. No more outhouses for us. We hadn't lived there long when he had a stroke at work one night and was hospitalized. I'll never forget waiting for him on the porch. I stayed out there until my grandma made me come inside. In the middle of the night, the phone rang and I was rushed to a relative's house so they could take Grandma to the hospital to be with him. A few months later, Daddy died from the pneumonia that overtook him there. I know deep inside of me there is still a little girl waiting on the porch for a goodnight kiss.

Later, we lived with my mother, who had remarried a man everyone called "Pete." For a long time I didn't know what to call him. Pete was not my father; only Daddy could fill those shoes. I was confused when our mother started talking of how Pete wanted to legally adopt my sister and me. He was a man in his thirties and, with us, he suddenly had a full family after our younger brother was born. A second son soon followed. Mom wanted us all to have the same last name as we entered a new community. I remember a judge asking us if we knew what it meant to be adopted. He explained that Pete would claim us as his own and provide for us and take care of us. It meant he would now be our father.

I'm not sure, exactly, when I got comfortable enough with the situation to call him Dad, but it finally happened. I worked it out in my young mind that there would only ever be one Daddy in my life, but he was gone, and I ought to be able to make room for a dad in another part of my heart.

Dad was a truck driver and then a construction worker. Once, he returned from a long haul with a gift for my sister and me: little gold pins in the shape of our names. I learned then that he thought of us even while he was on the road. I also remember family vacations in our Ford station wagon (six of us plus luggage) to Hershey, Pennsylvania, Niagara Falls, and a weeklong stay at a cottage on Lake Erie.

It was Dad who became "Grandpa Pete" to my own little girl, Michele, during her brief lifetime. She had spinal muscular atrophy (SMA) and used a wheelchair, and I sensed a special compassion in my dad whenever he spent time with her. Since we lived in another state much of that time, I kept him informed about our lives through letters. A Korean-conflict era army veteran, Dad came across as gruff to a lot of people but he was a big pussycat. His sentimentality surprised me, however, when upon his death, my siblings found a stack of my letters he'd saved and stuffed in a cereal box. He'd also kept an article I'd written, and framed it. It was one of my first published pieces. I didn't even remember sending it. The things he'd saved from each of his kids demonstrated the depth of his love and pride in our accomplishments.

I count myself lucky in another way. I experienced yet another father-daughter relationship when my husband Gordy's father, Butch, took me in as one of his own. Gordy was the first of the children to marry and shortly after we did, we left home to live on the Michigan State University campus. Gordy remembered some rockier times between him and his father, as sometimes happens with men who have difficulty expressing their feelings. But I recall occasions when I'd overhear Butch bragging to his friends about "my son, the doctor," who had a Ph.D. He may have had difficulty telling his son how he felt, but sometimes with tears in his eyes, he'd tell me how proud he was of his son.

Michele's birth further softened Butch. He'd make sure there was a piece of candy in his pocket or lunch pail for her to find whenever she visited. An annual Christmas gift, just for me from him, was a perennial can of peanuts or cashews. He's gone now, too, but I'll always consider him another of my dads.

* * *

I'm finding that God uses these unique relationships as a metaphor to describe what it's like to have a Father in heaven, a God who brings together all the nurturing qualities we may have been introduced to by our earthly father—and others who've sung the paternal song over us. I feel abundantly blessed to have known such father-to-child love from not just one, but several father figures in my one lifetime.

Author Bios

Jenne Acevedo is a writer, speaker, and substitute teacher. She lives in Chandler, Arizona with her husband and three children. She is an avid reader who loves studying God's Word, traveling, baking, and entertaining in her home. Encouraging women to find their worth and hope in Christ is her passion. Visit her at: www.jenneacevedo.com

Cona F. ("Faye") Gregory-Adams is an award-winning writer of poetry, children's books, nonfiction, and short fiction. Published in newspapers, magazines, poetry journals and anthologies, Faye served as Missouri's Senior Poet Laureate in 2010 and 2012. View her work at www.fayeadams.com, or email her at writer@fayeadams.com

Sylvia Adams is author of a novel, a poetry collection, an award-winning chapbook, and a children's book. A writing instructor, book reviewer, and former poetry columnist for *The Ottawa Citizen,* she is a founding member of Canada's Field Stone Poets. As *Adar Press*, she edits and publishes chapbook anthologies by her poetry groups. www.sylviaadams.ca

Millie Barger, an 89-year-old great-grandmother, had her first poem published at age 16. She has been a member of Phoenix Christian Writers' Fellowship for more than 30 years and has written 10 books and hundreds of articles.

Liz Barton is a retired elementary teacher who has been married to her husband for over forty years. They have three grown children, four grandchildren, and one black, mostly-Lab dog. She is learning to play the violin and hopes someday to master it enough to allow someone else to listen.

Mansoor Behnam is an experimental writer and filmmaker. His short films have been screened in several film festivals and his last untitled poem was published in "That Not Forgotten," *Anthology of Poetry, Prose and Artwork*, Hidden Brook Press, 2012. He is currently a third year PhD student of Cultural Studies at Queen's University and planning to publish his novella *This Is The Way I Disappear.*

Stephanie Bell-Boissonneault undertook her formal training in creative writing courses at Concordia and McGill, and has participated in writing/reading groups for over 30 years. Raising her family in Montréal, she and her husband now live near Campbellford continuing their passion for historical house restoration, gourmet cooking, and organically grown vegetables. Stephanie also participates in local community and family activities.

Maggie Brackley lives in Markham, Ontario. She enjoys writing about her travels as well as memoirs of her varied family. Previously published works include "How Sweet It Was" (*Grandmother, Mother and Me* anthology), as well as publication in on-line magazines.

Heide Brown loves living on Gabriola Island, B.C., almost as much as she loves writing, painting, hooking rag-rugs and sharing her life with family, friends, and The Gabriola Commons, which she co-founded.

Debbie Carpenter is retired from the children's ministries staff at her church in Tucson, Arizona. She enjoys writing devotional pieces and has published many. She is married with two adult children and their husbands, and four grandchildren who spice up her life.

Elynne Chaplik-Aleskow is a Pushcart Prize nominated author and award-winning educator and broadcaster. She is founding general manager of WYCC-TV/PBS and distinguished professor emeritus of Wright College in Chicago. Her stories and essays have been published in numerous anthologies and magazines. Her husband Richard is her muse. Visit:
http://LookAroundMe.blogspot.com.

Sue Chenette, a classical pianist as well as a poet, is the author of *Slender Human Weight* and *The Bones of His Being*, both from Guernica Editions, and of three chapbooks: *Solitude in Cloud and Sun*, *A Transport of Grief*, and *The Time Between Us*, which won the Canadian Poetry Association's Shaunt Basmajian Award

Karen Sue Chmielewski, Jackson, Michigan, is single mother of one daughter, and grandmother of two grandsons. She is an administrative professional, Microsoft software specialist, and an active member of the American Society of Administrative Professionals. Singer by hobby with a deep love for the art of music

Theodore Michael Christou is an Assistant Professor of education at Queen's University. He is the author of two books. The first is a work of nonfiction titled *Progressive Education* (University of Toronto Press, 2012). The second is a book of verse titled *an overbearing eye* (Hidden Brook Press, 2012).

Ruth Clarke is the author of five books and has published a number of short stories. She has written for newspapers and magazines, was editor of *Pacific Pearl*, an English magazine in Mexico, has edited a novel and a cookbook. Ruth has also worked for Canadian publishing companies, the Writers' Union, Canada Council, and she co-founded Cannon Book Distribution.

Carolyn Brown Copeland has been a member of the Phoenix Christian Writers' Club for more than 30 years, being published in more than 100 different magazines and newspapers in the United States and Canada. And yes, when her dad died in 1988, he had told all his four children that he loved them.

Linda Grace Cousins is a mother and a lover of books and writing. From a very young age, she knew she had a story or two to tell. She lives in Whitby, Ontario with her teenage son and Yorki Poo, Reese, who keeps everyone in line.

Dorothy Cox-Rothwell was previously involved in family business and now pursues her interests in writing and art. She is a Spiritualist Minister with two grown children and five grandchildren. Married to John Rothwell, she is also a Reiki Master.

Benjamin Creighton is a writer and teacher from Ontario, Canada.

Joanne Culley is a writer and DVD producer whose articles have appeared in the *Globe and Mail.* Her documentaries include *Be My Baby*, *Put the Brakes on Bullying*, and *Breaking New Ground: Contemporary Canadian Architecture*. She was the winner of the Media/Television Award for "In Celebration of Women". Visit www.joanneculley-mediaproductions.com.

Don E. Cunningham, Prescott Valley, Arizona, is the author of *Divorce and Remarriage Made Beautiful in His Time* (Tate Publishing), and several chapbooks of poetry, short stories, and essays. A retired social worker and licensed minister, he currently conducts a telephone pastoral care ministry at his local church.

Nancy Dobbins has taught all ages for over 25 years and has had articles published in regional publications. She has also taught on Divine Health and has had a number of devotionals published in the book *Spirit Aflame.*

J. Graham Ducker is a retired kindergarten teacher. His memoir *Don't Wake the Teacher* was published in 2004, and his poetry book *Observations of Heart and Mind* was published in 2006. *The Elephant That Wanted to Join the Circus* and *Why Pigs Have Curly Tails* were both published in 2011.

Terri Elders, a lifelong writer and editor, lives near Colville, Washington, with two dogs and three cats. Her stories have appeared in dozens of periodicals and anthologies, including two previous Hidden Brook Press collections. She blogs at atouchoftarragon.blogspot.com.

Patricia Anne Elford is a minister, an educator and presenter, editor, award-winning poet and writer in many *genres.* Her work continues to be published on line and in periodicals, anthologies and literary journals and displayed *(framed, not graffiti)* in such places as a tearoom and Fashion Design Studio www.janaemiliafashion.com.

Diane K. Ellenwood resides in southeast Michigan. She has published a children's book, *The MisAdventures of Three Amigos*, and has stories included in anthologies, *Celebrating Christmas* and *I Choose You* and writes devotionals for a Christian newsletter, EACM Roseville, Michigan.

Daniela Elza's work has appeared nationally and internationally in over 80 publications. *the weight of dew*, her debut poetry collection, was published by Mother Tongue Publishing (2012). The two poems here come from her latest book, *milk tooth bane bone* (Leaf Press, 2013). Daniela lives and writes in Vancouver.

Linda Rose Etter, Adrian, Michigan, taught school for 36 years in Michigan after graduating from Huntington College. In 2011 she published a devotional book, *Listen To HIS Heartbeat.* She also has stories in two anthology books. Her website is: www.etterlinda.com

Rona Evartt is a single mother of four grown daughters and two amazing grandchildren. She has taught at-risk teens in various settings in public schools and is working on several books to be used for curriculum specifically for them. She is also working on two novels.

Raymond Fenech from Malta embarked on his writing career as a freelance journalist at 18 and worked for the leading newspapers, *The Times* and *Sunday Times.* He edited two nationwide distributed magazines, *The Globe Trotter* and *Living 2000.* His work has been featured in several publications in 12 countries. His book *Blood Lines* is available on Amazon.

George W. Frey grew up in a Methodist parsonage in Tennessee, studied music, earned a graduate degree in voice, traveled with his family on music concerts and only began writing Christian fiction two years ago. He and his wife have made Arizona their home for 45 years.

Corinne D. Furtney is an elementary school teacher and volunteers with the youth in her church. She became interested in writing at an early age and also enjoys baking, travelling, and spending time with her family.

Joyce Gero, contributor to several anthologies, is an office administrative professional, a volunteer with diverse community organizations, and webmaster/Facebook administrator for a local service organization. Surrounded by unfinished craft projects and an eclectic collection of books, she lives in Truro, Nova Scotia, on Canada's East Coast.

Donna Clark Goodrich is a freelance writer, editor, proofreader, and conference instructor. The author of 24 books and over 700 published manuscripts, she lives with her husband of 53 years in Mesa, Arizona. Contact her at: dgood648@aol.com, www.thewritersfriend.net, or read her weekly writers' blog on Mondays at: http://donna-goodrich.blogspot.com

Sonja Grgar is a writer and journalist who lives in Surrey, BC. She is passionate about exploring complex themes in her prose and poetry. Her work was published in *The Globe and Mail*, broadcast on radio and television, and featured in the *That Not Forgotten*, an anthology published by Hidden Brook Press, 2012.

Effie-Alean Gross, Fountain Hills, Arizona, is a writer and speaker. She has a master's degree in English from Drake University in Des Moines, Iowa, and teaches writing at a community college near Phoenix. Effie enjoys her family, travel, and writing historical fiction from the WWII era. Visit her at: www.EffieGross.com or her blog at: www.kilroywashereusa.wordpress.com

Richard M. Grove, find his many books of poetry, prose and photography on Amazon. President of the Canada Cuba Literary Alliance, Board of Director of IFPOR – International Festival of Poetry of Resistance, former president of the Canadian Poetry Association, former vice-president of the Canadian Authors Association, Toronto. www.HiddenBrookPress.com

Sue Hardesty lives in Northwest Arkansas, is semi-retired and has three grown children and several grand, and great-grandchildren. She has several short stories published in anthologies and is working on her first novel.

Gillian Harding-Russell has had poems published in the anthologies *Poet to Poet* (Guernica, 2012), *That Not Forgotten* (Hiddenbrook, 2012), and another accepted for publication in the anthology *I Found It At the Movies* (Guernica, 2013). Her manuscript "We came to find what was real, and to be afraid" won 2nd place in the Gritlit 2012 contest. http://hardingrussell.wordpress.com

Christine Henderson: Christine Henderson has won awards locally and nationally for her short stories. Her inspirational stories have been published in several anthologies about growing up and in daily devotional guides. She has written several children's picture book stories and is currently finishing up a contemporary romance novel.

Helen Hoover enjoys sewing, knitting, and traveling. As retirees, she and her husband volunteer at various organizations. Their four grandchildren and three great-grandchildren give them great joy. Helen's devotions and personal stories are published in books and Christian hand-out papers.

Gay Ingram began her writing career as a result of a passionate interest in herbs. A creative writing course offered by Tyler Junior College launched Ms. Ingram into fiction writing. Her articles and short stories have appeared in numerous publications. She has had several novels published. Her newest publication, *Second Time Around*, was released in Nov. 2012. Her books can be seen on her website: www.pineywoods-books.webs.com and at Amazon.com.

Linda Jett writes, grandmothers, and practices therapeutic massage from her home in Newberg, Oregon. Her work has appeared in a variety of anthologies.

Vivekanand Jha, MA and Ph. D in English, is a translator, editor and award winning poet from India. He is the author of 05 books of poetry. He has also authored one critical book and edited nine critical anthologies on Indian English Writing. His poems have been published in more than 100 magazines and 25 anthologies round the world.

Jane Jimenez, a mother of two, lives with husband and supporter Victor in metro Phoenix, Arizona. As a freelance writer, Jane is dedicated to issues of importance to women and the family. Her work has appeared in local and national publications, with a special focus on changing sexual mores that began in the 60s.

Connie Johnson has published poems in *Sandcutters* (Arizona State Poetry Society), *Vista*, *Leaves of Poetry* (Anthology), *Fresh Ink*, and *Wingtips*. Her memoir was coauthored with her sister. She reads with *The Mad Women Poets* in Prescott, Arizona.

Brett Johnston is an electrical engineer and freelance writer living in Arizona. He continues to pursue his love of woodworking and throughout the years has created numerous custom projects for businesses and homes.

Shane Joseph is the author of three previous novels and a collection of short stories. His work *After the Flood* won the best futuristic/fantasy novel award at the Canadian Christian Writing Awards in 2010, and his short fiction has appeared in international literary journals and anthologies. For details see www.shanejoseph.com

Deb Kemper, freelance writer and poet, hails from northwest Florida. She now lives in Kansas City, Missouri, with her husband and two dogs. Internationally published, *Mallory Ridge* and *Keeping Reggie's Widow* are available on Amazon. Visit her website at www.DebKemper.com.

Patricia Kirby is an artist and a retired internal communications professional and nonfiction writer. Dabbling in poetry since moving to Ottawa in 2002, she has been published electronically in *Bywords* as well as in several collections with the Pachyderm Poets.

Glenn Kletke was born in Manitoba, now lives and writes in Kanata, Ontario. Pioneer of the framed glosa form, his most recent collection of poems is "Bones On A Bed Of Blue."

Alice Klies has enjoyed writing life stories from a very early age. After joining American Christian Writers Association and Wordweavers she was encouraged by fellow writers to publish. Her articles have been appeared in *Angels On Earth, Wordsmith Journal* and anthologies *God Still Meets Needs; Grandmother, Mother and Me*; and *Women Inspire Faith.*

Kristi Lewis writes: My mother bought me my first journal when I was 11 and I've written ever since. Recently my Opa asked me to edit his memoirs— I hope to have them printed for him to give to his loved ones by the end of this year. I've never tried having any of my work published.

Martha E. Link is a baby boomer who grew up on the prairie. A bookworm, she has developed many other creative talents. Her greatest passion has always been writing. Currently working on her first novel, Martha belongs to The Campbellford Writer's Group. She also attends Ursula Pflug's Loyalist College writing workshop.

Claudia Loopstra, a retired photographer, is a writer of short stories and poetry. Currently, she is writing a book about her life growing up in the household of an alcoholic father. Claudia is married with two children and has six grandchildren.

Brendalyn Crudup Martin is a published devotional and poetry writer with work appearing in *Chicken Soup for the soul*, other anthologies, and online sites. She is the Poet Laureate of the Arizona Supreme Court, a member of the Phoenix Christian Writers Club, and editor of Inspired Christian Newsletter.

Leila Mason has a degree in English and Occupational Therapy. Now a retired therapist she is reaching into her English background to write historical memoirs of family life in small town Ontario. She resides on a hobby farm in the hamlet of Claremont with her husband and several pets.

Connie Kinnell McKinney was born in Hornell, New York and raised in different areas of New York and Massachusetts before attending Cottey College in Nevada, Missouri. She now resides with her husband in Carthage, Missouri where she enjoys spending time with her four grown children and their families.

Cynthia Mendenhall, a wondering and wandering Life Coach and Teacher-at-Large, is new to writing and to Phoenix. She passionately helps others take control of their lives and to think differently about their futures. Her latest secret: she carries her new harmonica everywhere and plays it in traffic.

Gail Murray, strongly influenced by Keats to capture the essence of the moment, writes in response to her natural and emotional environment. Her poems have been published in Arborealis, CAA's *Wordscape*, and online at *CommuterLit.com.* Creative nonfiction/profile/travel pieces have appeared in *The Globe and Mail*, *Trellis,* and *NOW Magazine.*

Bonnie Nish is founder and Executive Director of Pandora's Collective Outreach Society, a charitable organization in the literary arts based in Vancouver British Columbia. Bonnie has a Masters in Arts Education from Simon Fraser University and is currently pursuing a PhD in Expressive Arts Therapy at the European Graduate School. Bonnie's first book of poetry *Love and Bones* will be released by Karma Press in September 2013. www.bonnienish.com

Honey Novick is a singer/songwriter/voice teacher/poet. She believes that winter never fails to turn into spring and loves to smell the lilacs. She appreciates her grandfather and loves her father. www.honeynovick.com

Andrea Arthur Owan, Tucson, Arizona, is a writer, speaker and educator. Her nonfiction and fiction work has appeared in a variety of Christian and secular publications. Her blog, http://brokenheartsredeemed.blogspot.com, is dedicated to helping parents, siblings and family heal emotionally, physically and spiritually from the premature loss of a child during pregnancy or at birth.

Nora Peacock, a freelance writer, lives in Newberg, Oregon. The 2012 Silver Prize Winner of the Oregon Women's Report contest for inspirational writing, she has also written for Gary Chapman's *Love is A Verb* and *Love is A Verb Devotional.*

Cherry Pedrick lives in Washington State with her husband and cats. She enjoys church, family, friends and volunteer work. She is the coauthor of 7 books, including *The OCD Workbook* and *The Habit Change Workbook*. www.CherryPedrick.com.

Tammy Pfaff is a freelance writer living in Prospect Park, Pennsylvania, with her husband and four children. She studies Journalism at DCCC and is a member of Christian Writers Fellowship of Philadelphia, hoping to encourage others through her writing. Learn more about Tammy at www.tammypfaff.com.

Jaclyn Piudik—recipient of a New York Times Fellowship for Creative Writing and Academy of American Poets' Sellers Award—is the author of two chapbooks, *Of Gazelles Unheard* and *The Tao of Loathliness* (fooliar press). Her poems have appeared in numerous anthologies and journals, including *The New Quarterly*, *Columbia Poetry Review*, and *Barrow Street.*

Jan K. Potter, homemaker/freelance writer, resides in Phoenix, Arizona with her husband of 44 years. Her articles have appeared in many magazines and compilation books, and she is currently writing a novel for teenagers.

Bea Purcell was born and grew up in the Philippines. She moved to the United States after marrying an American who served in the U.S. Air Force, and retired after a career of more than 24 years in the screen printing industry.

Felicity Sidnell Reid is a retired teacher, author of a variety of educational materials and text books, who now lives in Colborne, Ontario and writes fiction, poetry and occasional memoir which has been published in anthologies, newspapers and on-line.

Joanne Sandlin published her first children's book in 2012 as well as continuing to write a recipe column in the *Prescott Daily Courier*. She is inspired by membership in the Northern Arizona Word Weavers.

Debbie Schmid, award-winning author, has written four books including two best sellers and numerous articles for various publications. Throughout the years, she's been a keynote speaker at ladies' retreats and church seminars. Debbie also enjoys leading Bible studies, mentoring young Christians, and nurturing hurting individuals.

K.V. Skene's latest publications include *Love in the (Irrational) Imperfect*, Hidden Brook Press (Canada) 2006 and *You Can Almost Hear Their Voices*, Indigo Dreams Publishing (UK) 2010. After over 18 years as an expat in England, including a year in Ireland, KV now lives and writes from Toronto.

Gloria I. Taylor enjoys Scottish Country Dancing and Irish Set Dancing as well as writing poetry. She is a retired FSL, ESL teacher and loves fishing.

Connie Poole Wesala, Gilbert, Arizona, was previously published in Hidden Brook Press anthologies. Her short stories, poetry, and nonfiction have been published in several literary journals. She placed second in Fiction in a 2012 college writing contest, and second in Nonfiction in 2013. Connie is currently working on a historic novel. Her blog can be viewed at conniewesala.com

Cass Wessel, author, contributes to online devotionals, print media, and anthologies, such as *Grandmother, Mother and Me.* She belongs to ACFW, Ancestry.com, and the Forest and Clarion County Historical Societies. Her website, "Words About the Word" and her blog "The Word Heart Written" are found at www.wordsabouttheword.com.

Deb Wuethrich, Adrian, Michigan, is a staff writer at the *Tecumseh Herald* in Tecumseh, Michigan. She has contributed to several anthologies and is a 2003 recipient of an Amy Award of Outstanding Merit.

Carolyn Hei-Kyoung You is a poet and writer who lives in Kingston, Ontario. Her father is a keen observer of birds, baseball, markets, weather. Together they have watched blue jays in winter and seen the Blue Jays' summer stock rise in 1992.

Another
Hidden Brook Press anthology
edited by
Donna Clark Goodrich

Celebrating Christmas
with Memories, Poetry, and Good Food

ISBN 978-1-897475-80-5

Another
Hidden Brook Press anthology
edited by
Donna Clark Goodrich

Grandmother, Mother and Me

with Memories, Poetry, and Good Food

ISBN 978-1-897475-94-2

Order these or other Hidden Brook Press books from
any **Amazon** or
many other e-stores around the world.
Use the ISBN when looking for a book.

To save shipping

order from your local bookstore. Just give them the title and ISBN. Your retailer will order directly from their Ingram distribution account or if they are a new Ingram client they can contact Ingram at 800-937-0152.

www.ingramcontent.com/pod-product-compliance
Lightning Source LLC
Chambersburg PA
CBHW070626170726
48291CB00003B/894

* 9 7 8 1 9 2 7 7 2 5 0 7 8 *